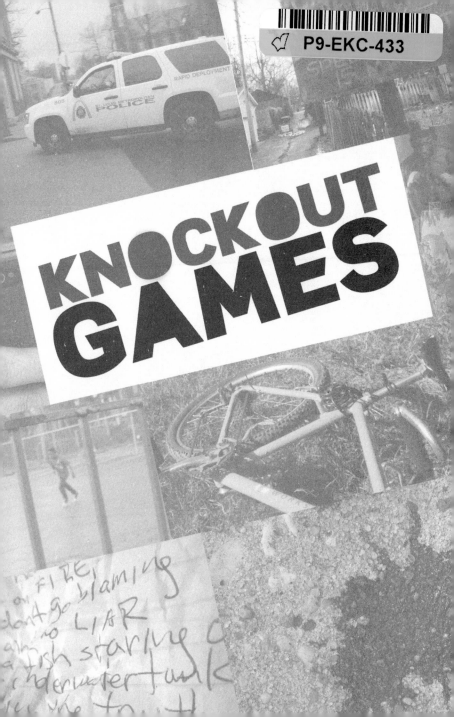

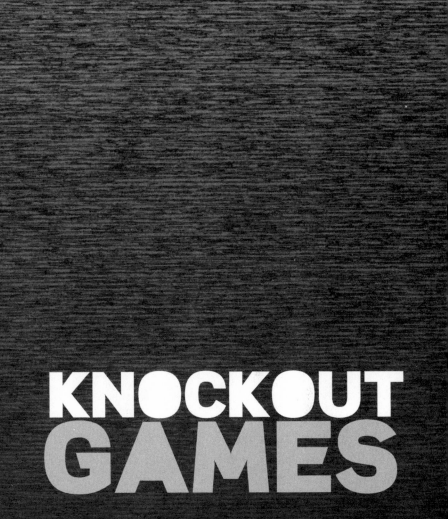

KNOCKOUT
GAMES

G. NERI

carolrhoda LAB

MINNEAPOLIS

Carolrhoda Lab™
An imprint of Carolrhoda Books
A division of Lerner Publishing Group, Inc.
241 First Avenue North
Minneapolis, MN 55401 USA

For reading levels and more information, look up this title at
www.lernerbooks.com.

Front Cover: © Giliane E. Mansfeldt Photography (fists); © Cocoon/Photodisc/Getty Images (eye); © Paul Bradbury/OJO Images/Getty Images (hooded sweatshirt); © iStockphoto.com/kyoshino (static).

Back cover and interior images: © Greg Neri (note, sorry, surveillance tape, drink, zipper, lockers, wrestlers, finger tattoo, assembly of kids, kissing, crumpled flyer).

All other images via Creative Commons by 2.0: © Elvert Xavier Barnes Photography (candle); © Mathias Klang (surveillance sign); © Jamiecat (boxer); © andrewmalone (playground); © Thunderchild7 (bloody hand); © Thomas Anderson/PhotoDu. de/CreativeDomainPhotography.com (parking lot); © klynslis (shopping cart); © whiteafrican (phone); © MoonSoleil (redhead); © Joe (arch); © Martin Pulaski/flickr. com (man in shirt); © Stephan Ridgway (casket); © gm.newsted (cityscape); © mhiguera (exploded balloon); © Buzz Farmers (hands holding phone); © Paul Sableman (kid, caution sign, alley way, fire hydrant,); © KOMUnews (sheriff); © ukhomeoffice (arrest); © dvs (shadows); © Paul Sableman/St. Louis Metropolitan Police (police car); © Oliver Ruhm (bike); © Norlando Pobre (cigarette); © David Lofink (red ants); © H. Powers (Chihuahua); © Ano Lobb (Do not chew), © k. dordy (bald head); © Daniel X. O'Neil (white orb); © Mary Roy (gun); © Frank Hebbert (cleaning bucket).

Main body text set in Janson Text LT Std 10/14.
Typeface provided by Linotype AG.

Library of Congress Cataloging-in-Publication Data

Neri, Greg.
    Knockout Games / by G. Neri.
      pages cm
    Summary: As a group of urban teenagers in a gang called the TKO Club makes random attacks on bystanders, Erica, who is dating one of the gang's members, wrestles with her dark side and "good kid" identity.
    ISBN 978–1–4677–3269–7 (trade hard cover : alk. paper)
    ISBN 978–1–4677–4627–4 (eBook)
    [1. Violence—Fiction. 2. Gangs—Fiction.] I. Title.
PZ7.N4377478Kn 2014
[Fic]—dc23   2013036855

Manufactured in the United States of America
1 – BP – 7/15/14

For Carrie Dietz

"You've got to destroy a few lives on the way to where you want to get."
—Joe Frank, radio artist

PROLOGUE

It came out of nowhere.

The sound of Nikes charging across asphalt—
the bounce of baby fat in the black kid's face—
the meat of his fist smashing into a random stranger's jaw—
I heard the *SMACK!* from where I was standing.

Through my lens, I saw the stranger's cigarette fly out of frame, his eyes rolling back into his head—

And then he just fell.

Hard.

The guy's head bounced off the sidewalk with a *thunk* as the boy yelled "Knockout!" His friends rushed in and jumped all over him like he'd just scored the game-winning touchdown.

I stared at the man on the ground with my camera, his eyes gazing at the sky, blood trickling from his mouth. He looked like a character in a movie.

But this was real. It was on my screen. But it was real.

To the boys, it was just a game. Some called it One Hit or Quit, most just called it the Knockout Game. One kid, an eighth-grader with a crooked smile and ketchup stains on his school uniform, noticed the man's eyes were still open. He grinned at me, the white girl with the camera, and jumped on the man's head like it was a balloon that needed popping.

The Knockout King would be proud.

1

(months earlier)

"Pain is a gift," Mom whispered.

There was a ringing in my ears; my face burned like someone had just smacked me. But it was only her words that stung. She was going on and on—about how we were leaving Dad, about how we were moving to St. Louis, and how we were going to leave everything behind to start over, just the two of us.

I felt sick.

We were sitting by the overgrown pool at our house in Little Rock. I tried to focus on the ripples in the water, but the wind was kicking up and my eyes were getting wet.

"Things will get better, Erica," she told me, trying to make it hurt less. I didn't believe her.

"It's not your fault," she said, but I knew somehow it probably was. It's been my fault a lot lately.

I leaned over the edge of the pool until I dropped straight into the deep end. I didn't care that I was wearing clothes. I let myself sink to the bottom and watched the surface bob and weave. I could see Mom up there, distorted and all bent out of shape. She was yelling at me until Dad came out. They started fighting again.

Fuck 'em. The water was freezing, but I could stay down here forever. The cold stung for a few seconds, then I felt the pain slowly floating floating away. Who needed it? The numbness came and it felt good to be underwater where everything was blue and quiet and I didn't have to feel anything anymore . . .

If pain was a gift, then it sucked ass.

2

Right before I was cast into exile, Dad gave me one of those mini HD video cameras for my birthday. I guess he felt guilty for splitting up the family.

"You always liked movies," he said, searching for a way in. "I thought . . . maybe you could make your own. Maybe send me some about St. Louis." He gazed at me with those gray-blue eyes of his, hoping it would help get me on his side. The camera looked tiny, engulfed in his thick fingers.

"Why don't you just come and see it for yourself," I shot back.

He winced, brushing his rough reddish hair off his forehead. "I will, Erica. When you and your mom are settled . . ." His voice trailed off and I knew it wasn't going to happen.

He tried to smile, something I hadn't seen him do for a while. He pressed the camera into my hands and neither of us knew what to say. I spotted my name and phone number engraved into the bottom of it, next to a little heart. He was a bail bondsman who was used to dealing with drug addicts, liars, and thieves. He was not used to saying good-bye to his daughter.

I wanted to smash that camera into a thousand pieces. But I took it and turned on him without a hug, running straight to the car, where Mom was already gunning the engine.

***

The drive took seven hours. Mom didn't say much, just let the wind howl through the windows as if it would blow away the past. Normally, her hair was tied back tight in a bun; now she let it fly wild. Her pale blue eyes were fixed on the horizon, searching for something. Maybe a new beginning.

Through my new camera, I watched the Midwest rush by, but refused to record anything because that's what Dad would've wanted. The camera had one of those flip viewfinders so you could point the camera at yourself and see what you were filming.

I didn't like what I saw.

"This thing makes me look fat," I said to myself.

"You look like a real girl," answered Mom.

I turned the camera off. "A real fat girl, you mean."

"No, a *real* girl. Not some skinny, anorexic home wrecker—" she caught herself, and didn't say anything more.

She was all tensed up, so I rested my head against the window and stared at myself in the side view mirror. I'm big for my age I guess, but that wasn't the thing that ruined my freshman year.

It was the red hair. In grade school, it was cute. Got called leprechaun, the usual little-kid crap. But by my freshman year when I really hit puberty, I blew up and everything got bigger—my butt, my breasts. I tried dying my hair but the red made every color muddy, so I just cut it short and took to wearing hoodies and baggie clothes—mostly to piss Dad off once it was clear things were coming to an end.

It's not like anyone was ever going to ask me out or anything.

***

When we finally reached St. Louis, we had to go downtown to pick up the key to our place. We had to drive by the only thing I remembered about the city, its one real tourist attraction: the Gateway Arch. A couple years ago, we drove here just to go up in that thing. It was Dad's idea of a weekend getaway. He talked the whole way out about having gone up there when he was a kid and how you could see forever out of those tiny windows. Told the whole history of how it was built and this crazy elevator system they had that worked like a Ferris wheel and how once you got up there, it felt like there was no way this thing should be standing.

He'd planned it so we'd arrive just before sunset because that was the perfect moment—Magic Hour. But by the time we got there, we found out the thing was closed due to renovations. Mom was pissed he hadn't checked online. We had a silent dinner, then they decided to head all the way home rather than spend the night in a hotel.

That was the last trip we took together.

"We could go up in the Arch," I said as we drove by it now.

She didn't even look at it.

We stood in front of our new "home."

"Wow, a brick house," I said. If there's one thing I knew about St. Louis, it's that everything was made out of bricks. Every house was brick. Even some of the streets were brick.

"Matches your hair," she said. A joke.

If the house didn't look abandoned, I might have laughed.

Our area was called Tower Grove. Most of it was filled with these stately old buildings and majestic parks filled with grand old trees. It's just that our street looked like it had missed the parade.

"Do we really have to stay here?" I asked, hoping we could upgrade.

"It was cheap. Right now, that's important."

We were right in the middle of the city, but you couldn't tell by standing on this block. A lot of the houses had been torn down and the wild grass had taken over the empty lots around it again. Some of the other houses that remained were boarded up, standing alone like random tombstones in an abandoned cemetery.

"Can't Dad pay more? Doesn't he owe us?"

She nodded. "Problem is, he owes the IRS more. If he hadn't . . . spent it, believe me, we wouldn't be staying here."

By "spent," she meant gambled away. And not just on football games. I guessed home wreckers too.

We didn't even get the whole house. It was divided up, so we were crammed up in the attic rooms. When we got inside, it smelled musty, like an old museum.

We dragged our stuff inside, piled up the boxes and ate

some OK Chinese food. After I set up the blow-up mattress, I locked myself into the extra bedroom and listened to Mom pacing the floor until I fell asleep.

Welcome to St. Louis.

3

It was October. The air was harsh, the streets littered with orange leaves piling up in the gutters. I'd missed the first five weeks of school. From the outside, Truman High looked like one of those Ivy League places—brick towers and stone columns, green grass and big knotty trees surrounding it. Inside had a warm glow to it, the sound of students bouncing off the wood floors and through its creaky hallways.

The metal detector should've been a warning, though.

"Hey, Red!" some girl hissed at me as she passed through security. She gave me a look that said *Good luck with that*—"that" being my whole appearance. She raised her hands in the air and turned around for the security guard. "Ain't you gonna frisk me?" she asked him. The guard ignored her like he'd heard that every morning of his life.

The school was almost all black kids. So not only did my red hair stand out, I felt I was the freak show coming to town. And that was before I had to put on that dumb school uniform. I refused to wear the dress, but the tan pants and white shirt didn't do me any favors.

The metal detector beeped and I had to stand there in front of everyone spread-eagled while that tired old security guy waved his wand over me. It beeped when he passed it over my butt several times. He raised his eyebrows, and I reached into my back pocket where my phone was.

"Can't use your phone in school," he said.

"It's my first day," I pleaded. "My mom might need to call me."

"No calls," he said. "That's the rule. Make sure it's off or we'll confiscate it."

"Can I just call my mom to tell her I made it?"

He gave me a look like he was ready to take it right there.

"It's alright," said a sharply dressed man standing in the middle of the hallway. He acted like he owned the place—dark-skinned, shaved head, goatee. He smiled and shook my hand. "A new face. Welcome to Truman. I'm Principal Evans. Miss . . . ?" He waited for me to answer.

"Asher. Erica."

"Oh, yes," he said, like he'd been warned. He looked me over, still holding my hand. I could see him calculating in his head as to whether I would be trouble or not. He made up his mind quickly. "Erica. You'll have to play some catch-up here. We've already been in session five weeks now."

"I know. It wasn't my fault," I said, looking at the floor.

"Nobody said it was," he answered. "I'd like you to go see Mr. Jamison during your free period. He'll give you the low-down on what to expect here. Me, I'll tell you what I tell everyone here: *Success onto you.* Reach high, respect yourself, and respect the other students, and we'll get on just fine."

He told me where my assigned homeroom was and on the way, I nearly ran into a big white giant of a man, standing in the middle of a traffic jam of students. He reminded me of a guard post—towering over everyone else, and had a wall eye which gave him the appearance of looking at two things at once. He had one big eye trained on me, while his other scanned the hallway for trouble. The ID card around his neck said *Mr. Jamison*.

He knew who I was. "I'll be seeing you later," he barked.

I sat in homeroom, trying to block out all the kids' stares. There was one other white girl in class, but she ignored me for some reason. The teacher pointed to the one empty seat and I thought she said, "There's your destiny." Then I realized she'd said, "There, next to Destiny," who was a big girl herself with chestnut skin and a tiny Band-Aid over one eyebrow, like a boxer. She rolled her eyes when she saw me coming her way. When I sat down, she put her hands over my head like she was feeling for heat. She whispered to her friends, "Ooh, this girl on fire!"

Funny.

***

A couple hours later, I sat in Mr. Jamison's office. It was immaculate—everything in its place, even his perfect crew cut. On his wall was a poster for something called "the Matrix." It wasn't a movie poster. It showed the different levels of discipline here at the school.

He leaned back in his chair; he was going to tell me a story. "When I came here three years ago, this school was a nightmare. In fact, it was the worst school in the city." He pointed to a framed newspaper clipping on the wall that said so. "The building was falling apart too—bad lighting and plumbing, overcrowded classrooms, and the bathrooms—they were a no-man's-land. Kids were getting bladder infections because they refused go in there for fear of getting jumped." He leaned forward and smacked a fly that happened to have landed on his desk. "That was before I was brought in." He picked up the dead fly and dropped it in the trash, then cleaned his hands with hand sanitizer. "I'm what you might call the *bad cop*—though Principal Evans doesn't like the idea of having cops stationed here."

"*Are* you a cop?" I asked.

He trained one eye on me while the other seemed to wander away. "I'm a specialist. The Discipline Specialist. And hopefully, this'll be the last conversation we'll have. If you find yourself sitting in this chair again, it'll mean you are one step away from being sent to one of the alternative schools."

I figured *alternative* did not mean groovy liberal arts school.

He was looking over my records from Little Rock. He noticed my grades had dropped a lot in the last two years, so I decided to cut him off. "My parents are getting divorced," I said, hoping it would explain everything.

He grunted. "This school is filled with single-parent kids," he said, making clear that was not an excuse. His one eye zeroed in on me. "So what's your story then?"

"Um . . ."

He was checking out my red hair. "You'll stand out here, but I'm guessing you already figured that one out. If you get bullied, you can see Alice Lee, next door. She's the art teacher, but because we cut so much of the art programs, she's now also the Safe Haven coordinator. She's the good cop. You get picked on, you see her."

He stood up suddenly, his fists leaning on the table. "But if you act out or get into fights with the other girls, you'll be mine. You act up in this neighborhood, I'll find you. You break the law outside of that, you'll *wish* you had me to deal with. Consider yourself warned," he said.

I nodded. I already didn't want to see him again.

***

We had art once a week. That was the first time I met Mrs. Lee. She was always on the move, her long graying hair floating behind her, her big round glasses making her eyes appear like an owl's—bright and laser-focused. But she was no school marm. There was an edge to her. She wore funky self-painted T-shirts with eyes or ears and sometimes mouths on them. She was all about the senses.

She already had her class divided into groups. I quickly found myself standing alone. Three white kids huddled in one corner around their art supplies. I walked over, but they closed ranks and made sure to ignore me. The black kids made up the rest of the groups and I knew I wasn't joining them.

That one black girl from my homeroom, Destiny Jones, had untied her hair and it kind of frizzed out. I couldn't help but gawk. She gave me all kinds of attitude just because I was looking at her. "You got something to say?"

"No."

"Well maybe you should take a picture. It'll last longer."

They busted up like that was the first time someone ever

said that. I felt I needed to say something back, so I chose "Why don't you?" as my official awesome comeback.

She gave me the stink eye and when Mrs. Lee wasn't looking, pulled out her phone and snapped a picture of me. "That's going on my Facebook page," she said all snarky, posting it right there. "There's a red giant in my class . . ." she said as she typed.

I looked to Mrs. Lee, who finally caught on and followed my eyes back to Destiny and her phone. "You know the rules: no phones in class. Give it."

She confiscated the phone and took it back to her desk.

Destiny shook her head at me. "You are so dead."

***

And it was like that for the next couple weeks. Nobody talked to me unless they were talking *at* me. Seemed as if everyone had grown up together in the Tower Grove area and as the official outsider, I was pretty much a target.

The only blond-haired boy in school saw me eating alone one day and stopped to talk. It was only when I saw his friends cracking up behind him that I understood he wasn't really asking me out to the upcoming Halloween dance.

Keep your eyes on the ground and don't talk to anyone became my new motto.

***

Mrs. Lee noticed I wasn't drawing in art class. She dropped a book on my desk. "Maybe your thing isn't drawing but some other medium."

The book was called *Video Art*. On the cover was a huge lens with an eye on it staring straight at me.

"So if you aren't going to make art today, at least you can *read* about some other forms. Maybe it'll inspire you." She tapped her finger on the cover of the book.

She headed back to the others and I put my head on my desk to close my eyes. I used to draw all the time. I'd spend days drawing these humongous *Where's Waldo*-like murals—you know, the ones so packed with people and places that you could just disappear into it. I even won a school art contest once. But then my family started to crash. One day, I just stared at that paper and nothing came out. It's been like that ever since.

I cracked open the book. The first picture I saw was of John Lennon. There was a picture of him and next to it was a picture of his butt! I shut the book quick. Mrs. Lee gave me a sly look.

After a minute, I opened it up again. I noticed a DVD inside the book cover. I don't know why but when Mrs. Lee turned away, I shoved the book into my backpack.

***

After school, Mom and I barely saw each other because the only shift she could get in her new job was the night shift. I felt like I was basically living alone and she was just dropping by for visits. To make up for it, she made me keep the Skype connection open on my computer so she could check in on me, and I could see her in the lab where she worked. That was the only way she'd do it. And even though I was fifteen, she made me connect at 10 p.m. when I was supposed to go to bed, just so she could watch me brush my teeth and hit the lights. I'd fall asleep to the glow of the computer, my mom staring into a microscope in an empty room on the other side.

***

My face time with Mom every day was a quick breakfast when she came home and before I caught the bus to school. And then an early dinner, around 4:30, when the reverse happened. We tried to have normal conversations but it always started with *So what's going on at school today?* or ended with *How was school today?* And when she caught on that school was a nightmare, she stopped asking, which left nothing for us to talk about.

I knew she felt the same way about her job, so I tried to be good. She worked for a genetics lab, mostly staring through a microscope all night, searching for faulty chromosomes (so couples would know who was coming up short in the baby making department, I guess). She dreamed of doing cancer research, but this is what she got stuck with for now.

***

The night I watched the DVD I took from art class changed everything. The John Lennon stuff was something he did with his wife Yoko. One video was an hour of him just smiling. It seemed stupid at first, but something about having John gaze at you for so long got under my skin. Another film, they shot over three hundred people's butts and that film was shown in museums! I didn't know you could do that kind of thing.

The DVD had all kinds of video pieces from the seventies

and eighties up until YouTube. Then I got it. Capturing everyday life and showing it in unusual ways—that was performance art.

I dug my video camera out of a box but I wasn't sure what to shoot. I liked holding it, though. It was all shiny and new and empty—a virgin waiting for something to happen. OK, maybe that's a bit dramatic, but I could picture the empty flash card in there, inviting me to put something on it. I remembered having that feeling every time I grabbed a blank piece of paper and how happy it made me after I covered every inch of that whiteness with something I'd created. It was a record of what I saw and how I saw it.

Now I just needed something to shoot.

4

I was sitting on the back stoop after a bad day at school, when I spotted a huge anthill in the dirt next to the stairs. Something about them made me angry all of a sudden. There were hundreds of them going about their business, day in and day out, doing their jobs, back and forth, back and forth. They never complained, never fell out of line. I wanted to step on them for it. I don't know why; it was just some primal thing, I guess. Put them out of their misery.

I stomped on a few and watched the panic set in. Suddenly, it was each ant for itself, struggling to flee the pandemonium. I'd upset the natural order.

It felt good.

It reminded me of one of those old monster movies. Only I was Godzilla.

I got out my camera again, and this time, I knew what to do. Watching those art vids on the DVD gave me ideas. So I began shooting a monster movie with me as Godzilla and the ants as the ones who got in the way. Godzilla stomped out all the ants, even the ones trying to escape. It was horrific and because my macro mode made it look cool, in super slo-mo, it was also kind of poetic.

I cut it together on my computer to some Japanese soundtrack remix I downloaded. It came out *good*. So I wanted to do some more. I started shooting a lot of weird stuff I saw around the neighborhood, just wandering around the overgrown lots and abandoned houses. I'd record them and make up stories about who lived there and what happened to them: *Lost his job and life savings. Robbed a bank and is on the run. Drug dealer/crack house raided by the cops. Family one day mysteriously disappeare*d . . . *dead and buried?* More likely is they just moved to the burbs like everyone else and nobody ever replaced them. It was as if somebody stomped on a few St. Louis ants, so the rest scattered.

During lunch break one day at school, I noticed that people behaved a lot like ants too—they were just bigger and wore clothes. We stood in line for food, shuffled back and forth to class, accepted our place in the clique order of things.

Every once in a while, someone broke free—dressed differently, skipped class, acted out against the Queen Bees. They'd get stomped for it—by teachers, school cops, bullies. And for those few moments, chaos broke free—students stopped what they were doing and refused to look away. They couldn't help it.

My camera had a good optical zoom, so I just started filming all this—especially the ones breaking the rules. Hiding behind my camera, I'd see all kinds of things. A couple making out by their lockers. A girl being hassled by Mr. Jamison for dressing too racy. The white kids trying to act black. Black kids crunking in the parking lot. Gay boys and goths getting in each other's faces. Nerds texting when they weren't supposed to. Staff cruising the halls looking for trouble. . . .

"What do you think you're doing?"

I panned my camera to the oversized head of Mr. Jamison, who was staring me down. His one crooked eye was checking out my camera.

"I'm just . . . filming."

"You can't just go around filming people here without their knowledge."

I blinked. "It's just . . . a class project. For Mrs. Lee. I'm not going to upload it or anything. I can stop. If you want."

He eyed me suspiciously. At least I think he did.

"If I see that camera again, I'll take it."

I nodded, put it away in my backpack.

Ant. Get back in line.

***

That Destiny Jones watched this go down and saw a way to get even for her phone. When she caught me filming one of her friends at lunch, she walked by and just snatched the camera out of my hands. She turned the camera on me.

"You know the rules: no cameras in school!" she said.

"Give it back." I tried to act calm.

"Hey, it took me three days to get *my* phone back," she said. "I think I can make some videos of my own for a few days."

"Give it back," I said again.

"Or what? You can't tell Mrs. Lee; she'll keep it."

"I said—"

She cut me off. "Uh, oh, she getting mad. She gonna turn into a one hitter-quitter!"

Her friends all thought that was funny. One of them piped in. "I wouldn't fight her if I was you. D here's a real boxer. She even took out one of them female cops in the ring at the Rec Center last week."

I didn't want to fight. I never hit anybody and I wasn't about to start now. I just wanted my camera back.

Destiny stepped up for a close-up. "Oh, I can see your veins popping with this zoom—"

I grabbed at the camera before she could finish her sentence. Next thing I knew, we were rolling on the ground, holding onto that thing like it was made of gold. Students came running, yelling "Fight!" and suddenly it was a scene from some jailhouse movie. I grabbed at her hair; she was trying to rip off my shirt. The kids loved it, but I didn't care. That camera was mine—

A pair of hands suddenly reached down and grabbed us both by the shoulder and pulled us up like we were dolls. Both hands belonged to Mr. Jamison.

Shit.

"You were warned," he said.

5

Destiny sat there glaring at me. I kept my eyes on Mr. Jamison, who was checking out my camera. "Erica, didn't we just talk about filming at school?" Destiny made a little satisfied sound.

"I . . ." I didn't want to see my camera taken away. "My dad gave that to me after we moved away. Then *she* took it from me." I didn't go into details, but I gave him a look that said it was my last memory of home.

He saw the inscription on the bottom and I saw a flicker of recognition in his eyes. Maybe he was a dad too. He turned his attention to Destiny. "I believe I was quite clear with you the last time you were here. You are now at level six. You know what that means?"

My eyes glanced up at the Matrix on the wall. LEVEL 6: *EXPULSION.*

Her face kind of dropped. I could see she hadn't thought it through. "But—"

Mr. Jamison was having none of it. "You had plenty of warnings. You had a copy of the discipline matrix. I had discussed it with you and your mother. What part of that wasn't clear?"

She was speechless. Her toughness vanished. I could see she didn't want to go.

"But—" she had no words.

"I'll be calling your mother to pick you up. You are to report to Grant Remedial after a six-day suspension. I'm going to have one of the secretaries clean out your locker and you'll wait here until you're picked up."

Destiny looked helpless as she fought back her tears. She was all talk and bluff before. Now she just seemed lost.

"It was my fault, Mr. Jamison," I found myself saying. I don't know why. I should have been happy to see her crash and burn, but there was something about her . . .

"*What?*" asked Jamison. He smelled a rat and turned to Destiny. "Is that true?"

Destiny looked at me and her eyes softened. "Yeah. What she said."

Jamison leaned back in his chair, staring at us both at the same time, one eye on each of us. "Do tell."

I swallowed. "Well, I guess I was filming her and—"

"No," Jamison interrupted. "I want to *her* tell it."

A fraction of a second of panic flashed in Destiny's eyes before I could see the actor in her take over. There's was a little shrug that said *sorry, this was your idea* before she launched into her story.

"Yeah . . . she was filming me and making all kinds of cracks about us, trying to get me all riled up on camera. She got in my face and I asked her to stop, but she wouldn't. I been trying to be nice to her with her being new and all, but she didn't want to be hanging with us none."

Mr. Jamison seemed amused by this. "And why do you think that was?"

She glared at me for a split second. "Maybe 'cause I'm black?"

I rolled my eyes. "What?"

"She may of called me the N-word, I'm not sure—"

I jumped up. "That's a lie!"

Destiny kind of cowered. "See? She's trying to hit me again—"

"Alright, alright, that's enough! Sit down, Erica," he said.

"But—"

His eye drilled into my head. "Sit. *Down*."

I sat.

He shook his head. "I don't even want to deal with you two right now. I'm calling both of your mothers—"

"What?" I protested. "It wasn't my fault!"

He cocked his head. "I thought you said it *was*?"

I stared at Destiny and shot her a message: *You owe me*. "I guess," I said.

"Detention, after school, for the next two days. The janitors are going to take a break. I hope you two like mopping."

"Is that even . . . legal?" I asked.

He rose up; he'd had enough. "Maybe you'd like to call your *lawyer*."

I backed off. "No, mopping sounds good."

***

Jamison was going to hold on to my camera for three days. Me and Destiny sat on the benches in the hallway waiting for our moms to pick us up. Mine would be pissed being woken up halfway through her sleep. I was trying to think of what to say when I saw Destiny staring at me.

"Why you do that for me?" she asked.

I shrugged. "Felt sorry for you, I guess."

She kind of laughed. "*You?* Felt sorry for *me?*"

Did I really have to say it? "You were about to cry—"

"I was not," she said, defiantly.

I rolled my eyes. Maybe I should've let her take the fall and have one less person making fun of me. But she quickly changed her tune.

"Thanks," she said quietly, surprising me for a second time.

I glanced up at her and her defiance was gone.

"I guess I owe you," she said.

"You think?"

Now she smiled. "I will try not to take your camera anymore."

"Wow. Thanks," I said, trying not to be too sarcastic. Then I thought some more about the session we just came out of. "Really? The N-word?"

She shrugged. "I figured it'd get a rise out of you. That was the only way to make it real. Sorry."

I didn't like being accused of being racist, but she was right. It had been my idea, and she sold it.

"Maybe we should take our act on the road," I said. She kind of smirked, but that was it. We sat there in silence till our moms came to get us. When my mom saw me in my ripped shirt and then saw Destiny with her defenses up again, I think she felt more sorry for me than mad.

***

The next day after school, we were mopping. It sucked. A lot. Destiny seemed to know what she was doing, and she gave me a few tips like I should wring all the water out first then it wouldn't be so damn heavy. I asked her how she knew that and she said her mom did custodial work, and she helped out on weekends.

She showed me the best way to cover a long hallway, and we split up. Every time we passed each other, I gave her a look, expecting her to say something, but she never did.

The afternoon after the mop marathon, Destiny seemed kind of down in the dumps and still not saying much. We were vacuuming in the library where the computers were. Mr. Jamison was in his office and there hadn't been a librarian in this room for two years. Destiny was watching me moving furniture around.

"I don't like your name," she said.

Did she want a fight? "What?"

She shrugged. "I mean, no offense, but Erica don't feel right for you."

"Like Destiny's a real name."

"Hey, mine fits my personality. Erica . . . don't match you," she said, matter-of-factly. "You need a nickname."

I warned her. "Don't even think about calling me Red."

"Too obvious." Something caught her eye behind me and she suddenly grinned. "Think I'm gonna call you *Fish* from now on."

I turned around and saw a giant poster of *Nemo* staring out from a fish tank.

Gee, thanks.

"I been watching you ever since you came to Truman. All you do is sit there and look at people, filming them and what not. It's like that camera's your tank and you just watching everyone pass you by. And with that hair, you the same color as Nemo. *Fish*. Yeah, that's what you are."

"Wow. That's . . . deep . . ." I looked behind her and saw Oprah in one of those READ posters. " . . . Oprah."

She turned around and got the joke. "There's only one Oprah. And now, there's only one person called Fish." She seemed pleased with herself.

It was not exactly a good name for a girl, but she was talking to me as if we were just hanging out together after school.

"Hey, you wanna see something?" I asked.

She looked at me kind of funny, wondering what I could possibly want to show her.

I took a DVD I burned out of my backpack and held it in my hands, unsure. "It's a little movie I made. From all the stuff I been shooting."

She looked around. "Beats vacuuming, I guess."

It was just a short video about how school was really just one big ant pile. I intercut all that footage I'd shot at Truman together with the ant stuff from earlier and even threw in Jamison's mug for effect, all to some Russian marching music I'd found online. I turned off all the treble, cranked the bass, and made it into something bizarre and underwater-like.

Then she said something I'll never forget: "Whoa." And the look on her face told me she was kinda blown away by it. She thought it was strange and funny and . . . kinda beautiful.

She asked to see it a couple more times, then sat there staring at the blank screen.

"When you getting your camera back?" she asked.

"Tomorrow, I guess."

She nodded like she had a plan. "Maybe I could show you something too."

6

She didn't say anything more after that, only had a little grin on her face when I saw her in homeroom the next morning. I went to go talk to her before we sat down in our seats, but she turned back to her friends and I knew she had to pretend me and her were still enemies.

It kind of hurt, but I understood.

After school, I collected my camera and found Destiny waiting for me behind the cafeteria by the trash cans. I felt a little funny about what she might be showing me back there, but all she said was, "Follow me, Fish."

So I did.

We walked through Tower Grove, heading toward Grand Avenue. She made me walk a few feet behind her just in case one of her friends saw us.

"Where we going?" I asked.

"You'll see," she answered.

"Yeah, but—"

She stopped, squinting her eyes at me. "That thing, with

you stepping on the ants, being all Godzilla and shit, I get it. It's like a, how you call it—a metaphor, right? You wanna be in control; that's what your video is about, yeah?"

I hadn't thought about it like that. "I guess so."

"Well, then you'll fit right in." She started walking again.

We had been walking for almost half an hour, through parks and streets, even cutting through some alleys. She was looking for somebody, but didn't say who. We came out into a drugstore parking lot, when she suddenly stopped like she'd just seen a rare bird or something.

She pointed. "There."

I spotted a group of middle schoolers, still dressed in their school uniforms. Red shirts, tan pants, white shoes. "Tokers," she said.

I didn't know what that meant, but she told me I should get my camera out. "You want me to record them?"

These boys looked big for their age—sweaty, husky thirteen-year-olds—full of energy and always pushing each other around like boys do. Most of them were black. But there were a couple of Hispanic wannabes too. They were all trying to act older, arguing and pointing at people from behind a blue Prius.

"Are they some kind of a gang?" I joked.

"*Please*, girl. Just do that thing you do with your camera. It'll be better than those ants of yours."

She nudged me closer and I could hear them arguing:

"Him."

"Who?"

"Dat guy over there. The white dude with the hat."

"That old fool? I thought we didn't do old heads?"

I remember glancing at Destiny and then I whispered, "What are we doing?"

All she said was, "You'll see. Start filming."

I shrugged. Recording a bunch of middle schoolers arguing? Yeah, it was kinda funny, I guess. But I expected more. I turned my camera on and zoomed in anyway.

"You're gonna make this look *good*, right?" she whispered back, like she didn't want to scare them off. "I mean, you should see the shit Prince tries to shoot with his dumb phone cam, all shaky and shit. Sometimes, he gets so caught up in it, he don't even see what he's shooting, and all you get is the street. You got one of them shaky cam things on there, the one that smoothes it all out if you have to run?"

"Why would we be running?" I asked.

"Oh you know, they just playing games on people—pranks. Sometimes you gotta take off pretty quick, but that's usually the funniest part. That shit you can put on your Facebook page and get tons of views with. That's how you make friends."

"I don't have a Facebook page."

She looked at me like I had said *I don't have a TV.* And I wasn't about to say that either.

She whipped out her phone. "We'll see about that. Keep filming."

She started tapping away at her phone.

"I thought Facebook was uncool," I said.

She smirked. "All the better for this kinda thing."

"But what am I doing?"

"Just follow their lead," she said. "Do this right and you'll get on his good side. Got it?"

"Who?"

"What?" she said.

"Who are you talking about?" I said back.

"The Knockout King, who else?"

That was the first I heard of the Knockout King. "What is that, a boxer?" I asked.

That was funny to her. "You'll see, Fish," she said. "These guys are cool. This'll be better than reality TV."

I watched the boys arguing over the people they were spying on. One said he didn't like that guy's shirt; another said the dude reminded him of some guy on TV. Another said that guy looked like a wuss. They might as well be fighting over *Yu-Gi-Oh!* cards.

Then one of them, a kid taller than me with nappy hair with a comb sticking out of the back, noticed me and my camera and stood up like I was a threat to him. "Whaddaya think you doin'?" he asked, his hand balled up into a fist.

"Shut up, C-Jay. She's with me," said Destiny without even looking up from her phone.

He seemed confused. "Why you bring a white girl here?"

Now she looked up. "That's TKO business and none of yours. Just pretend she ain't here."

C-Jay scowled and went back to his group. Pretty soon they were arguing again, but C-Jay kept an eye out on me.

"What's TKO?" I asked.

"It's our little club we started at the Rec Center. We sometimes take boxing lessons there."

When she saw me looking puzzled, she added, "TKO. Technical Knock Out. *Boom!*" She threw a jab at me and laughed when I flinched. "You should try it some time; you got the size."

"I don't fight."

She raised an eyebrow. "That's not how I heard it." Then I remembered our little bout at school.

Destiny started going on about the Tokers, how they were always trying to impress the King. I asked her why she called them Tokers. They didn't seem like potheads to me.

"Toker. TKO member. They get high on the hit too, I guess," she joked, raising her fist. "And in between, they sit around bored with the munchies."

Still, I had no idea why a bunch of middle schoolers were scoping out people walking down the street on a Friday afternoon. I didn't see any water balloons or anything. I remember wondering what were they going to do—jump out and scare them?

When they zeroed in on someone, I quickly learned. Through my viewfinder, I followed their pointed fingers to their target. He was some kitchen worker at the pizza place across the street taking a smoking break. He was older, looked like he'd been doing that job for a long time. When he lit his cigarette, I noticed flour on his hands and face, probably from rolling pizza dough.

I panned back and the boys were all huddled together. Finally, C-Jay stood up and began walking across the road. He had this kind of looping walk, and he still had his baby fat which made him look like a giant baby. I thought he was going to steal that guy's wallet or something. I zoomed in closer. Then suddenly he was running full speed at the guy and—

I didn't see it coming. I almost dropped the camera when he raised his fist. "He's gonna hit that guy . . . " I thought.

Destiny grabbed my camera and brought it back to my eye.

"You're gonna miss the best part—"

I zoomed in right as C-Jay's fist sailed through the air and I could hear the *smack!* from here. A puff of flour lingered in the air and the guy just dropped like a mannequin that fell to pieces. When I heard that clunk of his head bouncing off the sidewalk, I almost puked.

"Knockout!" the boys yelled as they raced across the street. Destiny pushed me along right beside them, and I went on autopilot as I captured them doing their end zone dance and high-fiving each other. Out of the corner of my eye, I saw some passersby quickly move away like nothing happened.

I felt dizzy and out of focus, like I'd been hit.

"Yo, white girl," one of 'em said. I guess that'd be me. "Take our picture for the Knockout King!" They posed by the body like it was some game trophy and I recorded them. My stomach tightened; I wanted to leave. Finally, satisfied they'd completed their mission, the boys walked off, leaving me staring at a smoking cigarette butt on the ground next to my feet.

"Get a close-up," Destiny whispered in my ear and next thing I knew, the camera pushed in on the man's face. He was still breathing. Barely.

There was something strange about looking at him so close up. It was like when you pass a car wreck and you don't want to stare, but you can't turn away either. You're caught staring even if you don't want to. And I guess I was staring for too long because I didn't notice Destiny tugging on my arm.

"Hey, Fish, you got your shot, now let's get outta here." Destiny playfully slapped me in the back of the head. "He'll be OK; he's just napping. Come on."

She pulled me along, but I kept glancing back over my

shoulder as we caught up to the others. Some lady was kneeling next to the man, pleading into her cell phone, her face full of panic.

Nobody came after us.

It was a beautiful fall day—the bright white sun, a flawless blue sky. But all I could see in my mind was the red blood dripping from the man's mouth.

Destiny beamed, all teeth, warming her face in the sun. She has that dark hazelnut skin that glows when the light hits it. The long shadows of the boys danced ahead of us on the sidewalk.

"That was crazy, right?" she asked. I could feel her eyes on me even if I kept mine glued to my viewfinder.

"Yeah," I sputtered, out of breath. I'd forgotten to breathe after seeing that man's face. The oxygen flooded back into my head, little spots floating in my eyes.

"You OK?" she laughed.

I wasn't sure. All my senses were hyperawake. Goose bumps on my forearms, the hair rising on the back of my neck. Everything felt brighter, more sharp. I even noticed my hand hurt from holding the camera too tight.

"You probably got some good shit, right, Fish? Man, C-Jay sure connected with that one! I didn't think he'd come through, but that boy got *pop!*" she yelled at the crew of middle schoolers.

I turned my camera back on them. They were so happy now, jumping around and reliving the moment. Before they'd been regular boys, bored and arguing with each other. But now . . .

"That was crazy," I said out loud again, to no one.

7

Walking home that day was the first time I ever really noticed the Eyez.

Some graffiti artist had painted strange eyes all around the neighborhood. Some were small, gazing at you from a fire hydrant or mailbox. Others were big, staring at you from the side of a building or on a tree. They kinda blended in, so I'd never paid them any mind. But today, they seemed to be watching me. Every block that I passed, those eyez were popping out to me. *Did someone just put them up or did I just never notice them before?* It was kind of creepy. I walked faster, kept my eyes on the ground. But even there, I saw a pair staring at me from a crosswalk.

Destiny wanted to come over to my place, but I said something lame like *an artist needs to work alone.* The truth was, watching the footage on my computer made my mind reel. Getting caught up in the action was one thing. Seeing it on your computer was another. Did I really want to make this video?

I'd skipped my 4:30 dinner with Mom routine and said I

had a lot of homework to do. Somehow I let it slip that I was out videotaping with Destiny and she got all excited that I might have a real friend.

Maybe Mom was right because as soon as I went into my room, Destiny texted me. Nobody ever texted me, except Mom when she was checking in. Destiny kept poking me every twenty minutes or so, asking if she could come by. It had been a long time since anybody that wasn't related to me showed an interest.

It felt good.

Eventually, she sent me the password and a link to a Facebook page she'd created for me. It was called Fish Films and was described as "Life Underwater."

Destiny was the only one who friended me. Suddenly, I didn't mind her calling me Fish. It was her special name for me, which meant we had some sort of connection and that she would bring me into her crew. I guess that made us friends.

It said so on my Facebook page.

I minimized the browser and stared at the frozen image of C-Jay's fist flying through the air about to knock this guy out. This was something different, that's for sure. I thought about a quote I read in that book Mrs. Lee gave me where some artist summed up his artistic mission in life: "*Capture something different and people will remember you.*"

People would remember me for this.

It'd take a lot of work with this rough footage of my first Knockout Game. Maybe I could make that my style—out of control mayhem put to some mad rap or punk—raw and on edge. Still, I didn't want her seeing anything until it was memorable. Even if it took all night.

I texted back: *"All gud things cum 2 those who w8."*

It was Friday, so I could stay up all night working on this video. I loaded up on Mom's coffee and dove in.

***

Next thing I knew, the front door was opening. My head was resting on the keyboard. I remembered I was editing, but what was Mom doing home? Did she forget something? Then I noticed a little sliver of daylight creeping across my bed.

Morning.

Shit, was I late for school? I jumped up—then remembered it was Saturday. Whoa. That had never happened before. I guess I had been in the zone. I squinted at my video editor and saw that I had compiled a two-minute video. Outside, Mom shuffled about. It was only a matter of time till she knocked. And then, she'd get all curious. . . .

I somehow caught a second wind and quickly uploaded the video to my Facebook page for Destiny to look at. She was my only friend, so no one else would see it. She could check out this version and then I'd tweak it later. I remembered doing all kinds of crazy stuff with the footage. Mostly playing with that shot of the fist rushing at the guy, over and over, using different filters and speeds and colors. It was almost like a hallucination. I guess staying up all night made me hallucinate, but now I was crashing big time. I sent her a message, even as my eyes began to droop. I hoped she'd like it.

Mom and I usually had breakfast together before she went to bed, but I couldn't keep my eyes open a second longer. My face barely hit the pillow before I was asleep.

***

My head was buzzing. I dreamt I was being chased by bees.

It was my phone.

I leaned over and checked the ID. Only three people ever appeared on that screen.

Destiny. She texted: *"Get up! Check yur FB page."*

I stumbled out of bed over to my computer and tapped the space bar. My Facebook page was still up, but there was no difference.

Then it refreshed. There was a message from Destiny.

And *forty-six* friend requests.

WTF?

I read Destiny's message: "I shared your vid. That was fucking amazing, Fish. You're good, bitch! I got like 50 comments already and I'm sure people will be friending you too. The King LOVED it. He wants to meet with you later today. We're going out for Chinese, so meet us at the Chung King Palace at 4. Damn girl, you a hit!"

I read the comments on her share. They said things like:

"OMFG TKO 4ever!"

"Damn, boy got bang!"

"Knockout King krew rulz!"

Stuff like that.

I loved the ones that talked about how fucking great the video was. Someone said it made them cry it was so funny and so fucking awesome at the same time. Nobody had ever said anything like that about something I'd made.

Watching my movie again was a trip. I had slowed things down, added this weird music and sound effects (you can find pretty much anything online) then speeded it up before key moments—an adrenaline rush. It was like being on drugs. Or at least what I imagine that to feel like.

As I lay in bed, staring at the ceiling, a strange feeling came over me. I felt warm inside, a little fire burning in my stomach.

The only time I could remember feeling like that was about two years ago when I made a drawing for my dad for his fiftieth birthday. He had been in a bad mood all day, angry at himself for getting old, I guess. But when he unwrapped my present; he kept staring at it until his eyes started getting all misty. The drawing showed me, Mom, and him fishing on Lake Maumelle. That was our last good vacation together. He had it framed.

It was a good feeling knowing you could make a person feel something—good or bad, happy or sad. That wasn't art. It was power.

8

When I walked into the Chung King Palace, I spotted the crew right away. They were all gathered around watching something on a smart phone, entranced by some spell that had come over them. Then all of sudden, they cried out at the same time: "KNOCKOUT!"

My video. Between all the hooting and hollering, Destiny noticed me standing in the doorway. She smiled and nodded her head in approval.

A tiny Chihuahua came out from under the table and wandered over to me. I kneeled down and he licked my hand. He was wearing a dog collar that had a gold 314 badge on it.

The dog was taken with my camera, so I did what I always do: I recorded him.

I could see my reflection in his big eyes. He saw his reflection in my lens too. We gawked at each other for about fifteen seconds when I saw a pair of red Jordan high tops come into frame.

"He likes you." The guy's voice was soft, but had a little rasp to it.

I didn't look up. "What's his name?"

He cleared his throat. "Boner."

Now I looked up. The first thing I saw were his fists. Scarred on the knuckles from some ancient fights. But it was the tattoos on them that caught my attention. One said *K.O.* The other had a crown.

"Dude loves bones," he clarified.

I didn't ask him what kind of bones his dog loved. The guy seemed unbelievably tall from down here—lean and wiry but even with his oversized Muhammad Ali shirt, I could tell he had muscles. He looked like a senior in high school, but he stood there like he owned the place.

When he kneeled down to pick up Boner, my breath stopped short. He took one look at me and that's when I saw he had the most piercing green eyes I'd ever seen. I almost didn't notice he was black.

"You're pretty good with that thing, Fish."

"What?"

He smiled. His teeth were as piecing as his eyes. "The camera."

"Oh . . . thanks," I said. Maybe I blushed.

"So why's that one better than my phone cam?" he asked, holding up his smart phone.

I knew this—I'd looked it up when I was figuring out how to work the camera. "Uh, well, it's um, HD and it shoots thirty frames a second, so the images and colors are better, I guess. Brighter. And um . . ."

He kept staring at me in a way that no boy ever did. I wasn't used to it.

"And uh, it doesn't blur when you move it like phone cams

do and its real good in low light."

Those green eyes of his drilled right into me like lasers, and in that few seconds he seemed to know everything about me. I couldn't take it. I looked back down into my camera and started babbling faster.

"It holds about an hour of footage and it's got stereo sound, um, a 12x zoom, all these, like, cool filters and stuff and its own built-in editing software—"

"You got a real name, Fish?" he interrupted.

"Yeah." I was still thinking what to say next about the camera, so I forgot to answer him until I heard him kinda laugh. Duh.

I cleared my throat, "Erica." I was breathing hard, so I tried to slow down and act somewhat human. "But only my mom calls me that. Oh, and my dad too." My focus shifted back to his fists again.

"E-ri-caaa . . ." he rolled it around on his tongue. "Hmm. You probably guessed I'm the Knockout King." He rubbed his right knuckle, then glanced back to see if anyone was listening. The whole crew was staring back.

He relished the attention. Not just theirs, mine too. He leaned in and whispered. "How 'bout you call me Kalvin, and I'll call you Erica?"

"Sure," I said, unsure.

"Just not in front of them, right? They all call me K." He was checking out my red hair, as if he'd never seen anyone with red hair before. He even reached out and gently pulled back my hoodie. His eyes lit up. "Nice."

I almost fell over.

"Don't seem right calling a girl Fish."

I nodded. I was not used to talking to boys. And definitely not black boys, though he could've been a mix. He had a kind of exotic look about him: green eyes, light-skinned, but with those nappy short dreads and full lips, he was definitely at least part black. What else, I didn't dare ask.

"I really dug what you did," he said. "Your video, I mean. That shit was fire. But you still got room to expand your visual vocabulary, ya feel me?" He nudged my shoe.

I did. "I wasn't even finished. I just uploaded it for Destiny to see is all. I didn't think anyone else would watch it. She didn't even tell me what I was gonna be shooting, so it was kind of all on the fly. I can do better."

He nodded, impressed. "Good. I like a girl who thinks she can do better. Some of these clowns think just because you do something once makes you king of the world. They don't realize someone's always gonna be bucking for your spot. To keep on top, you gotta keep pushing, keep trying to surprise 'em, ya know?"

I knew.

"You'll be better prepared next time. Then we'll see what you can really do." He stood up and offered me his hand.

Next time? I thought.

His hand engulfed mine. It was all rough on the outside; he'd seen battles. But his inside palm was soft. He pulled me up and his height caught me by surprise. He seemed about two feet taller than me.

He was used to it. "Why don't you come and have some egg rolls with us?"

I turned off my camera and gazed at the table. Everyone was watching us. Destiny looked a little unsure.

"OK," I answered.

He walked back to the table. I followed. I kept waiting for the other shoe to drop, the one where they all make fun of me. All the boys stared at me and I noticed I was the only white person there.

One of them, a skinny runt with cornrows trying to act bigger than he was, took offense. "How come you letting this white girl sit with us?"

Everyone froze. Kalvin didn't say anything. Instead, this Latino guy who was dressed like a rapper in a shiny purple track suit, hauled off and slapped the kid upside the head.

"Tyreese, if you disrespect our guest, you disrespect the King here. You should know better."

Tyreese lowered his head. "Sorry, K," he said. Kalvin looked at him and then gestured toward me.

He shrugged. "Sorry, white girl," he said.

Kalvin busted up, then everyone laughed. "He means well. But he's only twelve and kids can be fuckin' idiots sometimes."

"Especially Ty here," added the Latino guy.

"Now this guy," Kalvin put his hand on the Latino guy's shoulder. "This is Prince Rodriguez, my number two, my main *ese*. He thinks he's black, but don't tell him otherwise. He can't help it if he's a wetback."

Prince didn't mind Kalvin's jab, but he narrowed his eyes at me. He had kind of a mohawk thing going. He acted tough, but even I could tell he was just following K's orders.

"*Que 'onda, Heina?* Your vid was alright, I guess. I don't know why nobody likes mine. This phone has seen things—" Some of the older guys groaned as he held up his purple phone.

"Yeah, your mother's pink stinky!" cracked Tyreese.

"Shorty never learns," said Prince, slapping the kid upside the head again. "Who calls it that—but you know what? You wished you'd seen my mother's pink stinky. Then you'd know where greatness came from, *homes*."

That was wrong on so many levels but nobody questioned it.

Kalvin grinned, put his arm around him. "Prince is his real name too. I think his mom saw that movie *Purple Rain* about twenty times before he was born."

"I never saw it, but my Mom tried to show it to me once," I said.

K tried to suppress a laugh. "You hear that—her moms and you got the same taste!"

Prince rolled his eyes. "Well, she got good taste then, *ese*. Are you kidding? That movie's a classic. A little too gay, but there's no denying—that *chulo* Prince got mad skills."

We sat and ate lo mein and dumplings and fried rice. We had ourselves a party. Kalvin had snuck in some beer and poured some for everyone! I didn't really drink so much. Sometimes my dad offered me a sip of his, but it always tasted too bitter to me. But somehow here, it tasted sweeter.

The King paid for everyone. I liked that. He was taking care of his boys. I don't know where he got his money. I don't remember them stealing from the pizza guy. But everybody was happy, so I just went with it. Destiny kept an eye on me, but seemed kind of quiet.

I noticed the owner watching us. Maybe Kalvin knew him, but I'd think having middle schoolers drinking beer in public would be a bad thing. He wasn't Chinese and he wore these big glasses that made it obvious he was keeping an eye on us. He just stood there behind the counter pretending to work, but I could tell he was just waiting for us to leave.

It was like TKO owned the joint. Sitting at the right hand of the Knockout King was definitely better than sitting home alone or wandering the city by myself.

Tyreese looked at me like he wanted to say something. He was going to ruin it, tell me that it was all a joke, or something. He leaned over to me and said in a tiny voice, "I guess you OK for a girl."

9

It began the next day, Sunday.

Destiny texted me that the crew was hyped up on the video and wanted to play again. "*Fish gotta swim*," she texted. I wasn't sure what she meant.

Then she added, "*K wants u there.*"

I got ready quick.

They wanted to meet over by The Loop, which was a local hot spot. I went down once with Mom—it was packed with too many teens and tourists for her. Seemed like a crazy place to play the Knockout Game.

But that's what made it exciting.

Mom had read in the paper about some attack on Grand Avenue by a group of young hoodlums. They called it a flash mob. "You better be careful, Erica. They say that pizza man might have brain damage from the attack." She sighed, shaking her head. "Sometimes I wonder why we came here. . . ."

When she said brain damage, I had a weird feeling in my head, like a dull burning sensation in the back of my brain.

I didn't want to think about that man and wiped him from my thoughts, but not before wondering if someday she'd read about me.

***

We met by the Chuck Berry statue. Destiny was there with some of the Tokers. Chuck Berry was some kind of St. Louis hero. They said he invented rock 'n' roll. I'd never heard of him.

I was a little nervous. There were no Eyez watching us but the cops were out in force among all the regular people walking around The Loop, shopping, enjoying their Sunday. It was stupid to try something here. We'd get caught for sure—

"Er-i-caaa . . ." a funny voice said behind me. Then I felt a cold nose on my cheek.

Out of the corner of my eye, I saw Boner's big eyes dancing next to mine. He was excited (though I didn't want to see if he was excited like his name).

Kalvin was holding him up to me, talking in a funny voice like a dog might. "Erica. Will you kiss me? *Huh, huh, huh?*"

Hearing that come out of his mouth made my mind go blank. I tried not to blush.

Kalvin laughed. "I'm just shitting you. You don't have to kiss the dog. Got your camera?"

I held it up.

"Good. Come get a shot of us in front of this statue."

He gathered everyone up just like a tourist family posing in front of a monument. He put a nervous Boner up on Chuck's head. Everyone thought it was funny, but I rescued him after I got the shot.

We walked around, cruised in and out of the stores there—a comic book store, a record store, a sports shoe store. Grabbed some ice cream at Ben and Jerry's.

After a while, we seemed like regular people too.

***

The Tokers cruised to a less crowded part of the Loop, toward a parking lot off to the side. I was lagging behind, recording tourists shopping and teens hanging out listening to their iPods. I tried not to judge too much *what* I was filming—some of the vids on that DVD were tough to watch but it was all symbolic—animals being experimented on, people dying of AIDS, a woman who used blood to paint with—I guess that made it art. Maybe it was too much to think I was like them, but I was doing something different. And that's what Mrs. Lee was talking about.

When we caught up, Kalvin had his crew in a circle around him. He looked like a coach in a huddle before the big game. "Alright, who gonna be a man today?" he asked.

The Tokers all raised their hands, jostling for his attention. "Let's see," he said, his eyes studying them closely. I got in there with my camera, catching the excitement in their eyes.

Kalvin picked a Toker called Doughboy. He was my height, but must've weighed over two hundred pounds. And it wasn't muscle.

"I'm gonna be MVP today!" he piped up.

Prince interrupted, "Didn't work out that way last week, did it, *ese*? Most Valuable *Punk*, is more like it."

Kalvin put his hand on Doughboy's shoulder. "Don't listen

to him. You fall down; you get back up and try again, yeah?"

I zoomed in on Doughboy's pinched face. His eyes darted around, unsure. He nodded, his voice cracking, "I'll do right by you, K."

Kalvin waved his fist up to Doughboy's mug. "Just remember: the bigger they are, the harder they fall."

He pretended to pop Doughboy in the jaw and Doughboy made a cartoon face like a character who got hit with a frying pan and was seeing stars. "But in your case, you better not fall on the dude. You might kill him."

Everyone busted up laughing. They all looked up to the Knockout King, and he liked being the center of attention.

Destiny couldn't make it, so it was interesting to get a glimpse into this all-guys world, something girls hardly ever see. Kalvin walked Doughboy away from the others, pumping up his confidence as they moved around the parking lot. I stepped in close enough to hear.

They stopped when they spotted a guy getting out of a powder blue Honda. The target was some sensitive college-type. He wore a sweater and Converse shoes, a pretty-boy haircut, and shaved eyebrows. He did not look like he'd put up a fight.

"Him." The King had spoken. "One hit or quit."

They bumped fists.

"Better get him a blanket and pillow; he gonna say g'nite," I heard Doughboy say. He started making his way over to the unsuspecting guy.

"Check this shit out," said Kalvin. "Better than anything you'll catch on HBO."

I knew what was coming up, but I tried not to think about it too much. I went into Fish-mode. Like Destiny said, my camera gave me a protective shield, like I was safe underwater in my tank, staring out at the world. I was just observing this weird scene unfolding in front of me. It was so unreal, it might as well have been a movie already.

I followed Doughboy from the next row over as he snuck around in between cars. When he picked up speed, so did I, though that wasn't hard since he didn't run that fast.

The action was quick and awkward. This time I came up right behind Doughboy and got close up in the heat of it all. He was slow, though, bouncing up out of breath. You could hear him wheezing. The college guy heard him too. When Doughboy swung, the college guy ducked. His fist barely grazed him. The target panicked and ran. Unfortunately, the other Tokers caught up to him.

They pushed college boy to the ground, where he rolled up like an armadillo. The boys played him like a soccer ball.

I'm making art, I told myself.

A security guard came out of nowhere, yelling at us. He was huge—a grown-up Doughboy—his ginormous mass jiggling under his windbreaker. This is where the running part came in. The boys took off laughing at the guard. Kalvin wanted me to keep shooting, which I did as I ran away. The security guard was slow. Too many frozen custards and butter cakes.

After a couple of blocks, he gave up and we stood across the street egging him on. He flipped us off, which made for a great shot. When he started back, the boys thought it'd be funny to play the Game on him.

The security guard started running. He didn't get far.

Doughboy knew he had to make up for his failure. He had

been so winded that he'd just stayed behind and the security guard hadn't noticed.

Doughboy popped out from behind a van and clocked him good. I just happened to have had my camera pointing that way when it happened.

The boys all leapt in the air and yelled, "Knockout!" They ran over, crowded around him, celebrating and whooping it up, patting Doughboy on the back of his head.

There were real cops to avoid, so we headed into an alley. Kalvin raised Doughboy's arm and shouted into the camera. "The Champ! You my MVP today, Toker!"

Doughboy beamed. There was no higher compliment. It was a great ending to my movie.

10

That video was an even bigger hit than the first. I made it all slick and action-packed with fast cuts and house music, like the crew was a bunch of rabid dogs on the hunt. Then as a joke, I did a remix from the guard point of view, but this time I speeded the chase up, made it black and white, and put some scratchy filter over it to make it into a silent movie. With some old-timey music, I knew the guys would bust a gut laughing at it. They loved it.

I got more friend requests. I began to wonder what'd happen if the wrong person saw it, but Destiny said that's why they used Facebook—this was an underground club, *invite only* screenings. As in, if you only invite friends, no one else will see it.

The TKO Club met up every few days for a bit of mayhem and adventure after school. In between, me and Destiny started hanging out more. She even came over one day after school. I could see she was kind of surprised by where I lived, but I guessed she'd seen worse.

I showed her the videos I was working on and she made some good comments—what she liked, what could be different. She kind of pushed me to go deeper, not to repeat myself or rely on cheap video effects. She had a point, but it didn't mean I liked being criticized.

I left her in my room to see if we had any eats. When I came back with some cereal, I found her on the floor, going through my old drawings that were still packed away in some boxes.

"What are you doing?" I asked, more than a little pissed.

"*You* made these?" she said, like she couldn't believe it.

I put down the food and got on my knees, gathering up the drawings. "That's old. I don't do that stuff anymore."

"Why not?" she asked, surprised.

I got stuck on that question.

She picked up a pretty big one that was a detailed dissection of my old school in Little Rock. In every room, hallway or courtyard, something was going on. Me, I was hanging out in the cafeteria with my only friends. I remembered that one taking me a good month to finish. "Fish, these are amazing. Is there anything you *can't* do?"

"Yeah, look like a supermodel." I rolled up the drawings and shoved them into a drawer in my dresser. "Who said you could go through my things anyways?" I crossed my arms and felt my nails biting into my skin.

She crinkled her brow. "I thought we were friends. Friends share."

I felt the tension in my hands melt. "Still . . . you shouldn't go through my personal stuff. You want me prying into your past?"

She turned gray.

I laughed. "Exactly, right?"

"They're just drawings," she said. "I wish I could draw like that."

Me too, I thought.

***

I had to admit, next to the excitement of the TKO Club, school started to drag for me. I saw Destiny all the time which was cool, though sometimes at school, she still had to lay low and pretend me and her weren't so close. I understood. Mrs. Lee had heard about our fight, of course, and pulled me aside to ask if I wanted to change classes so Destiny couldn't bully me. I almost laughed at that, but tried to act stoic and said that I could handle it. "Well, that's what I like to hear," she said. "People should stand up to adversity and take the higher ground. Good for you."

I'd spot Prince too, from time to time, in the hallway. He always gave me a bit of a hard time, but kept his distance. I never saw Kalvin there, though. I asked Destiny about it, but she just shrugged and said, "K and school don't mix."

I was starting to understand why. School was predictable. You got good grades, graduated, got a job. At least that's what my parents hoped for. But I wasn't so sure now. I didn't know what I wanted anymore. Ever since we got to St. Louis, I was just . . . surviving, getting by. Trying not to be an ant. With TKO, it was the opposite. Every time was unpredictable, crazy, or full of chaos. School just seemed boring in comparison. It was hard to get your blood pumping about American history or algebra. What was the point?

Each time the club met up, I could feel the adrenaline rush. I found myself getting excited just by the idea of hanging with the boys—I became someone else for a few hours. And being someone else was good.

Sometimes, Kalvin would take us places just to have fun—the roller rink, Taco Bell, the park. He wasn't planning any Knockout Games, just treating his crew as family. For Halloween, he made all the Tokers dress up in costumes—mostly ninjas or superstar athletes—and took us trick-or-treating around the nice neighborhoods in Tower Grove Heights. He dressed up as Muhammad Ali with some funny, oversized boxing gloves. He suggested I go as Red Sonja, the only redheaded action figure he knew of. I felt ridiculous, but he couldn't stop smiling when he saw me decked out. I figured if he liked it, I must be making it work. When the sun went down and we roamed the streets, I thought maybe it was all just a setup, especially after they followed this one guy dressed as a clown. But it was for real. Kalvin made sure everyone watched out for the little kids and said thank you when they got candy. Including me.

I liked watching Kalvin taking care of everyone, making sure they were having a good time. He always kept his eye out for trouble too—cops, even gangs. *Real gangs*, he'd call them. I asked him what the difference was and he looked at me like I was ignorant or something. "Northside, gangs. Southside, just clubs. They're into crack dealing and killing over turf. We're a crew. My guy's don't even steal a dime off their targets. We're just into proving ourselves and having fun."

And they had a lot of fun.

Other times, when they played the game, I was scared that we'd get caught. But in a weird way, that felt good too.

Like going to a scary movie that makes you scream feels good sometimes.

Once Kalvin pulled me aside after I showed him a particularly good video. He put his arm around my neck, pulled me into a playful headlock. "I had my doubts about you at first, Erica. But you proving yourself to be solid. Some of these mutts can't handle it, but you can. You alright. For a white girl, I mean."

I pulled myself out of his grip and hit him in the arm. I meant it to be playful, but for a second, I thought I'd made a big mistake. Then he laughed it off.

"Girl got spunk. Not bad."

I tried hitting him again, but he blocked me.

"But you hit like a girl. I could fix that."

"Maybe I like hitting like a girl."

I took a swing and he grabbed my fist. He smiled, examining my hand closely. "You got good hands. Meaty. Like the rest of you."

"Thanks," I said sarcastically.

He flipped my hand over, studying my palm. "Nah, that's a good thing. Shows you're a fighter. Most girls got small dainty hands and shit." He closed my hand into a fist, then took that fist and popped it into his palm a few times, making a soft slapping noise. "Solid. You probably don't realize your own strength. Ever hit anyone before?"

I pulled my fist away. "Yeah, you." I popped him in the gut.

When he glared at me, I added, "You'd never hit a girl, would you?"

He smiled. "Only if she deserved it."

I tried to sucker punch him, but he ducked it easily.

"You gotta hit with your body." He showed me, faking a hit and throwing his whole body into it—legs, shoulder, arm. "Boom. You'd be down for the count with that."

He spent a few moments showing me how, walking behind me and guiding my body into a hit. I felt his chest on my back, his arms around me. He might be tall and lean, but he was built.

He made me hit him in the stomach a few times. He didn't wince, but it did hurt . . .

Me.

11

In between, we met up some afternoons at Prince's house. He had a giant video system in his basement where we'd gather to screen movies on his overhead projector.

Destiny even played some of mine on the big screen. The HD looked great, like real movies up there. It was cool, watching the others watch my flicks. They even acted out ideas for future videos.

Kalvin loved to download streaming movies and show them to us. The boys always wanted to watch a *Fast & Furious* or *Transformers* movie—some big action flick. But Kalvin had a taste for great old movies that he came across. He *hated* movies where the white character "saved" the black person or ones where the black guy always died first. That was Hollywood's idea of the world order, he'd say.

Action was great—he loved an explosion as much as the others, but the old movies he picked were different. He said if you wanted to learn how to do things right, you had to study the past. And not history-past, like in school. Movie-past was better because it felt more real. The funny thing was, he only wanted to show us the best parts, usually the first part of the flick. So we only watched the beginnings of movies.

We saw the beginning of this crazy British movie called *A Clockwork Orange*. This was not a movie my mom would ever let me see. Kalvin showed us the opening, over and over—from the first beat of that weird synth music and that jarring close-up of Alex, staring directly at you for the longest time, talking that strange gooblygoo talk of his—sucking me into his world. It was a real horror show, full of ultraviolence and anarchy. But I couldn't tear my eyes away from it. It was the first time I noticed what a filmmaker could do and how they controlled *how* you felt. The movie was filled with shock and laughs, but it was stunningly shot with classical music over it. Horrifying acts were suddenly strangely beautiful and you could almost understand how Alex and his droogs saw the world. It was their playground, their rules, their game. And we were playing with them, whether we liked it or not. That movie blew me away because even though I thought *this is so wrong*, I found myself liking it. A lot.

We also watched fun movies like *Butch Cassidy and the Sundance Kid*. That one was full of outlaws and big heists, something the boys really got into. It was a buddy movie—two guys against the world. But the bad guys were the good guys—you rooted for them. And you hated the good guys. Again, everything was upside down. Prince liked it so much, he started calling himself Sundance, though he dropped it when Kalvin didn't want to be called Butch. He said Butch had a different meaning these days.

One time, when there were just a few of us and Destiny wasn't around, Kalvin put on a movie called *Bonnie and Clyde*. He sat next to me. Our knees touched. The movie was weird, about this waitress who suddenly starts going with this gangster, just to escape her boring life. When they started robbing banks, it got pretty exciting. I was worried for Bonnie, but you could see her getting sucked into it—the glamour, the danger, the excitement—who could blame her? It looked like fun.

Out of the corner of my eye, I could see Kalvin looking at me every now and then. He stopped the movie after about half an hour.

"So how come I never heard of these movies?" I asked him.

" 'Cause nobody ever bothered to show them to you before me."

"Yeah, and who showed you—Prince?"

"Yeah, right. Even though he likes *Purple Rain*, he don't know the good stuff," he said, offended at the idea. "There was this teacher at Truman, kind of weird but she was ok. When I got in trouble a couple times, she secretly gave me a list of great movies to watch on my own. She thought I needed to be challenged, that the thoughts in my head could be expanded."

"What was her name?"

He brushed it off like he'd forgotten. "Doesn't matter. She was a little off, but it was a place to start. Then I looked movies up on my own and found even more. I started showing them to these clowns so they could see the bigger picture."

"And what is the bigger picture? You don't even show us the whole movie," I challenged him.

He scoffed. "Endings are for idiots. Just because the heroes of the movie don't live by 'The Rules,' Hollywood says they gotta suffer so they can show the audience you can't live like that. Well, fuck that. Beginnings are always a lot better."

"Says you."

He laughed. "You know, you don't realize it, but you're making your own movie. 'Bout us. And one day in the future, some kid here in St. Louis will see it and say, *Damn! That TKO Club is fire!*"

"Maybe. Or they'll get you in trouble."

He shrugged. "No. 'Cause everyone knows if they open their mouth, they gotta deal with the Double Trouble!" He held out his fists and began boxing right in front of my face. He got close enough for me to feel the wind from a right jab.

***

A couple days later, Kalvin texted me on Saturday when I was hanging out with Destiny. It felt good when I saw his name on the caller ID.

Kalvin said he had gotten some new ideas after our last talk. He had been watching some nature film about cheetahs and thought a moving target might be a challenge. I reminded him about chasing the security guard and he said, *no, something faster.*

He told us to meet the crew down near the bike paths in Tower Grove Park. The Tokers were hanging out behind some of those giant old trees you see everywhere here. He told me to position myself down aways on a grassy hill.

I waited on the top of the hill. Destiny lay on the grass with me. I felt like a sniper gazing through my zoom lens as I watched the bikers speeding by on the path.

"I told him about your drawings," she said.

My heart skipped a beat. "Why would you do that?"

"He wants to see them. Maybe you could invite him over—"

She was testing me. I gave her the stink eye.

She grinned. "I'm not lying. Just sayin'. . . "

I fiddled with my camera. She could see I was embarrassed, so she changed the subject. She nudged me in the shoulder. "You always film the Tokers, but you never point that thing at me. I got moves too."

She posed like a supermodel and I recorded her for a minute, doing my fashion photo talk: "Yeah, baby, make love to the lens."

She fell down on the grass and we busted up laughing. It was definitely a girlfriend moment. We lay on our stomachs on a low hill and observed the boys waiting to pounce.

"How come we're the only girls and we're stuck out here?" I asked.

"Dunno," she shrugged. "Maybe 'cause most girls don't like to fight?"

"How did you get in, then?" I asked.

She frowned. "My brother. He used to be TKO top dawg. He was close with K. One day, my mom told him that he had to watch me. I was twelve. Neither of us wanted to hang with each other, but he took me along with him. And you know how it is, guys love to show off when a girl is around, 'specially one as fine as me." She gave me her straightest face. "Why you never laugh when I'm joking?"

"Sorry."

I peered through my viewfinder and spotted a couple of the boys peeking from between some trees.

"Anyways," she continued. "I caught K's eye. He liked me and kinda took me under his wing. My bro didn't like that and threatened to whup me if I came back. I didn't know what was up with him, and later I figured it was because he didn't want K hitting on me. But I wasn't about to let my brother tell me what to do! I'd already seen what they was doing and told him that I'd be happy to tell momma what he been up to. He let me come back and I been there ever since."

"You didn't tell me your brother was here. Which one is he?"

She stewed. "He left."

"Well, when is he coming back?"

She shrugged. "I mean, he ain't here no more. He said he outgrew it. To him, it was a stupid thing only kids do."

I could see she was pissed. "And he doesn't mind you being here?" I asked.

"He ain't around to stop me—oh dang, look!"

There was action. I trained my lens on one of the Tokers. He sprinted out of the trees and was quickly on the heels of a biker with the fancy racing clothes you see around. It *was* like a nature film—a cheetah pursuing his prey. The kid caught up to the biker and swung, but hit the dude's helmet by accident. The biker freaked and took off, barely escaping the three or four others chasing him. Eventually, they all gave up.

They tried a few more times, failing over and over until finally they just drove some guy into the bushes and attacked him in a frenzy.

It made for a crazy movie. I added some narration from a nature film I downloaded about cheetahs. I did quick cuts and made all the failures dramatic, until the exciting climax when they captured their target.

It was wild.

12

We were on the bus over to Benton Park. The Rec Center had a gym where K and some of the Tokers boxed. It was a run-down brick building left over from another time. Somebody had spray painted a "W" in front of the sign so it read WRec Center. It was like out of some old movie—even had a salty old guy in there with a whistle—your typical hard-fought movie coach who'd seen a million boxing matches. His face was all knots and full of what my mom called "character." He had a bunch a guys doing exercises with these big heavy leather balls, throwing them at each other and doing squats and stuff. All the while he was walking back and forth blowing his whistle and talking.

"Use your fists in the ring, not the street!"

"Yes, Teacher Man!" they all shouted back like they were in the army.

"Be disciplined in your work and you will be a champion in life *and* in the ring! Do you doubt me?"

"No, Teacher Man!"

"Do you believe you have the will to succeed?

"Yes, Teacher Man!"

And on and on he went. While he had them doing laps around the gym, he spotted us and wandered over.

"My Million Dollar Baby!" he said to Destiny. "Where you been hiding yourself? I've been waiting for you to get in the ring again and show these boys what it takes!"

She checked her nails. "Nah, I'm retired. Once you KO a cop, you can't go nowhere but down. I just like to watch now."

He nodded. "You and me both." He noticed me and gave me the once-over. "Fresh meat?"

"Her? Nah, she ain't the punching type. More like a wrestler." She winked at me.

"You never know..." He checked my arm muscles. "You could use some work, but you got heft." He slapped me on the thigh. "Solid. I like it."

I gave him the evil eye. "Do that again and you'll see how much heft I got."

"That's the spirit, ladies!" Teacher Man boomed. "Use that attitude in the ring! Join us anytime, darling!"

Destiny shook her head. "We ain't here to box, old man."

"No, she's here to see the champ," interrupted the Knockout King, who was standing there covered in sweat... and yeah, looking more than a little hot.

"Girls are not good for a boxer, Mr. Barnes," said Teacher Man as he headed back to his guys.

Kalvin shook his head. "Don't pay him no mind, Fish. Teacher Man is a funny guy. But he watches out for us. Keeps me out of trouble... at least as much as he can."

"Watch out for that one, ladies!" Teacher Man shouted. "He'll sucker punch you every time."

Kalvin rolled his eyes. "So, you came to see the King do his thing."

"You going to get in the ring?" I asked.

"Shoulda been here an hour ago. I flattened one of these clowns like Ali. Float like a butterfly..." he danced around, shadowboxing.

"Right," said Destiny. "You said you had plans for us this afternoon?"

"Yeah, just give me twenty minutes. Wait over in the video room . . . and make sure them shorties ain't playing no video games."

The video room was some kind of training spot for screening fight videos. It was clear they didn't know Kalvin's instructions because the room had been taken over by six or seven Tokers all playing this game called Splatterhouse. It was the goriest video game I ever saw, filled with blood and ripping people in half and all kinds of unimaginable things. Seeing all these boys playing was a trip. Giggles filled the room whenever someone's head exploded.

They made room for me to play. Kalvin wasn't going to be there for awhile, so I sat down with them. I had to admit, it was kind of fun. If anyone tried something on me, that's what I'd do to them—rip out their spine or cut them in two. But after a few rounds, it became too much. There's only so much spine ripping I can take.

Instead, I just talked to them while they played, taking out my camera without them noticing (which wasn't too hard since their eyes were glued to the screen). I felt it might be good material to sprinkle into the videos. "So how's it feel to rip someone's spine out?" I asked.

I got all kinds of answers. "Like a badass!" "Like I'm immortal." "Like I can do no wrong!" Things like that.

I asked them if Knockout was like playing videos, but for real. Most of them liked that comparison. But really, they did it because they liked proving themselves to Kalvin.

"What's playing Knockout mean to you?" I asked.

They didn't really have an answer. "I dunno. It's a game. We play it when we bored."

I asked Tyreese if he wanted to be like Kalvin.

He stopped playing, his eyes darting back and forth. "Nobody can be like K. He the One, like the dude in *The Matrix*."

So if they can't be like Kalvin, then what? Did they have dreams of becoming something when they grew up? None of them said *go to college*, *get a job*, or anything like that. They all laughed like the thought was stupid that they might grow up and become something else.

C-Jay made a face. "What'chu wanna know my dream for? What's yours?"

I couldn't answer. It had been so long since I had one, I didn't even want to think about it.

They went back to their games and I filmed Kalvin working out through the window instead. He was all muscle, lean and tough. The way he attacked that punching bag was pretty amazing. I could see he had some kind of demons he was working out—that bag was gonna come off its chain from how hard he was hitting it. I could see him becoming a boxer or one of those mixed martial arts guys.

"So when does he ever play Knockout?" I asked Destiny.

"K? He doesn't play anymore. He's more of a. . . coach, like Teacher Man, I guess. It just got old, having people trying to dethrone you all the time. I think he even got a ulcer or something 'cause for a while, all he drank was milk."

"I don't see him getting worried about things."

She scoffed. "Yeah, on the outside. But between you and me, he's sensitive. Last KO he ever did, the target pulled a gun on him. K just snatched it from him and threatened to shoot him. But he couldn't. He was no gangbanger. He just walked away and said, 'That's it.' "

"So what, he retired? Why have a club, then?"

She watched him pummel the punching bag. "Rival clubs started coming up, copycats. Even some group of white kids in the burbs slumming like they something. K got pride. So he had the idea of creating his own club where he'd train these Tokers and that's when he got his mojo back. More satisfying, I guess."

About thirty minutes later, Kalvin emerged, drenched in sweat. He smelled like some kind of wet cat, his eyes burning as he watched the Tokers playing their game. Pissed, he marched over and yanked the plug from the TV. They protested but shut up real quick when they saw he meant business. "Video games are for pussies. You need to be in the fight for real. Breathe it in. Feel your fist as it cracks somebody's skull. *Then* you'll know you're alive. This"—he knocked the controls out of C-Jay's hands—"is not what we do. Now let's go out and have some *real* fun."

13

There was something in the air that afternoon. It smelled like fire. We descended into an old neighborhood park like a pack of lions heading out for a feeding frenzy. I found myself moving deeper into the pack, closer to Kalvin, as we kicked up leaves in our wake. They were hunting for new targets. Me, I was hunting for the right image, trying to make each video fresh and different. I wanted the viewer to feel they were right in the action—the sweat, the taste of blood, the shock of the punch, the thrill of it all.

Kalvin and Prince stopped the group at the swing set. That was a great contrast—them strategizing on the playground. It was all a game. There were only a couple of toddlers there, but when their moms saw us coming, they cleared out. As they did, Destiny's phone went off. When she saw the caller ID, she stopped in her tracks. She went kind of pale, then answered—taking off in the other direction.

"Where you going?" I asked. But she ignored me and kept moving, listening to the caller on the phone. I let her go and refocused on the group.

Kalvin eased himself into one of the swings and watched Prince.

Prince asked, "So what's the plan, *jefe*?"

Kalvin nodded to himself, deep in thought. "Today's your day, P. You decide."

Prince was caught off guard, his mind obviously churning, trying to decide if Kalvin was serious or not. When K didn't bat an eye, Prince finally beamed like he'd been handed command of a ship. "*Orale*, Tokeheads, listen up!"

The crew looked at each other, unsure. Prince surveyed the park like he was buying time. Maybe he didn't know what to say.

Kalvin rolled his eyes. "Are we gonna do this or what? Or should I ask Fish to take over?"

That settled it. Prince stood there awkwardly for a few seconds, then turned to inspire his troops.

There were six Tokers. Different from yesterday, except for C-Jay. Prince picked the smallest one. "You. Tyrone."

"Tyreese," he answered.

"'*Spensa*—my bad," he said. "Now come here, Tyrone."

I took out my camera and decided not to use my zoom. Today, I'd get right into the action. I was right up in his face. I could see through the lens that he was scared, but he put up a good front.

"Ignore her," Prince said. "You wanna be in the TKO Club, right?"

He nodded. "Yeah."

"You ready to man up, *ese*?"

He puffed out his chest to prove it. "Bring it."

Prince laughed. "A'ight." He scoped out the park, saw one of those guys with a metal detector sweeping the grass for lost quarters. "Him."

Tyreese frowned. "Man, he got on a headset. I might hurt my hand on that thing."

Prince rolled his eyes. "*Chingada*, are you kidding me? Don't hit his headset, then!"

"What if he move when I swing?"

"Jesus, you want me to hold that *pendejo* for you?" Prince had had enough. "You know what? Fuck it. I have another idea."

I was focused on this kid's eyes darting around when I heard Prince say, "Fish."

I looked up. "What?"

"Come here."

I glanced over at Kalvin, but all he did was motion with his head for me to go. I looked to Destiny for support. "What're you afraid of? Prince Rodriguez?"

Fine. I walked up to him. "What?"

Prince motioned to the metal detector guy. "Go ask that dude for a cigarette."

"I don't smoke."

He gazed at me like I was the stupid one. "You're the, what you call it—the diversion. You ask him for a cigarette and he won't be able to hear you then he'll take off his headset. Then baby Tyrone here can do his thing."

"It's Tyreese!" he said.

"You're making this too complicated," I said. "Why don't you just pick another guy?" I asked.

He was annoyed. "*Nena*, you're a girl. He'll answer you. He's probably the kind of guy who digs the fatties—"

74

"Don't." I gave him the stare down. *Don't mess with the Fish.*

He backed off. "My bad." He shuffled in place, resigning himself to my protest. "Look, just do this, please, and don't make me look like a douche," he said softly.

"Too late." I sighed and started walking toward the metal detector man.

"Hey, gimme your camera," he said. "I'll shoot you."

There was zero chance of that. I headed down, Tyreese on my heels. When I was about ten feet away, I circled around so I wouldn't be sneaking up on the guy. Tyreese stopped.

The man was about fifty, balding with beady eyes. He was scowling at a stray cat who was rubbing up against his leg and getting in the way of his work. When the cat didn't take the hint, the guy booted it away. Nice.

He wasn't paying any attention to me, so I waved at him, pursed my lips, and held my fingers up to them. He ignored me.

"Hey!" I said.

His eyes drifted up toward me. "What?"

"You got a cigarette?" I asked.

Annoyed at being disturbed from his precious work, he looked like he was going to kick me too. "What?"

I rolled my eyes, motioned for him to take off his headset.

He stopped his little beeping machine and pushed his headset off his ear. "I don't give money to homeless kids."

That was Tyreese's opening. He just stood there.

"I'm not homeless." I had to stall. "Uh, what are you searching for, gold?" I asked, staring at Tyreese, who finally got the hint.

Before the man could answer, Tyreese jumped into action. The man saw my reaction to Tyreese charging and swung around just in time to see the shortie's fist coming his way.

BAM.

When the guy ducked, Tyreese hit the man's headset anyway. They both cried out at the same time.

"Fuck!"

"Fuck!"

The man went down to one knee. Tyreese was rubbing his hand. Prince yelled, "Finish him!" He held the other Tokers back. In the middle of all this, I spotted K recording the whole thing with his phone, trying not to shake too much from laughing. *Fucker*, I thought.

The guy suddenly grabbed his metal detector and rose up to smash Tyreese in the face. In that fraction of a second, everything went white—my head felt like it was on fire and a roar came out of me that shocked me.

I saw red. It was coming out of someone's face. My fist was wailing on the guy's face, smashing his nose. The blood shocked me and at the same time, the heat from it set something off in me that I didn't expect.

I felt like lightning hit me—everything went quiet and it was like I was seeing myself through the camera. I don't know how many times I hit him. When the guy fell over, the boys broke free and ran up to me yelling "KNOCKOUT!"

They jumped all over me and suddenly we all tumbled over in a big ball of sweaty boys and excitement. I was buried beneath them, smothered by their laughter and bodies. I had no idea what was going on, but someone started throwing them off me and then Kalvin pulled me out, grinning ear to ear.

I kind of stumbled away from the pile and fell to the ground and jumped up again dazed, but happy. The Tokers were laughing their asses off, doing victory bumps. I saw the man lying on the ground, groaning. Some of the Tokers were still doing a number on him.

I saw the blood on my fist and was gonna be sick. An arm reached out and grabbed me, pulling me in tight.

"I got you, girl," said Kalvin, holding me close to his chest.

"Did you see it?" I said.

He hustled me away as the boys scattered. "See what?"

"The lightning."

He smiled in recognition. "Yeah, I saw it. Crazy, right?"

14

It wasn't like I fainted or anything. Or even passed out. It's more that I went into a hyper state so pumped with adrenaline that my head short-circuited. I could hear the Tokers hooting and hollering in the background. And I could feel the Knock-out King's arm holding me tight. But other than that, I was somewhere else.

We were walking and walking, and it was starting to get dark outside; then we were inside and suddenly, I felt a jolt and there I was again, sitting on someone's bed, and that someone was in the shower.

Something was going on outside and I walked over to the window and saw I was in a small apartment building. The window overlooked the rooftop of a lower story and there was Prince in the middle of a bunch of Tokers on the roof deck as the sun was setting. Tyreese was standing next to him, looking small. C-Jay and Doughboy were wearing boxing gloves.

I thought maybe they were training or something, but as soon as Prince left the ring, C-Jay and Doughboy went at

Tyreese. They circled around him like wolves. I thought he was gonna piss his pants. Suddenly C-Jay lurched and got him good on the side of the face. Doughboy quickly landed a punch to his stomach. Tyreese's knees buckled.

I guess that's what you get when you fail your mission. Harsh.

The shower stopped. I heard Kalvin's voice in the bathroom—singing. I couldn't make out the song. I was in his room, his apartment. I remembered him pulling me along, totally out of it.

His room was just like any young guy's. Posters of LeBron, rappers and MMA fighters, and of course, swimsuit models. The guys on his wall were all black, the girls all white. Underneath those, there were some framed pictures on his shelf—him and Teacher Man outside a boxing ring. K had a medal around his neck. There was a middle-school graduation picture of him next to it, where he was all dressed up and beaming—the kid next door. And then there was one ripped in half and pinned to the wall. He looked about twelve. He was standing on that roof, with a white man's arm around his neck, the man's face torn out.

I heard a commotion outside and I peeked out the window again. Tyreese was lying on the ground, the other two hovering over him. C-Jay kneeled and propped him up. He was woozy, bleeding from the nose. The guys were cheering him on and slowly, he got up onto his knees. Finally, he stood and shook it off. The crew rushed in, patting him on the back and head— he'd survived.

"He has work to do, but he's got spirit," said Kalvin.

He was standing right behind me. I could feel the heat

from the shower coming off his body. "You alright?" he asked.

I nodded, a bit woozy.

He was naked except for the towel around his waist. "Let me look at you."

He turned me around to face him. I had to rest my hand on his shoulder to steady myself, but it stung like hell and I pulled it back. It looked swollen.

He held my hand gently, looking at both sides like he was a doctor. When he touched my knuckles, I flinched. He pulled on each finger, one by one. That didn't hurt so bad.

Turning my hand over, he pressed on the top of my palm.

"I don't know what happened back there," I said.

He smiled. "What happened was you finished the job when little Ty couldn't."

K curled my hand into a fist. I winced from the pain. "I had to do something. The guy was gonna smash him with his metal detector."

"All I know is you finished that dude off." He soothed my hand by blowing on it.

"Someone had to," I said. But now I was worried. "What if . . . he goes to the police?"

"Oh, he's definitely going to the police," said Kalvin. "Thing is, when you get knocked out, you don't remember a thing. Last thing he probably remembers is looking for some old coins or something."

"Or some strange girl with red hair coming up to him trying to bum a cigarette."

He shrugged. "Hey, no one's ID'd us yet. I don't think it'll start with you. Can you imagine him saying he was knocked out by some *girl*?"

That still didn't make me feel any better. "Do you think he went to the hospital?"

"What do you care what happens to him? You don't know him. He could be a child abuser for all you know."

"Or he could've been a war veteran or something . . . "

Kalvin made a dour face. "Just stop talking. You're still probably in shock. Come here." He led me to his bed and sat me down. "Don't worry so much about it." He shuffled through his nightstand until he found a prescription bottle of something. "Percodan," he said. "Take this; it'll help." He handed me two pills and a bottle of water. I did what he said.

He had an ice pack in a mini fridge by his bed and put it on my hand. "Bruised, but not broken. It'll hurt for a while. But you'll get used to it."

"I hope not," I said.

We sat there awkwardly on his bed. I'd never been on a half-naked guy's bed before. I didn't know what to do with myself.

"Hey, you wanna see it?"

My jaw dropped. "Um . . . "

He smiled. "The video, fool." He dug around in his pants pocket and pulled out his phone.

"I don't think so."

"Come on, you were amazing." He pressed play and there I was talking to the metal detector guy. The camera was behind Tyreese. When he froze up, I saw Kalvin's hand come in and give him a push.

"Who said you could record this?"

"What? You can record us, but I can't shoot you? Besides, this is a moment to remember. The moment where the queen rose up! I knew you had it in you."

My face felt hot. It was weird being on the other side of the camera for once—all I could think of was how fat I looked.

In the video, Tyreese ran at the guy, popped him in the face and then howled like he'd hit a wall. I could hear Kalvin and them laughing as Tyreese rolled around holding his hand.

Then Prince said, "Oh, shit, check it out. That old fucker's fighting back!"

I saw him grab his metal detector and raise it over his head to smack Tyreese. That's when I lost it. The guy's head just snapped back when I popped him from the side, just like Kalvin showed me. I put my whole body into it—*Pow!* He fell to his knees.

"Holy shit!" K shouted. The crew was hopped up excited, snorting hysterically at the sight of me smacking this old guy.

I kept going at him until he hit the ground. Everyone rushed in. The camera came straight at me and it was like watching a different person. My eyes were all wide-eyed and wild, and then suddenly, I was buried in a pile of boys. The camera went crazy for a few seconds, pointing at the sky and the ground until after I emerged from the pile, pulled out by Kalvin. I kept hitting at the air and stumbling around. Kalvin was chasing me around, "Hold up, hold up. I got ya!" The camera went all wonky and the next image was of him holding me up to the camera. "The new heavyweight champ!"

Kalvin put the phone down on the bed. "Looks like I taught you something."

"I never hit anyone before," I mumbled. He took my hand and stroked it softly.

"There's nothing like it, right? The energy . . . surges through your body and you feel like you can do . . . anything," he whispered, almost to himself. "That's the lightning. That's what you felt back there."

"Adrenaline," I said.

"No." He traced his finger up my arm. "My pops used to say there's a warrior spirit trapped in all of us. Some use it; most don't. But when you whup someone good, that spirit gets knocked out of them and the warrior who hit 'em takes on that power. That's the surge you felt. You took that dude's power."

I knew that was bullshit, but I couldn't deny this crazy feeling I had: I *did* take that guy's power. I could almost feel it coursing through my blood—I was somebody to be reckoned with.

Next thing I knew, his lips were on mine. Just like that. My mind kinda went blank but I found myself kissing back. I didn't really know what to do. I wondered if I was kissing him right, but he was like a dancer, leading me, showing me what to do and I just sank into those lips of his. His arms held me close, his body on mine—but he didn't try to force anything.

I couldn't tell him I was a virgin, but he probably sensed I was uptight. I kissed him a little too hard and our teeth hit. I pulled back embarrassed, but he didn't seem to care. He was all clean and smelled good, and I was still sweaty from the park but he seemed to like that. I let him guide me. His hand drifted down, and I found myself grabbing his wrist when it got to my waist. He eased up. That surprised me, him taking it slow and easy. I liked that.

As soon as it felt like we were just going to make out, I relaxed. I mean, he was naked except for his towel. And I could *feel* his . . . you know. . . on my leg, but even that didn't freak me out too much. His kissing put me back at ease.

The only thought in my head, besides how nice this felt, was to flash back to a couple of months ago, when I was so alone floating at the bottom of that pool.

For once, I felt like I belonged.

15

When me and the Knockout King emerged from the door that led out to the roof, the boys all looked at us with a funny expression. They were huddled around a metal trash can, their eyes lit up by the fire. Boner came panting up to Kalvin, relieved to see his master.

"What are they staring at?" I said.

Kalvin picked up Boner and whispered into my ear. "You."

When they lowered their eyes, I felt like royalty.

Kalvin broke the spell. "Who wants some Kool-Aid?" Hands shot up. They may be tough Tokers, but inside, they were still kids.

We sat around the fire drinking Kool-Aid and eating Doritos. Me and the King sat on a utility box and Prince squatted with the minions looking none too pleased.

"What's his deal?" I asked.

"Oh, he's just bein' Prince is all. He get jealous easily. It's that hot Latino blood, I guess."

"About what?"

"Not what. Who. Just ignore him; he'll get over it."

He surveyed the scene, me by his side. His eyes connected with Tyreese and he nodded his approval. "I was twelve when I started training out here, just like these guys. Pops taught me to fight right where they are now. It was either fight or get thrown off."

"I don't think so," I said.

"For real. He used to whup my butt, but one day I got better of him and he stopped training me. I started going to the gym and Teacher Man turned me into a boxer. But hitting a bag gets boring pretty quick."

He watched two of the Tokers going at it over the last of the Doritos. That made him grin. "Back in the day, me and this other dude named Tuffy . . . we were hanging out with nothing to do. We joked around, talking about all the people that passed us on the street. Then one guy gave us a look like he didn't like us and I said something like, 'Man, I'd like to pop that dude.' "

"And did you?" I asked.

He shrugged. "I didn't have a good reason, but I was bragging about how I could take that guy down in one blow, and ol' Tuffy said, 'So what're you waiting for?' I had no choice then, so I walked up behind the guy as he's waiting at a crosswalk. I just whacked him in the side of the head. Only problem was, being thirteen, I wasn't so buffed out like now and it just pissed him off. He chased us for a whole block before we jumped some fences and lost him."

He laughed at the memory, raising his cup for a toast. "Here's to ol' Tuff," he said. "My former right hand, my ex-CEO, and brother of badass!"

Prince overheard him. That didn't help his mood any.

Kalvin ignored him. "I didn't hit someone again till after—you know, after my pops was gone."

"Your dad died?" I asked.

He didn't say anything, but a darkness passed through his face. He was staring at Prince and then his eyes lit up again. "When word got out, young Prince here showed up looking to prove himself. Little wetback kid trying to sling it like us. Now normally, blacks and Latinos hate each other's guts. But you know what? He proved his worth. I'm a equal opportunity guy when it comes to people willing to prove themselves."

He raised his cup to Prince, who toasted back. "He knows I love him like a brother," said K. "And man, did we have us some times. But by the time I got to Truman High, I kinda outgrew it. I liked getting these Tokers going and training them and whatnot. It's like raising little pit bulls."

It was nice hearing him talk. Part of me wished I was shooting this, but the other part was just glad to be sitting here with him. "Sounds . . . nice?"

He gave me a sour look. "Nice? I don't know about that. But most of these Tokers don't got dads, so I feel I'm giving 'em something I didn't have. You know . . . direction. Something to feel part of."

I found myself staring at his lips while he talked. There was something odd about his teeth. The front four were whiter than the rest.

He caught me staring at his mouth. "What?"

"Are those . . . fake teeth?"

He was a little embarrassed, but just shook his head and kissed me, his mouth opened wide. Someone dropped their Kool-Aid. I felt Kalvin's tongue pushing and then—

"Jesus!" I pulled away and spit something on the ground. His four front teeth.

Kalvin fell on the ground cackling. The others caught on and C-Jay ran over and picked up the teeth and held them up to me. "These yours?"

"That's . . . disgusting."

"You asked!" Kalvin said, his face red from laughing so hard.

I flipped them both off. "I'm going."

"Come on!" I heard him say. "I thought you liked my smile!"

"Not in my mouth."

"Let her go," said Prince.

Kalvin waved him off and caught me at the door with his hand on my shoulder. "Come on," he said softly. "Are you really mad or just showing off?"

I turned and stared into his green eyes. "That *was* disgusting."

"Yeah, I guess it was. I'm sorry."

I softened.

"But you gotta admit, it was funny, right?"

I shrugged. It was. "Only for sick minds."

"Sick minds think alike." He nudged me. "So we good?"

"Maybe."

Then before he kissed me, I slipped out of his hold and walked down the stairs. He watched me walk away. "Hard to get. Good move."

He was grinning, his four front teeth missing.

16

I woke up the next morning, the sun falling on my face. As I stretched out on my bed, I actually felt different. When I glanced in the mirror, I even looked a little different. My skin kind of glowed. Or maybe it was just because I couldn't stop smiling.

All day at school, I kept thinking of Kalvin. Destiny had heard rumors and tried interrogating me, but it got her nowhere.

I interrogated her back about her mystery call at the park, but she just said it was a family thing. She'd heard about the Metal Detector Man. "I guess you one of us now." She didn't seem too pleased about it, though.

After school, I had some errands I had to run for Mom, but I knew I'd make a pit stop at a certain person's apartment.

***

Kalvin lived across from an old brick church. The neighborhood was not bad, all lawns and charming houses. K lived in a small yellow-bricked apartment complex on the corner. When I spotted him, he was standing on the stoop of his building. Prince and some of the crew were standing on the steps talking to some older white guy wearing a bright red shirt. The man was in his fifties, with sad but intense eyes. He was also pointing a bulky old video camera at K.

As I got closer, I realized the guy wasn't exactly talking. More like yelling. At them.

His red T-shirt sported the phrase, "We Are Watching" in big letters over a giant eye. They reminded me of the graffiti Eyez I had seen painted around the neighborhoods, always watching.

The first thing I heard him saying was: "You need to educate yourself!" He was hiding behind his camera, his free hand waving in the air. "You people are trapped in the prison mindset of self-hatred. Knock out your ignorance and not the people who can't defend themselves."

K stood there with his arms crossed and a slightly amused look on his face. "What do you mean 'you people'?" Boner snapped at the man. The Tokers circled him—hyenas ready to pounce.

The man ignored them. "I was with the Marines, man. I've been around; I know what conflict is. But those people fought for a cause. You're just wasting time. I know you are smarter than that. You're the leader here, I can see. And I see you. The camera sees you. Why not teach these young people to fight with their minds instead of their fists? Otherwise, you're just a racist thug."

I took out my camera. This is not something you see every day, so I wanted to document it. K noticed me, then whispered something to Prince, who called his boys back into the house.

"Racist? What the fuck are you talking about? I'm *black*." He poked his finger into the guy's shoulder.

The man didn't care. He kept railing at Kalvin. "Racism cuts both ways, brother. There's a race war going on in this country. You're targeting white people, and that's what we call a hate crime."

"Whoa, *whoa*—" said Kalvin. "We don't target white people, *brother*. Because *we* haven't done anything. And even if I did, I wouldn't hit a white person just 'cause they're white. I got nothing against white people. Some of my best friends are white. He snuck a quick glance at me.

So how 'bout we look at you instead?" Kalvin took a step toward him. "You're just like the cops—profiling us 'cause *we're* black. You see a black teen and you think *oh, he's out to get me!* But really, it's you, creating paranoia and hate."

The man wouldn't back down. "Don't try to put some spin on your thuggery. You're targeting white people and taking out your hate on them! Can't you see that?"

Kalvin eyed him coldly. "I see a white man who knows he's the minority now. Who's afraid, now that the power's out of his hands, from the White House to the streets. Maybe when you were young, this neighborhood was all-white, and you had your way. Well, I'm the president here and you and your little club with your red shirts surveilling us like we're a bunch of dogs to be kept down, that ain't gonna fly. Not anymore."

Even from here, I could see the man's face turning red. If he was a cartoon, he'd have steam coming out of his ears. He had to fight to regain his calm.

"Your time . . . will come," he spat. "Sooner or later, we'll get you in action on tape and that'll be it. All your fancy rationale will mean squat and all that will speak is the violence you and your homies lay on the rest of us. The whole neighborhood is watching you, whether you like it or not. We're not going away." He held up his camera. "I'm not going away. We already have tape of all of you looking for targets."

K had heard enough. "Them's big words." He grabbed the camera right out of the man's hands. He had very fast hands, boxer's hands. The man was shocked and stammered on as K popped the tape out of the camera, using his body to keep the man from grabbing it back. "By the way, videotape's kinda outdated. You might consider joining us here in the future." He cracked the cassette on the railing and unspooled the tape. Then he smiled and tossed the camera back at the man.

"Don't you know about backing up your work? Otherwise you might accidentally delete it." K threw a handful of discarded tape in the air and let it rain down on the man before tossing the cassette to the side. He turned and went inside, shutting the door in the guy's face.

The man pulled the tape off his head angrily. I almost laughed, but then he just stood there for a few seconds, fuming. He was about to bang on the door then stopped, his fist frozen in midair. Finally, he flipped off the door in frustration and stormed back to the street.

He saw me with my camera. I quickly turned it off and shoved it in the pocket of my hoodie.

"Did you see that? Idiots and thugs. Just walking all over us without fear of prosecution."

He reached into his bag, pulled out a flyer and handed one to me. "I'm running the neighborhood watch group. We need more people on the streets to keep us safe. Come to the rally. We need your support." He pointed to my camera. "I see you have one too. Good. The more eyes out there, the better. Together, we'll make a difference."

I watched him walk away. "Check out our website!" he said over his shoulder. I studied the flyer.

It was for a rally tomorrow in front of the church here. *Knockout Violence!* it said.

I watched him hurry down the street handing out flyers to anyone who'd stop to talk. Then he turned and walked up to a small brick house. An older lady with long graying hair and round glasses was planting sunflowers in the front yard. When they kissed, I recognized her: Mrs. Lee.

***

"Don't worry about him," said Kalvin, leaning out a second-story window. "Just an old crank getting in people's business. Got turned down by the cops, kicked out of the war. Now he thinks he's a vigilante taking on the young punks who fuck everything up."

"You mean you?"

"Smartass. That includes you too, don't forget that. And did you notice how in *his* eyes, a white girl gets a pass every time?"

I didn't know what to say to that.

"So, you just gonna stand there, or are you coming up?"

I stared down at the flyer, folded it up, and pocketed it.

That man got me a little rattled. "I got some stuff to do. I just . . . wanted to stop by."

"What for?"

"I don't know. Just . . . to say hi."

"Oh. . . hey."

I waved. "Hi."

He shook his head, laughing. "You're funny, Fish. You're looking pretty good, though. You dress up for me?"

I shuffled my feet. Maybe, a little.

"Mm-mmm," he said smiling. "You sure you don't wanna come up for a bit?"

I did but . . . "Maybe later?"

He shrugged. "OK, then. Text me; I got something coming up you should come to."

He waved and disappeared from sight.

I could feel that flyer burning a hole in my pocket. It made me uneasy; the bruises on my knuckles began to ache.

I started walking the other way. I needed to clear my mind. I glanced back at Kalvin's apartment. I thought I saw Destiny peeking out the window, but I could've been wrong.

17

All that night, I kept thinking about Mrs. Lee's boyfriend or husband or whatever he was. It was one thing to see a mention in the paper. But now, people were looking at TKO. Maybe he was just a crank, somebody who thought he could rid the world of everything he thought was bad. But he had a big mouth and sometimes big mouths get heard. Which meant that if K and the boys ever got caught, I'd get caught too.

I stared at the flyer again. It said things like: *BLACK ON WHITE CRIME! SPEAK OUT! TAKE BACK OUR NEIGHBORHOODS!* They called us *mindless* and *criminal* too. It made us look like we were some thugs roaming the streets, raping and pillaging. Were we? I mean old people are always complaining about young people—the music is too loud; they're into drugs and sex and video games. Knockout was just another game compared to the guys on my corner who were actual crackheads and dealers or gangbangers or whatever. They actually killed people. How come *they* weren't being hunted down? OK, I knew that was bullshit but still, compared to what some others were doing . . .

On the flyer, I noticed a link to a Facebook page. I was curious, so I looked it up.

The group page was called *Knockout Violence!* There was a picture of a group of people who called themselves The Watchers (as in, we're watching you) all wearing those red shirts with eyes on them. That man was front and center. His name was Joe Lee and he was a medic in the Iraq war who'd been injured and now is all about helping fight for a strong community. There was a page about the protest, followed by links to news coverage of different attacks that had happened. These attacks went back several years. I read a few of them and it made me upset.

At the bottom of the page was a YouTube video with the man's face on it. My cursor hovered over the PLAY button and finally, I just clicked on it.

The man was sitting at his desk, an American flag behind him.

"My name is Joe Lee. I'm a former medic for the Marines and head of the neighborhood watch committee for the Tower Grove area. I want to be clear up front: we are a group of concerned citizens who are *not* willing to stand by while our way of life is slowly being destroyed. It is being shattered by random attacks on white citizens by black perpetrators." He paused dramatically. "There, I said it. This is not some crazy right-wing conspiracy from Fox News. In fact, I wish you could hear about it on Fox News, or any news, but the media refuses to call a spade a spade, because it's not PC to say *black-on-white* crime. But the facts are what they are. If you are white, you need to be on alert. It doesn't matter if you are young or old, male or female. If you live in St. Louis, particularly—"

Here, he unfolded a homemade map of St. Louis. He had circled several neighborhoods in red. "If you live in one of these five neighborhoods: Compton Heights, Oak Hill, Shaw, Tower Grove East, and South. These are the hot spots for black-on-white crime that is being perpetrated by a gang of bored teenagers who get their kicks inflicting horrifying violence on random white victims."

WTF? This was crazy. My first thoughts were that Kalvin was right: this guy's a crank. But then the more I thought about it, doubt crept in. All our targets had been white. Every. Single. One.

I shared the link with Destiny and said, "Is this true? Are we really what he says we are?" I clicked send.

I went back and saw a link to a video page. It was filled with videos that The Watchers had made. They followed young black men and documented their movements. More than a few showed Kalvin and members of the TKO. Some showed evidence that Kalvin was messing with them—leaving rude comments on their Facebook page or dog shit on Joe Lee's front doorstep. There were all kinds of comments and once they got started, the commenters became really vicious—against us.

I freaked out when I saw a video with *me* in it from the back. The woman who was filming commented to someone how sad it was to see a white girl get mixed up in all of this.

At least they hadn't caught us playing Knockout. Yet.

Suddenly, there was a *ping!*—a message from Kalvin Barnes, right on time, like he knew what I was thinking.

I took a deep breath, opened it.

"Don't let that fool scare you off. He's just making noise. Guys like that tend to get caught for doing something stupid.

They always do." He added a link to an article about The Watchers, which mentioned a bit about Joe's troubled past—being dishonorably discharged from the service and annoying the city council with baseless claims on the so-called race war.

Destiny must've forwarded my message.

I stared at Kalvin's profile picture. It didn't occur to me that he had his own Facebook page since he always posted from the TKO Club page. His profile pic looked like one of those stock pictures, all bright-eyed and smiling, just the nicest guy in the world.

But when I began scrolling his info, I got this weird feeling down my spine. Was this even the same person?

Name: Kalvin Octavius Barnes

Job: community organizer, youth activist

Studies at: University of Missouri

From: Saint Louis, Missouri

Knows: Russian, Arabic, kung fu, sword fighting, and deep-sea diving

He had to be messing around. I guess anyone can say anything they want about themselves online or just reinvent themselves. Was this the version of himself that he wanted to be? Or just a cover?

There were a bunch of pictures, and they were definitely of him. There was even a cute one of him and Boner. I knew he was NOT going to university, but whatever. Maybe that was just a cover for him not being at school.

There were pictures of him with some of the Tokers I recognized. He looked like a big brother, taking them for pizza, posing in a gym dressed like a boxer. And then some of girls that looked like more than friends.

Including one of *me*, a still he lifted from the park video.

Another image showed him and a younger looking Destiny. They were standing next to another guy who looked kind of like her—her brother? I noticed K had his hand on her ass. Brother was not smiling.

One of the weirdest touches was at the end of his list of favorites. His favorite quote kind of gave me a chill: *A disobedient child shall not live his or her days to the end.*

18

A day passed. I thought of Kalvin a lot, but kept to myself, trying to figure out what it all meant. Were we *going together* now? Was that a onetime thing? I wanted to talk to Destiny, but there was something going on there I wasn't quite sure about.

In art class, I still didn't feel like drawing anything, but I had worked up the nerve to finally show Mrs. Lee some of my non-TKO videos, like the ant one and some of the ones I made about my neighborhood. I'd given her a DVD to watch at home, and when she saw me, she made a beeline for my desk.

"Erica! Your videos are quite good. I *knew* you had an artist's eye. You're a rebel; I can see that. Keep going. I want to see more!"

I didn't think she meant my TKO videos. Speaking of artistic eye, she was wearing that T-shirt with all the mouths and ears and eyes on them. "Are you the one who makes those Eyez all over the neighborhood?" I asked.

She blushed and looked around. She looked a little rattled.

"I just made one and my husband kind of co-opted it for his own purposes. It's interesting to see them posted around, but, as a teacher, I'm not supposed to be doing graffiti art. . . . "

"You're a rebel too, I guess. I met your husband—"

This rattled her even more. "You met Joe?"

"He handed me a flyer."

"Oh," she nodded, unsure. "He's really the rebel. I just try to keep him grounded."

"Do you believe in his cause?"

She paused for a long beat, choosing her words carefully. "I believe you need to stand up for what you believe in and that people have a right to be safe in their own neighborhoods. He's more the activist. I try to work from the other side, through art and education. I try not to pick fights."

***

On the second day, I decided to talk to Destiny. I spotted her from my locker but she was with her "other" friends. So I waited, and while I was standing at my locker, this white girl from my homeroom came over. She was the skinny blonde who always ignored me in class. But today, she wanted to talk. I think her name was Autumn.

"Maybe she don't want to be your friend anymore," she said, nodding at Destiny's clique. I wasn't sure she was even talking to me, but there was no one else around.

"You talking to me?" I asked. I didn't look at her because, first of all, I felt even fatter standing next to her. Secondly, I didn't know her. She was in one of my classes, but we never said hi or anything.

Destiny was watching me out of the corner of her eye. I just shrugged. "At least she talks to me," I said under my breath.

"Yeah, but why would you want to talk to her?" the girl said.

This is not how I imagined our first conversation would go. "You know this is the first time you ever spoke to me, right?" I said louder. "Destiny is my friend, that's why."

She rolled her eyes. "Isn't she the one that you got in a fight with?"

I turned back to my locker. It was true; that's how we met.

"Maybe you haven't noticed, but about 80 percent of the kids here are not like us," she said.

"What do you mean, *us*?" I was nothing like her.

She frowned. "You know, *us*." She held out her arm next to mine.

Her arm was delicate and pure, with manicured finger-nails. I didn't have to hold up mine for comparison. Mine was thick, with scratches on it. My nails were chewed as short as they could be.

"You mean people with arms?"

"No, idiot. Didn't anybody tell you, you have to hang with your own people?"

I kind of laughed in her face.

"No, I must have missed *that* announcement. All I know is since I been here the last two months, nobody but Destiny has given me the time of day. If you or your *white* sisterhood had bothered—"

"Problem?" Destiny had snuck up behind this girl.

The girl glared at Destiny, then back at me. "Yeah." She just shook her head and left. I heard her mutter "wigger," and I almost went after her.

Destiny grabbed my arm. "Hold on there, girl. She's just jealous, don't you see? Let it go."

I was thinking that girl would make an excellent target for a Knockout Game. I could see my fist wiping that perfect makeup off her face, her head flying into the lockers—.

"Hey, are you with me?" Destiny stared into my eyes. "You been hanging low last coupla days. S'up?" she asked.

"I was about to say the same to you. You seemed kinda stressed last time I saw you. Why'd you leave us in the park?"

"Family stuff. You know how it is."

I did. I wasn't gonna press her on it.

"I saw Kalvin yesterday." She watched me for any kind of reaction. I played it cool. "Seems Kalvin likes having you around."

I tried to read her face. "Is that OK?" I asked. "I mean, with you."

She made a funny noise in her throat. "Hmph. Who invited you to join TKO?"

Trick question? "You did?"

"OK then." Matter settled.

I turned back to my locker. "So how come you passed my message on to Kalvin?"

She acted confused.

"Facebook?" I reminded her.

"Oh that. I just wanted him to know you were worried is all. He 'asked' me to keep an eye on you."

"What's that mean?"

"Nothing." She sighed and relaxed her stance. "Look, K's got something in store for that guy, Joe Lee. Gonna crash his 'rally' this week. Let him know he ain't afraid. And he wants you there too. But only if you record it and don't knock the crap outta some old dude."

I scowled at her. "You think I wanted to do that?"

"Just don't do it again. It's not your style."

"But it's yours?"

For a second she looked like the old Destiny, ready to take me out. But I must have looked overly concerned because instead, she pulled me into a hug which she never did at school. "You alright, Fish. You just new to all a this."

***

Walking home, I wasn't sure what to think. Destiny told me more about Kalvin: that he was just messing with people on his Facebook page, that he'd been suspended six months ago because supposedly some Knockout Games happened near Truman and he was under investigation.

"No way Kalvin's comin' back to school," said Destiny answering my unasked question.

My phone buzzed in my pocket.

Speak of the devil. I was not playing hard to get; I guess I was just a little bit confused. On the fifth ring, I answered.

"Hey you," K said. "What're you doing?"

I was trying to think of an excuse, but my mind was blank. "Walking home from school."

"Hmm." There was silence on the other end. "School."

"How are you?" I asked. So lame.

"How am I? I'm just wondering where you been. At first I figured maybe I had scared you off or something."

I shook my head. "No. Nothing like that."

There was a pause on his end. "Then I thought maybe you didn't like kissing me or something."

My face felt hot. "No... I—I like that part."

It was true.

"Good. 'Cause my Boner misses you."

"*What?*"

"My dog, Erica. What were you thinking?"

I smiled. Bad joke. Still . . .

I heard him sigh. "So, is it those neighborhood watchers and the rally and all that?"

"Well . . ." I hesitated. "It did kinda throw me."

He paused for a beat. "Like I said, don't worry about that, I have an idea how to take care of them."

Images of Kalvin shooting Joe Lee flashed through my head.

"Water balloons," he said.

"What?"

"It's Friday. They're having their *Knockout Violence!* rally tonight, right? I had this idea maybe we could hang on top of my building and give them a real St. Louis welcome."

Water balloons? "Really?" I asked.

"Yeah, why not? It'll show the media that we're just a bunch of kids having fun. What's more kidlike than a water balloon fight?"

"We could use pies," I suggested. I'd seen that on TV.

"Pies," he scoffed. "Too messy. Plus, we'd have to be on the ground. This way, they won't see it coming. So, you in?"

Water balloons I could deal with. "I guess."

"She guesses," he said off phone to someone else. "Whatever. Be at my house at seven. Afterwards, maybe we could do something . . . *else*," he added, suggestively.

"Like what?" I asked, all innocent.

"Well, you haven't shown me those drawings you done. Maybe I could come over. . . . "

Fat chance. "We'll see. . . . "

"Yeah, we will," he said. "Lates."

He hung up. I was still blushing.

19

The night air was cold and crisp, so we could hear the noise from a couple blocks away. A man's voice on a bullhorn: "It's time to stand up and fight for your rights! What do we want?" Then the response: "Justice!"

"When do we want it?"

"Now!"

I had my camera out when me and Destiny turned the corner, and the first thing I saw was about sixty people huddled in front of the church on the corner. Joe Lee was on top of the church steps. Standing behind him, Mrs. Lee was scanning the crowd nervously.

When Joe leaned over and whispered in her ear, I wondered how much she was like him, or maybe, he was like her and I just didn't see it. She leaned into his ear and seemed worried about something. He nodded and stroked her arm trying to ease her concerns. Finally, he raised his bullhorn and spoke.

"St. Louis was once one of America's most beautiful cities," he said. "Beautiful brick buildings, a glorious history in baseball, and the Gateway Arch. Am I right? Now, it's known as one of America's most dangerous cities."

He scanned the crowd, saw people nodding. "These seemingly random attacks are going on in our own neighborhoods—and the perps are not just a bunch of gangbangers whose after school programs have been cut or can't find work to keep them busy. This is about boredom and violence, and how violence is the only thing that snaps these kids out of their video game stupor. And the sad truth is, it's only our black youth that are playing the Knockout Game, attacking white victims and getting away with it because they are just 'kids.' "

There was a murmur running through the crowd. Some clapped; others looked unsure. "Now I'm no racist. I love black people. Some of my St. Louis heroes are black: Lou Brock, Miles Davis, Maya Angelou, Scott Joplin. These people represented their race—and us—proudly. But something has gone terribly wrong in the last decade or so. Yes, there is a black president. But even he is powerless against this rising tide of aimless violence in our youth. People don't feel safe anymore. Our neighborhoods have been taken from us by thugs."

I scanned the crowd. They did not look like militants, just normal white people—neighbors.

"The city will tell you they are doing what they can," said Joe, pointing to two cops standing under a streetlight. "But it's not enough to stem the tide. We, the people, must be vigilant. We, the people, must protect our own from these thugs. We have tried to reach out—through education, after school programs. I personally have tried to talk to many of the black youth around here, and my dear wife," he looked over at Mrs. Lee, "has done more than her fair share of trying to open young people's eyes through art and education." She seemed embarrassed by the attention.

"But there comes a time when we, the people, must stop being victims and start taking *action*! If the police can't help— and I see no evidence that they can—the time for talking must stop and we, the people, will start taking things into our own hands! *We* must make our streets safe. *We* must take control of our lives. *We* must make change. That is why we've formed an action group of neighborhood watch patrols to keep our citizens safe!"

The crowd roared. Many were holding up signs: WE WANT OUR NEIGHBORHOOD BACK! MAKE OUR STREETS SAFE FOR OUR CHILDREN! and ATTACK ME AND YOU WILL MEET THE WRONG END OF MY .44!

"Pretty powerful stuff, huh?"

I glanced up from my camera to see the pizza guy standing next to me. I froze. I hadn't recognized him because of the winter cap he was wearing. But he wasn't looking at me. His eyes were glued on the speaker. I nodded, staring at his face. The last time I saw him, I thought he was dead. Now he had a bandage over his eye and wore a neck brace. He was leaning on a crutch.

Paranoid, I scanned the crowd and saw a few more of our "targets" in the audience. I elbowed Destiny and when she saw the pizza guy, she pulled me to the back. We spotted the two cops and threw our hoodies over our heads, walking as fast as we could toward Kalvin's building, which overlooked the street corner.

"That was close," she said.

The front door was open. I stopped her before we went up. "Are we really going to do this?" I asked.

"We're doing what Kalvin wants us to do. Don't worry, nobody's gonna get hurt. Just fighting fire with water." She made a splashing sound.

We ran up to the third story, where his apartment was. There was a piece of paper taped to the door with an arrow pointing toward the roof deck.

The roof door was ajar. I heard whispering and the sounds of things being moved. I was about to poke my head out when Doughboy came up from behind me.

"Out the way! Ammo comin' in!"

He was carrying a garbage bag over his shoulder. He swung the door open, and I saw the crew in the dark lined up behind the edge of the rooftop. Doughboy dropped the bag and water balloons came tumbling out of it.

"Careful, *ese*!" hissed Prince. "Don't fuckin' waste 'em." He picked up a water balloon and nailed Doughboy in the chest. *Whap!* Drenched.

"Hey bitch, that's cold!" He picked up a balloon and everyone dove in and scrambled for the rest.

"Chill!" Everyone froze. It was Kalvin, sitting on a chair behind the open door.

"What the fuck? This ain't playtime. We're here to make a point."

He walked out and saw us standing in the doorway. "Hey girls. Just in time. Make sure you get my good side, Fish." He winked, then turned his attention to his minions.

"Listen up. They gonna be marching down this street in a few minutes and when we see ol' Joe Lee pass by with his big ol' bullhorn, we gonna let him have it, *comprende*?"

"Why we don't all just go down there and play Knockout?" Prince muttered. "A few KOs, *that* would make a statement."

Kalvin nodded. "Yeah, a stupid one. We got to be cool, Prince. Can't be doing the obvious. They expect us to act like animals or something. We got to show them it's all a joke to us."

Prince was flustered. "Well, that *cabron* is wrong. I ain't no stinkin' animal."

Kalvin took the water balloon from Prince and rolled it in his hands. "Damn straight. Now let's show these fuckers what we got."

They ducked behind the barrier armed with balloons. Kalvin noticed me standing there. "You too, girls."

Destiny grabbed a couple of balloons and held one out for me.

"But I'm gonna record this," I protested, holding up my camera.

"Don't be a wuss." She tossed me a balloon. I let go of the camera to catch it. Luckily, the camera was strapped to my wrist.

"Just throw with one hand and shoot with the other," she added.

We sat with our backs on the barrier and I pointed my camera down the line. It was like one of those war movies where they were getting ready to attack. C-Jay sat next to me, drawing a face on a balloon with a Sharpie pen. "Who's that?" I asked.

"It's me! That dude's gonna look up and see me coming for him!" he said, all excited.

"There's a couple cops down there," I told Kalvin.

"*Eh*," he scoffed. "Mall cops looking for overtime. Besides, we're hidden by the dark up here. No one will know where the attack came from."

I listened to the chants coming from down the street and tilted my camera up and over the ledge to see. Sure enough, they were on the march. Joe Lee was in front, chanting on his bullhorn: "What do we want?"

"Justice!"

"When do we want it?"

"Now!"

That last chant came right as they marched in front of our building.

Kalvin rose up. "You heard 'em. They want it now. Well, let's give it to 'em!"

We all rose up, arms cocked, ready for battle.

"Fire!" he hissed. Nobody saw the cloud of water balloons coming their way.

I let mine fly first, just so I could see what I was filming. It was blind luck that it headed straight at Joe Lee. The last thing I heard him say into the bullhorn was: "Shit!"

Bullseye. The balloon exploded on his chest, the others splattered the crowd around him, dousing some of the candles the marchers had. The boys stayed calm and before the crowd could run, the second round was in the air and headed their way.

The crowd scattered like ants. Nobody seemed to know where the balloons came from, pointing up in different directions into the darkness.

When someone pointed our way, some of the boys panicked. "Dang, we gotta get outta here!" said Tyreese. Within three seconds, they were all running back down the stairs. Destiny and Prince were right behind them, laughing. I got up to leave, but Kalvin grabbed my arm.

"Stay," he said, as a dare. My feet were ready to move, but he had so much confidence in his eyes, I stayed put.

Prince lingered by the door. "*Orale!* Come on, K. They're coming."

Kalvin walked up to Prince and put his hand on his shoulder. "You go on ahead. I'll catch you later. Make sure everyone goes out the back." He gently pushed him through the door and closed it behind him. Prince started to say, "But—," and then the door clicked shut. The last thing I saw was Destiny, down the hallway, looking confused.

"Uh . . . what are we doing?" I asked, panic starting to rise in my throat.

"Wait." He grinned, grabbing the chair he'd been sitting on. He jammed it under the doorknob good and tight. There was a cement planter sitting to the side. "Come on, help me." It was heavy, but we managed to slide it over in front of the door. "Let's see them get through that!" he said.

There was no other way out. The buildings next door were shorter or taller than ours and there was no fire escape leading up here.

Kalvin took an apple out of his jacket pocket, polished it on his shirt, and took a bite as he watched the scene below. A few Tokers made their way out the front, busting past people coming in. The cops gave a halfhearted chase. Mrs. Lee now had the bullhorn and was pleading for people to stay focused.

I peeked over the ledge right when Joe looked up where we were. We both ducked down out of sight.

"He saw us!" I panicked.

"No, he didn't. It's too dark up here."

We waited and listened. Kalvin calmly took a bite of his apple and offered it to me.

I heard steps. Someone was running up the stairs. "He's coming!" I hissed, about to run for it.

"Ooooh . . ." he said, pretending to be scared. He held on to my arm so I couldn't bolt—not that there was anywhere to go. "Chill. Don't you trust me?"

The doorknob moved. Someone pushed on the door; luckily, it didn't budge.

"Kalvin . . ." I said nervously. Kalvin giggled like it was no big thing.

Somebody rattled the door and started pushing on it. Hard.

"What?" he whispered. "We got the roof to ourselves." Kalvin regarded me with those green eyes of his and held out the apple for me. This was nuts, but he just didn't seem to care.

I had to admit, it was kind of exciting.

I took a bite of his apple as he held it, the juice dripping down my chin. He leaned in and licked it. The next thing I knew, we were kissing.

Someone kept banging on the door, cursing us, but those sounds disappeared from my mind as I felt his breath on mine. He kissed me deeply, his tongue doing all kinds of things that scattered my thoughts. I came up for air, out of breath.

"Kalvin . . ." was all I could manage to say.

He put his finger to my lips and gazed into my eyes. I was confused—should I give in and hope the cops don't come busting through? Should I let go and do whatever came next?

"Trust me," he whispered.

I held on to his hand. Suddenly, it felt like this could go

further. Everything felt heightened, more alive, like anything could happen.

I nodded, opened his hand and kissed his palm. I felt awkward doing it. It was something I saw on TV and thought was sexy. But he took my other hand and started doing the same thing and it sent a chill up my spine.

I was breathing harder and then I just had to grab him and hold him tight. He began kissing my neck and I couldn't help it, I started giggling. I didn't know what to do. But for every fumble I made, he made a gentle adjustment—he just showed me how to do it. Guiding me by the hand. I let him.

As we made our way to the ground, in the back of my mind I wasn't sure if I was I ready for this.

He pulled back softly and looked at me. "Are you scared?" he asked.

I wasn't sure what the right answer was. "I guess."

He stroked my hair. "We don't have to do anything if you don't want to." Right then the banging on the door stopped. Kalvin shrugged. "I guess he realized there was nothing going on here. . . . "

I eased up and held him close. Maybe I was ready to try. "Do you have any . . . " I couldn't even say the word.

"Condoms?" He gritted his teeth and shook his head. "Normally, I woulda come prepared, but I really wasn't expecting this. I guess I just got caught up in everything. . . . " He paused to think about it. "When did you have your . . . last period?" he asked, embarrassed.

"That's kinda personal, don't you think?"

He just raised his eyebrows as if to say *it doesn't get more personal than this*.

"Oh. Yeah, I guess . . . a week ago?"

"Mm," he said, unsure.

His body was pressed to mine, so I wasn't exactly thinking straight. "Maybe we could just do it . . . just a little?" I asked.

He smiled. "A little . . . is not so easy."

"It's my first time," I blurted out before I could stop myself.

I expected him to laugh, but he didn't. He kept stroking my hair. "I can be gentle, you know. The first time should be nice."

He kissed me softly on the cheek, caressing my hair, my face, my lips. Slowly, I could feel something building in me like a train. I kept wondering how much it was going to hurt, but everything else was feeling good.

"Give me your camera," he whispered into my ear.

"What?" I asked.

He smiled gently. "I want to record us."

That made me uneasy. "Why?"

"This will be a moment to remember, something just for us." He kissed me even deeper, his hand roaming my body and then stopped when it found the camera in my pocket.

"Nuh-uh," I said. "This is one video that is not happening."

He acted hurt. "Not even . . . for me?"

I shook my head. "Some things are off limits."

His other hand was resting on my heart. He could feel it pounding like it was going to jump out of my chest. He nodded.

"I need you to trust me," he whispered. "I'll take care of you." He kissed me softly and started to undo my pants.

I grabbed his hand.

"Just . . . relax," he whispered.

That's when his hand slid down into my panties.

Oh. So that's what that's like. I closed my eyes and melted into his body. I relaxed.

I could feel him doing something with his pants and I just let it happen.

"Are you OK?" he breathed into my ear as he pressed his body into mine. A "yes" escaped my lips even before I knew what he meant. Out of the corner of my eye, I saw him pull out his phone and set it against the wall next to us.

"I want to be able to see you when you're not with me."

"But—"

His mouth glided down to my breast and a white-hot flash engulfed my thoughts. "It's just for me, for my eyes only," he said, but before I could protest, his other hand slid off my pants, and I lost control. "You're the only one," he said as the stars started spinning.

I wanted to make him happy. I let him take me for a ride.

20

We spent the night on that roof. It was freezing, but our bodies gave off so much heat, we could've melted an iceberg. Kalvin grabbed some blankets from a storage box where he kept boxing gloves and stuff. He claimed in the summers, he and the crew would lie out under the sun. I found that hard to believe but at the moment, I didn't care.

We cuddled up under the stars and listened to all the hoopla on the street slowly die out, until it grew quiet. I had bled some, but the pain had been less than I'd expected. He had taken it slow and gentle, like he promised. It felt weird, but I liked that he took his time. We ended up doing more than just a little, but he said he had pulled out in time. And now, I guess I was no longer a virgin.

Even though the last thing I wanted to do was watch me fumble about, we watched the video. I could see it meant a lot to him. At first it felt super strange being in front of the camera, *especially* like that. Oh my God. My only thought was what if my parents saw this? But Kalvin was very reassuring. He said he'd send it to me, for my eyes only. This was our first real moment together and now it was captured forever.

A picture might have been better but I guess that's what people were doing these days. I just went along because I wanted him to feel happy, I guess.

"Don't go showing this to the guys or anything," I said, just to make sure.

He acted insulted. "I would never do that, Erica." I believed him.

***

I knew I should be home in case my mom Skyped me. I texted her saying that I was going to sleep and I'd see her in the morning. We hadn't Skyped for a while, so she should buy it.

"Say hi for me," said Kalvin.

I elbowed him. "Yeah, maybe you want to show her that video while you're at it?"

I'd spent years wondering what it would feel like to be with someone, but this was not what I expected—doing it outside with a black boy on a sex tape. Despite everything it took to get here, though, it felt surprisingly right. Except for the video part.

I spotted Boner watching us from the window above. He didn't yap or jump about like his usual self. At least he wasn't threatened by me.

Kalvin told me that when his dad died, he'd hide out here alone at night and watch the stars. He hoped maybe his dad was up there looking back. I joked that maybe he hadn't been alone up here, but he shook off the idea that he'd be out here with another girl.

In a quiet moment, he gazed at my skin under the moonlight. "It must be weird having white skin," he said. He confessed that he'd always wanted to be with a white girl, especially one with red hair. He'd had plenty of black girlfriends before, but when he saw me, even though I was hiding behind a camera and a hoodie, he had a feeling. Like I was just waiting for him.

"So you must like . . . big girls?" I asked, feeling the flab on my stomach.

"What?!" He laughed so hard he almost choked. "You think all black brothers dig big white women? Is that what you heard?"

I nodded.

He kissed me softly. "People are into things that are different from themselves, that's what draws us. You're about as different from me as I am from you. Opposites attract, right?" He stroked my hair. "Besides, you're just all woman, and I like that. Don't care for them skinny model types. I want a real woman, one that you can feel the weight of."

I poked him. "The weight of?"

He didn't back off. "That's right. And that hair? Come on, for real? It's like you're the sun or something. How many girls got real red hair? You don't need to hide it under that hoodie. Show yourself; be proud of who you are."

He was right. I was tired of hiding. "White boys never even look at me, unless they're making fun."

"Well, fuck 'em," he said angrily. "What do they know? They're into those cutesy little girls with their ponytails. That ain't a woman. *You're* what I want. I'll take you to any dance you like."

That meant a lot, even though I couldn't picture him in a

tux escorting me to the prom. But this was better. He held me tight and didn't say anything more, slowly falling asleep in my arms. For the longest time, I just watched his face.

He *was* different. That's what intrigued me. There was something dangerous about him, but I knew he had a sweet side too. That's what drew me in. Under the stars, I felt good to be next to him and yeah, maybe even good about myself. I pulled off the blanket and let myself be naked for all to see. It was dark out, so it wasn't that risky. I got goose bumps all over from the cold, but for the first time, I wasn't ashamed about what I looked like. Against his dark lean body, I was yin to his yang. Lightness and dark. A whole.

I covered us up and dozed off. I wasn't asleep very long before he started twitching and rolling about. Bad dreams. I looked closely at his face, trying to read his mind. I almost got elbowed in the face for it. I woke him up and he jumped with a start, his fists up and ready to attack. I had to call out his name a few times before he saw it was me, even though he was looking right at me. He was covered with sweat.

***

The sun slowly crept up on the horizon and I knew I should get home before Mom got there. He seemed sad to see me go, but he let me. "I still wanna see those drawings you made," he said.

I looked around and spotted the Sharpie C-Jay had used earlier. "Hold on," I said. I reached out and grabbed it, then slung his leg over my lap.

"What're you doing?" he laughed.

"Giving you something to remember me by." I looked up

and saw Boner still in the window. It took me about ten minutes to capture his likeness.

"Well?" I asked.

"That's some tat." He gazed at it, amazed. "It doesn't look like you, though."

I pushed him off me and got up. "Funny."

He touched the ink dog. "I'll never wash it."

"You better not," I said as I headed to the door with only thoughts of what we did just a few hours ago.

When I hit the street, the first thing I saw was a pair of those Eyez drawn in chalk on the sidewalk in front of Kalvin's building. They were watching, but did they see us? I felt invisible walking through the damage from last night—broken balloons, trampled signs, a few shattered car windows on the street—I just floated through it all. As I turned the corner, I glanced back at Kalvin's building.

He was still watching me from the roof.

***

Of course I barely beat Mom home. I didn't even have time to change. I was so flustered, I couldn't bear talking to her, scared I might reveal something by accident. So I said I had to go meet up with Destiny because of some video project that we were going to present on Monday. She asked when was I going to show her something and I said, "Soon."

Right as I was headed out, she stopped me.

"What happened to your hand?"

My fist was still puffy and bruised. "I . . . tripped. At school."

She touched it; it was still tender. "Are you OK? Do you need to see a doctor?"

I pulled my hand back. "No, the school nurse said it wasn't broken."

"Well, good. At least you'll be able to draw again."

She was always throwing in things like that out of nowhere as if the past was always on her mind. I didn't respond.

When she came in to hug me, her expression changed. Something was off. She looked me up and down like something was different.

"What?" I asked.

She kind of blushed and wouldn't say. I hurried out, embarrassed. At the bus stop, I smelled my collar. It smelled of Kalvin.

21

I spent the whole Sunday wandering the city alone. I tried hooking up with Destiny, but she was nowhere to be found. I thought about going over to Kalvin's, but part of me said I should play it cool and not be too eager. I knew boys didn't like that.

On Monday, a mandatory assembly in the cafeteria was suddenly scheduled. I needed to talk to somebody about the night before and there was only one person I was looking for: Destiny. But she wasn't in homeroom and didn't answer my texts. As soon as I walked into the cafeteria, there she was, sitting alone at one of the tables, staring at her phone.

I sat down next to her. She seemed distant, barely acknowledging my presence.

"Where were you this morning?" I asked, as the students filed in.

She kept staring at her phone, then barely said, "Something came up."

"Is everything OK?" I asked.

She shrugged. "I don't know, is it?"

I hated when people played games. "What are you talking about?"

She looked at me for the first time. It was a look I hadn't seen since she'd challenged me to a fight way back when. "Maybe you should ask Kalvin."

She was giving me all kinds of attitude. So I dished some back. "I would if he was here, but I'm asking you because you're in front of my face."

I could see the wheels spinning in her head. "You really don't know?"

"Jesus, Destiny. OK. Yeah I . . . stayed last night with Kalvin. I'm sorry if I . . . " *Fuck this.* "Look, you never said you and him were—"

She cut me off. "Were what?"

I glanced down at my hands, which were shaking. I had never been in the middle of something like this.

"God, you really were a virgin, weren't you?" she said.

WTF?

She was still fiddling with her phone. "Well, at least you'll be able to share the memories with your grandkids," she said all snarky.

Now I was really confused. "What are you *talking* about?"

She looked around. People were still settling in, talking and making jokes. No one was sitting next to us yet. She thought for a minute, then held her phone in front of my face. "Gotta say, though, his camera work is nowhere near yours." She pressed Play.

I stared at the video. It was me, out of focus and blurry, until the camera settled. Then I saw Kalvin on top on me. It was from the roof last night.

Holy shit.

I grabbed it from her and stopped the video. "Where did you get this?"

She leaned in. "Where do you *think*?"

I grabbed her arm. Angry tears rolled down my face. "No. Tell me. *Where* did you get this?"

She pushed my hands away. "Kalvin sent me a link."

"He *sent* this to you?" I couldn't believe it.

She took her phone from my hands. "Don't worry, I'm the only one who can see it on Facebook."

"It's on *Facebook*?" My mind was reeling. I grabbed my phone, tried to access my Facebook page. When it came up, there was no link to the video.

"Ladies, no phones! You know the rules." It was Mr. Jamison, patrolling the room with his crooked eyes. Destiny scratched her nose with her middle finger. Jamison moved on to the next offender.

She watched him go, then whispered, "Kalvin sent it to me. I had to look. I know he was just trying to push my buttons. But now I don't give a shit."

My first thought was, Did Kalvin use me to get back at her for some reason? "Destiny, I didn't—"

But before I could get into it, the principal tapped on the microphone. "Alright, settle down everyone. We have a special guest here and I need everyone's complete attention. What he has to say concerns all of you."

I shot a look at Destiny, but her eyes were glued to the stage where Principal Evans was watching over the crowd. Today he was all business. He stood next to another black man—older, calmer, and dressed like a businessman. He surveyed the room like he'd seen it all. I could see the badge on his belt from here.

Evans glared at us like we were all guilty. "What Mr. Graves has told me is extremely disturbing—"

That's when I noticed someone else had joined them onstage: Joe Lee.

Fuck me.

Someone cracked a joke, but I didn't hear it, just the laughter from a group to the right.

Evans snapped. "Hey. Hey! If I hear one more comment, you will have Mr. Jamison to deal with. And anyone here who has dealt with him personally, I'm pretty sure doesn't want a repeat of *that* scenario."

He stared down the jokester as if he was daring him to talk out again. "Do I make myself clear?" There was no response. "DO . . . I . . . MAKE . . . MYSELF . . . CLEAR?"

We all mumbled, "Yes, sir."

He scowled at us for what seemed like forever. I wanted to say something to Destiny, but it was so quiet, I was sure Evans would hear me.

"Good. This is Mr. Rodney Graves, a special investigator from the juvenile division. I know many of you know him because he's a strong member of this community and always out on the streets walking the walk. He's come here to Truman because he believes there's a serious problem that involves our students. Mr. Graves . . . "

Joe Lee was whispering something in the cop's ear as he stepped up to the mic. Nobody clapped. Joe hung back, his eyes surveying the crowd.

I pulled my hoodie up over my head.

The cop had a slight Southern accent and an easy way about

him. "How many of y'all know about the Knockout Game?"

I covered the bruises on my hand with my long sleeves.

We all glanced around at each other. He had no patience. "Come on, no one's being arrested here. I'd like to know. How many of you know about this game?"

A few hands went up. Then some more. He kept encouraging us, so after a few seconds about half the assembly had their hands up.

Me and Destiny kept ours down.

"About half of you have heard of this. How many of you think it sounds like fun?"

There were some giggles and smiles and even more hands went up, mostly from the boys showing off.

"Alright. It's just a game, right?"

Several jokers cheered.

"Yeah! I hear you," he said all folksy. Then he got serious. "Now how many of you have *played* the Knockout Game?"

There was about a second delay before all the hands came down. Graves laughed. "Well, I figured that. See, the thing is, it turns out this game, after years of defying any kind of pattern or stats that we could follow up on, now has a pattern that can be identified." His eyes carefully studied us. "There have been twelve attacks in the last four months. And if you charted these out on a map, do you know where ground zero for these attacks would be?"

No one raised their hands.

"You all sitting on it. This school. And the middle school next door." He let that sink in.

"There have been witnesses who have described kids wearing colors similar to the school uniforms here and at Joplin. So it doesn't take a genius to tell me that sooner or later, arrests will be made." He rubbed his chin like he was surveying his crops. "Sooner or later, a witness will be willing to stand up in court and the 'club' that some of you belong to will be locked up—and I'm not just talking juvie here. I'm talking being tried as *adults*. For first-degree assault. With a deadly weapon. That's fifteen to twenty years right there, yup. How many of you think *that* would be fun?"

No one.

"Mm. Didn't think so. In my experience, it's hard for y'all to put yourself in the other person's shoes. That's what you call *empathy*. But prison—that you can understand, am I right?"

No one moved, laughed, or joked around. "The rules are changing on your little game. So I'd suggest that you all realize NOW that maybe sending someone to the hospital for no reason other than getting your kicks is maybe *not* in your best interest."

He paused for a long time, looking everyone in the eye. I swear he stopped when his eyes met mine. "Now, last night, everything changed. There was a peaceful protest lead by Mr. Lee here and apparently, some of you decided it'd be a good time to stage . . . a water balloon fight."

Laughs broke out. Graves smiled and nodded along. "Pretty funny, right?"

Destiny looked at me grimly. I shrugged.

He continued. "The only problem is, in the middle of the melee that broke out last night, one of you decided to knock out a protester as he made his way through the crowd. Except *that* person, who's now in the hospital, is a city councilman. So now the mayor has decided to make this a high priority alert and arrests will be made. *Convictions* will be made."

My eyes shot around the room and I saw Prince, his head in his hands, a little more than worried. I nudged Destiny and she saw him too, but said nothing. Then I remembered: she left with him last night.

"Did you see it?" I asked. She didn't answer.

Joe came up and whispered something else in Graves's ear. Graves nodded. "There were witnesses this time, and despite prior descriptions of the group, the suspect is a non-black male, approximately sixteen, with short dark hair cut in a Mohawk fashion."

All eyes drifted Prince's way. He slowly pulled his hoodie over his head. He was probably pissed off at Kalvin and wanting to make his own statement. Well, he made it all right.

"Instead of showing witnesses the usual mug shot book to identify the perp, this time we have a new book." He held up the Truman yearbook. Murmurs broke out in the room. "This is serious business, people. Some down at the station think it's just a small group doing these crimes. Others think that as many as 15 percent of you and the middle school kids are playing. As far as I am concerned: You are all potential suspects. And we will find you and prosecute you. Right now, I'm your friend. I'm here to help and listen and keep you all out of juvie. That's my mission. The rest is up to you."

With that, he stepped back and let the words sink in. Everyone started talking at once. The teachers moved in and began dismissing the students.

I spotted Prince trying to slink out, only to be stopped by Mr. Jamison. He wanted a word. I watched as he walked him to the corner of the stage where Evans and Graves were waiting for him.

Shit.

"What are we gonna do?" I asked Destiny.

She looked at me as if it was all my fault. "You better stay away from TKO."

She got up and left with the rest. I wasn't sure if that was the advice of a friend, or a warning.

22

As soon as the last school bell rang, I set out for Kalvin's place. His house was a good mile away, but I didn't care. There was so much swirling in my brain. Walking would help clear my head.

I had to pass a couple of The Watchers to get to his apartment building. Right before I went in, I glanced back and saw them filming me. I ignored them. The front door to Kalvin's building was open as usual. I made my way up and stood in front of his place, ready to knock.

But what was I going to say? I was so pissed about the video and upset about the assembly, I didn't know where to begin. Rip his head off or hide in his arms?

Before I could come up with an answer, the front door swung open and a woman who was on her way out jumped back, startled by my presence.

"Oh, my! You scared me, honey," she laughed. "Who you? What can I do you for?"

She was dark skinned, much darker than Kalvin. Her kind brown eyes considered me closely behind her librarian specs.

"I'm sorry, I was looking for Kalvin. . . . "

She smiled when she saw my school shirt. "Oh, Truman. Hi, I'm Kalvin's mom."

"Uh, hi . . . I'm . . . Erica." I stood there awkwardly.

"Hello, Erica. Are you dropping off homework for Kalvin? He says he's keeping up while he's . . . you know . . . on leave," she shook her head. "Always a different friend showing up. . . . Glad you all can help him, though."

I sighed. "Is he here?"

"He'll be here in about fifteen minutes. Out walking that dog of his. You can come in and wait if you want to."

"Uh, no thanks; I can come back."

She took my hand. "Nonsense. Come on in; you must be thirsty."

I guess I was. She took me into the kitchen and sat me down, plying me with juice and cookies. Maybe I looked younger than I was, but I didn't care; I scarfed them down anyway.

"How is school, Erica?"

I was still surprised by her appearance. She seemed so homey, a good motherly type. Not like a woman who gave birth to the Knockout King. "Uh, fine."

"I haven't met you before, have I?" Then suddenly, something clicked when she noticed my red hair. "*Oooh.* You're *Erica.* . . . " she said, knowingly. She winked at me. "One of Kal's *special* friends."

What did that mean? I blushed, staring into my glass.

She smiled. "Oh, it's OK. He never introduces me to his girlfriends, so it's nice to finally meet one."

One?

"I shouldn't show you this," she whispered. She got up and

opened one of the kitchen drawers, pulling out a crumpled piece of paper. She smoothed it out on the counter and brought it gently over like it might crumble into nothing. "The reason I know your name is, I was cleaning his room the other day and when I emptied the trash, I found this."

She handed me the paper. It was in Kalvin's writing. "A poem?" I said, surprised.

"He was probably too embarrassed to show you. Still, you must be quite something to inspire him to write poetry again."

Again? "Kalvin wrote a poem? For *me*?"

My eyes quickly scanned the page.

Red hair flaming

Eyes on fire

She don't go blaming

She ain't no liar.

She a fish staring out

From her underwater tank

Recordin' the truth

Like its money in tha bank

She got weight to her

And I don't mean how much

She feel heavy inside

You can feel her touch

She suck the air out

from all 'round me

She ain't afraid

She see right thru me

She will say what up

Right to my face.

She keeps me real

She no basket case.

But that hair of hers

Is like a match—

One strike

And she'll burn ya

that'll be the last.

But for now

She my latest thing

She got weight to her

She my bling bling

Where did that come from? My anger kept falling away as I reread his words. But then it came rushing back when I thought about the video he sent to Destiny.

His mom paused thoughtfully. "It's nice to see him writing after all these years. He used to write me all kinda poems when he was little. His hero was Muhammad Ali. You know, *float like a butterfly, sting like a bee*?"

Kalvin, the boxing poet. This was getting too much.

"Yes, he had quite the way with words. 'Course I'm talking back when he was five, back when he was a happy little guy. He used to call them *pomes*. Wait here; I'll show you something else."

Then she just walked out of the room, leaving me there alone. Maybe she had to go to the bathroom. . . .

She returned a minute later with her iPad. "I just had these pictures transferred from my old scrapbooks. It's so much easier these days."

Two minutes in and she's showing me baby pictures. Not what I had in mind. . . .

The first one was with a boy around three, cute as can be, sitting on her lap.

Even then, his eyes were intense.

"Where did those eyes come from?" I said, pointing them out.

"That's all his father left him with, those eyes. Striking, isn't it? He was such a happy kid in those days. Interested in all kinds of things. Always asking questions, how to do this, how to do that. Just soaking it all in."

"And now?" I asked.

She shrugged, forwarded to the next image. It was a silhouette shot at sunset—Kalvin around six on the shoulders of a man—tall, big and muscled.

"His dad," she said. "He was trouble . . . but I was attracted to trouble back then, like any girl is. I was rebellious, mostly against my parents, I guess." She stared at the picture. "We had our moments. He was a good man, but also a hard man. He drove Kal to become tougher because he believed . . . that's what it took to survive. Then he left us."

I knew that story. "Yeah, he told me. I'm sorry for your loss. I know what it means not having a dad around."

She looked surprised. "Oh? Your daddy's in prison too?"

I was confused. "You mean he's not—"

I heard the front door open, the dog yapping. Kalvin was back. I shoved the poem in my pocket.

"Not what, honey?" she asked. She saw Kalvin coming, then glanced mischievously back at me. "Oh, he's not going to like this."

Kalvin took one look at me with his mom and her iPad and knew it wasn't good. He walked over and grabbed it from her.

"Kal! There's no harm in sharing pictures with your friend."

"Some things ain't for friends!" he said. He glared at me and saw that I was more pissed off than he was. He grunted. "So I suppose you got it in for me too. Come on." He walked toward his room.

His mom sighed. She was used to it. "You want some more juice, honey?"

"No, thank you, Mrs. Barnes. I'll have a few words for your Kal, then I'll be going."

She shook her head. "I wouldn't waste your breath. He won't listen anyways. He doesn't listen to anybody."

***

He was sitting on his bed, holding his dog in his lap, when I walked into his room. I shut the door behind me. It was a little weird with his mom just on the other side, but I needed to unload.

First the sex video, then lying about his dad?

I knew he knew what I was mad about, so I waited for him to explain himself.

He was all tensed up, looking guilty. "OK, I fucked up."

"Really? I'm trying to understand why someone sends a video of a girl he's just *fucked* to that girl's only friend! That's what I'm trying to get. I mean, maybe I could see you showing it to your perverted little pal Prince, which would still be fucked up—but Destiny?!"

He kept his eyes glued to the wall. "It was an accident."

My jaw dropped. "An *accident*? Oh, this should be good. Go ahead, tell me how a sex video of us gets sent to my best friend? Go ahead."

His face was burning up. "This app I got posts it to Facebook and then you just tag the person you want to see it. Your name is right next to hers. I accidentally clicked on hers thinking it was you. It was a mistake. Believe me, D told me off good."

I sat there with my jaw open. I didn't know whether to believe him or not. "How is that even possible?"

"I said I was sorry, OK?!"

I was fuming. "No, actually, you didn't."

He looked at me for the first time. "OK, then. Well I am. Sorry."

"Of all people, her. I mean, you two already have some

weird history going on. I could see you sending it to her just to piss her off—"

"She's just one of the guys to me now."

"OK. I'm not even going to comment on that," I said, shaking my head. "I told you I didn't want you to record us."

He blinked. "I thought you'd understand. You filmed the crew doing all kinds of things and shared it—"

"This is nothing like that! Jesus—that was . . . my first time." A tear escaped my eye, but I quickly wiped it away.

"I'm—"

I cut him off. "Give me your phone."

He saw he was going to lose this one. "Fine."

He pushed Boner away and reached into his pocket, tossing the phone to me. Boner scampered to his hiding spot in the closet.

I didn't have to search for the video; it was already opened on his screen. I didn't ever want to see it again.

I deleted the video and waited for the phone to process it. "This was not something for others to see!" I threw the phone at him. He didn't duck fast enough; it pinged off his chest.

"Fuck, girl. Get your shit together," he said, rubbing his shirt.

"Delete it from Facebook. Now!" I watched him do it. He knew better than to argue.

When it was done, he stuck his phone in his pocket. "You got no problem filming some dude getting laid out—"

"Yeah, well that's gonna change. What is wrong with you? I'm not just one of your slutty girlfriends. That was supposed to be . . . special!"

"Special? You been watching too much TV. This is real life. People do it all the time now."

"Real life? It's MY life!" I yelled. "It's my *fucking* life!"

He jumped up when I started yelling. "Whoa, whoa, whoa. Chill. My moms is out there."

"I don't care," I said, my eyes misting up again. I ignored it, not wanting to give him the satisfaction.

"Hey. I'm sorry. Really." He walked slowly toward me trying not to spook me. I flinched when his hand touched my arm. "I'm really sorry," he whispered. "That was stupid of me. Maybe part of me did want to show someone; I don't know."

Unbelievable. "*Did* you show it to Prince and those guys?"

He seemed upset. "No. No, I promised I wouldn't do that. . . ."

I closed my eyes. Part of me wanted to hold on to my anger and let it eat him alive. But there was still something about him holding me that calmed me down instead. "You two. . . have a messed up friendship."

He nodded. My arms were limp at my side; he held me close. We stood there for a minute until I finally raised my arms and pushed him away.

"And why did you lie to me about your dad being dead? What's that about? I felt like an idiot in front of your mom."

Kalvin scoffed. "I didn't lie . . . not exactly." He went to the window and gazed out. "He is dead—to me."

I was out of words. I stood there for at least a minute or two staring at his backside. Finally, I just said, "I don't know what he did to you that was so bad or why he's in prison, but you are your own person. Those Tokers look up to you. You could do something with that besides turning them into fighting machines. I'm starting to think Joe Lee is right. It

140

makes no sense what we're doing."

"What—you on his side now?"

"He came to our school today. With the police! So far, I can't say he's lied. I mean, I've only seen you guys pick white people as your targets. How can you go after white people and say you're in—say you like being with *me*?"

He laughed bitterly. "Because it ain't about race! You just been hyped up by those commenters on his website. They think this is some kind of *black-on-white* thing! Shit, Tokers is just looking for targets that won't fight back is all. Can't help it if white people can't fight. If it makes you feel better, we clocked a Asian dude a while back—"

"Whatever. We're putting people into the hospital. People are afraid to go out because of us. That guy may not be my kind of person, but I can understand how he just wants his life back. Maybe that's what I want too."

He was taken aback by that. "Did you even hear him at the rally? He didn't have a life before. Now he's somebody. He has people watching his videos. And how do you get more viewers? By calling it a race issue—"

This was going nowhere. "You're just making excuses." I pushed him away. "I'm leaving."

I had my hand on the knob when he said, "Wait."

I stood there in front of the door. I heard him open his dresser drawer and riffle through some junk. I glanced over my shoulder and saw him pulling out a bunch of DVDs in sleeves and flipping through them. He stopped suddenly when he came to what he was searching for.

He dropped the rest and stared at it like it was Kryptonite. "Fuck it."

He pulled out the DVD and stuck it into his laptop. While it was loading, someone started banging on the front door. He jumped. When the banging continued, his mom called out, "Kalvin?"

He kept his eyes locked on mine. "Just sit and watch this before you leave. I'll be right back." He paused next to me. "Whatever you wanna think, it's out of my hands."

23

Kalvin stepped out into the living room, where I saw his mom peering through the peephole in their front door. "Kalvin," she said again, a little more desperate.

He shut the bedroom door in front of me.

"Kalvin, get your butt over here," said a man's voice. It was coming from his laptop. I turned and saw a skinny little kid who was maybe twelve, with cornrows. His eyes seemed more brownish, but it was definitely Kalvin. Someone was recording him; it was a home movie. He didn't want to engage with the person behind the camera. "Come on, Kalvin. Time to man up!"

The camera turned to reveal the shooter—a white man in his early thirties, with thinning hair and a tattoo of a fist on his beefy arm. He had Kalvin's intense eyes. "Come on, kid. How you gonna learn anything way over there?"

I recognized the roof. The sky was cloudy and dark, on the verge of rain. Kalvin was smaller and skinnier, but still rough around the edges. He had sparring gloves on, but he hung back;

he wasn't sure he wanted to be there. Finally, the man coaxed him into coming up to the camera.

"Say hi, son."

He peered into the lens. "Hi, son." So I guess that was his dad then.

His dad pulled off his shirt, revealing plenty of tattoos and muscles. He set the camera down on something and walked into frame with Kalvin. No gloves on. "Hands up," he said.

Kalvin held up his arms like he was being robbed. His dad backhanded him in the stomach. Kalvin recoiled. "This is serious. You gotta learn to fight if you want to survive in this world. Otherwise, a person like you is gonna get his ass kicked good."

His dad leaned over him. "Knocking someone out is an art form. See, in a fight, you wanna punch at the guy's nose because his eyes will water up and then he can't see, and that's when you can really mess him up." He put his hand on Kalvin's shoulder. Kalvin tried to brush it off, but his dad was holding him tight. "But in the street, a punch to the jaw is a better place to start; it's on a hinge, so you won't hurt your hand. Avoid hitting somebody straight to the mouth. Because when they see it coming, they're gonna scream and then you're going get some teeth in your knuckles." He spoke from experience.

His dad faked a punch and Kalvin almost did scream. His dad shook his head, disappointed. "See? Now, listen to me, Kal. Because this is a skill you can use out there in the real world. Someone like you, a lazy no-good waste of space, you'll always be a target, but here's the good news: it's not so tough to knock someone out in one hit if you know *where* to hit. When someone gets knocked out by a punch, it's not just the impact from the hit." He put both his hands on Kalvin's head and shook

144

it. "It's their brain getting scrambled inside the skull from the hit." Dad slapped him upside the head. "Of course, in your case, there might not be much to scramble."

Kalvin was getting pissed off.

His dad cracked his neck and did some shoulder rolls to loosen up. "Surprise is the main thing. I mean if they see a punch coming, they tense up and get ready for the blow. But if it's a surprise attack, they're all relaxed and the neck is loose and *POW!*"

His dad suddenly popped him in the head. Kalvin dropped out of frame and hit the ground. His dad held his hands out flat. "How could you not see that coming after I just talked about surprise attacks?"

Kalvin tried sitting up. He was a bit woozy and holding his jaw. "Shake it off; you're OK. If I wanted you lights out, you'd be sleeping, ya feel me?"

Kalvin nodded, still dazed. "Now a hook to the side of the head is more likely to knock someone out than a straight punch to the face." His dad acted out each punch in slo-mo. Kalvin flinched when the fist got close to his face. "If you are in front of them, an uppercut under the chin is better than a straight punch, but not as good as a hook. A good sweet spot is a hook right on the end of the dude's chin. You OK?"

Kalvin seemed unsure. "Yeah . . . "

"Good. Now let me show you the ultimate knockout punch, which is a strike to the temple. But you have to be the right height to do this, because it's gotta be *just right* to work."

There was a jump in the video and it sped up for a minute. I could see Kalvin in fast motion getting up off the floor a couple times. Finally, it returned to normal speed.

Kalvin was hitting into his dad's hands, which he held up in front of K's face. He kept driving at him, yelling at his boy to hit harder, telling him he hit like a girl. Kalvin's face was getting all red, but that didn't stop his dad. It only got him going more. His dad pushed back every time Kalvin missed, slapping him and yelling in his face. "Come on! Put some man into it!"

I would've lost it by then. My cousin used to pretend to fight with me, and I remember wanting to pop him, but he was three years older and I never did get him back.

Sure enough, in the next moment, he caught his dad off guard and *WHAP!* Kalvin connected—I could hear the crunch of his dad's nose.

"Fuck!" his dad yelled. Kalvin had popped him pretty good, because his dad crouched down, holding his nose. He checked his hand and saw blood.

Kalvin stood there, thinking he showed his old man. His dad even smiled for a second, nodding—*now that's what I'm talking about.* But instead of clapping him on his back and calling it a day, he stood up, took two steps toward Kalvin and laid him out *cold.* The punch was so loud, it shocked me. Kalvin just dropped, the life leaving his body before it hit the ground.

His dad kneeled down and yelled into his face, "Don't you ever—!" He tried to calm himself down, but he was reeling in anger. Instead of feeling bad or carrying his son's body into the house, he hit him again in the face.

That's when my eyes bugged out. I mean, Kalvin was out cold and his dad was now beating his face raw. My gut twisted into a knot just watching it. Then he just stood up and yelled, "Next time you think about taking a pop at me, you better knock me out, because next time, there won't be a fuckin' next time!"

Then he just turned and walked into the building. The video kept running for another minute or so, and Kalvin did not move. If I hadn't seen him today, I'd have thought this kid was dead. My dad was tough. But he never hit me, never abused me. I hated him for leaving Mom, for ruining our lives, for making us leave Little Rock. But he never did anything like this.

After a minute, Kalvin started coming to, groaning and rolling on the ground. Finally, he rolled over and acted like he was gonna puke his guts out. Instead, he spat out blood. He saw something, then reached over and picked up a few teeth. Kalvin sat there for a few seconds gazing at them, running his tongue over his gums. But he didn't cry his eyes out, which I was doing just watching this. He slowly got up, stumbled toward the camera punch-drunk and laughing to himself. He got up close to the lens and smiled. He was missing his front teeth. Staring straight at the camera, he cackled, "I got you. I got you *good*."

The video stopped and it was only then that I heard a voice yelling in the next room. It was a man, but it wasn't Kalvin.

24

I cracked the door open just enough to see Mr. Jamison in the living room. He was towering over Kalvin, who was on the couch trying to play it cool. Boner growled at the intruder.

"You got no right to be here," said Kalvin. "You ain't a cop and I don't go to Truman anymore."

Jamison raised his eyebrows. "Oh, so you're admitting you no longer go to school. Does your mother know that?"

"Don't be playing my moms. She knows I'm good," Kalvin said.

Jamison smirked. "I seriously doubt that." Boner continued to growl, and Jamison seemed ready to strangle him.

Kalvin ignored him. "That dog is trained to kill, yo."

Jamison looked at Kalvin's mom. "Mrs. Barnes, I'm here as a favor. Next time it won't be me; it'll be SLPD. I'm trying to look out for my kids—" he stole a look at Kalvin, who was about to say something. "The kids at Truman, who have been involved in these Knockout Games."

Kalvin's mom piped in. "Kal don't go in for these kinds of

things. He works that all out at the Rec Center."

"Is that what he tells you?" He turned his attention back to Kalvin. "I don't know if you heard or not, but we had a little chat with Prince Rodriguez this afternoon. Know him?"

Kalvin shrugged.

"Yeah, apparently he was part of that whole water balloon incident last night—"

"For reals, Mr. Jamison?" interrupted Kalvin. "Why don't you arrest me for stealing lollipops?"

Jamison was not amused. "You know someone knocked out a city councilman that night?"

Kalvin looked confused.

Jamison brightened. "Oh, you haven't heard yet? Well, apparently your pal Prince was identified as a possible perp and in our discussions, one name kept coming up: the Knockout King. Ring any bells?"

"Yeah, it's one of those old-school video games my pops use ta play." He pretended to box from the couch.

"Nice tat," Jamison said, pointing at his fist. "Coincidence?"

Kalvin pulled his hand away. "You gonna have to do better than that."

His mom cut in. "He's a boxer, and you know it. He won a bunch of fights, so they started calling him that. I told him he shouldn't deface his body, but he was so proud."

Jamison glowered at him. "That's a nice story and I'm sure it'll play in front of a jury."

Again, Kalvin scoffed. "Ain't no juries in Family Court."

Jamison was impressed. "That's right, Kalvin, there aren't. But there are in *adult* court, which is where you'll end up, Einstein." Jamison leaned into his face. "Like father, like son. Do I have to explain it? The man beat it into you."

Kalvin jumped up off the couch, ready for action. Boner started barking. Kalvin's mom stepped between him and Jamison. "Kal, no! Don't let him make you do something stupid. He's just baiting you."

Kalvin calmed himself and held out his wrists. "You ain't got nothing on me; otherwise, you'd be here with a cop, arresting my ass now. So you just making noise is all."

Jamison stood up to his full height, one eye on Kalvin, one on his mom. "OK, tough guy, this is where we part, then. You had a chance to go to Grant Remedial and get back on track. But you've stayed away. And now, I don't have to bait you into doing something stupid. You'll screw up on your own and when that happens, the cops will be the ones standing here. Then, you won't be so cocky. You sure you have nothing to say to me? I'm your last chance."

Kalvin nodded. "Yeah. One thing. *Good-bye.*" He waved him off like a rich person waving off the help.

Jamison walked up to Kalvin's mom. "I know he's involved," he said. "The question is, are you going to help him by coming forward, or wait until somebody dies and he's charged for murder?"

She didn't say anything; she just opened the door for him to leave.

"Alright then," said Jamison. "My job is done here."

Kalvin ignored him. When the door closed and the footsteps drifted down the stairwell, Mrs. Barnes sat down next to him.

"Kal, I don't want to lose another person in this family to prison. If you have anything to say to me, please say it now. You know I'll back you. Are you involved in all this?"

Kalvin took a deep breath, even managed a smile. He put his hand on hers. "Mom, I ain't going to no jail. I ain't dealing; I ain't in a gang; and I ain't killed no one. And I plan to keep it that way. I'm gonna get back into school, graduate, and apply to college, like I said. That's bank, Mom. What he's saying . . . that's just lies. We're just messing around, having fun, and they don't like it. But I'm a good boy, Mama." On cue, Boner hopped up into Kalvin's lap and licked his face.

She patted his hand. "I know you are, son. As long as you're trying to better yourself, I'll be on your side."

"I did mess up one thing, though."

His mom lowered her head. "What's that, son?"

"I messed up with that girl in there. She trusted me and I kind of screwed it all up."

I almost believed him.

"Well, what do you do when you mess up, Kal?"

He knew the answer, which they said together like they'd practiced it a hundred times before.

"You make it better."

She stood. "I'm going to the store. You spend time with that girl and make things right, ya hear?"

"I will, Mom."

When she left, Kalvin just sat there petting his dog. After a minute, he said, "I know you're listening."

I opened the door and walked over to him, plopped down on the couch. This day just kept getting stranger and stranger. "What're you going to do?"

"About us?" He moved his hand over toward me, but I didn't take it.

"About the cops," I said.

151

That stopped him. He got up and went to the window, overlooking his kingdom. "I gotta do some cleaning up. Prince shouldn'ta disobeyed me. And Joe Lee, well, he'll have to learn that sometimes speaking out only makes things worse."

I got up to leave. He didn't move from the window. Before I stepped out the door, I asked, "Is it true you wrote a poem for me?"

He didn't even look at me. "I don't write poems. I take care of business. You do what you gotta do."

25

The next morning, I woke up antsy and paranoid. I hadn't slept much all night and when I did, all I had were weird dreams. I dreamt Kalvin's dad was teaching me how to fight. After he showed me a thing or two, he wanted me to prove myself by knocking out Kalvin. I couldn't bring myself to do it. "It's okay," he said. "He deserves it." When his dad yelled at me to do it, I jumped off the roof and landed in the park where the Metal Detector Man saw me and started chasing me, yelling, "You did it! I know it was you!"

I sat on my bed feeling like they were on to me. Who *they* were, I wasn't sure. Jamison? Kalvin? Rodney Graves said arrests would be made. Did they already know everything? I was about to call Destiny, but what if they tapped the phone? That was followed by, *How would they know to tap my phone?*

I was already late for school, but I got on to my Facebook page. First thing I did was delete any video that had anyone from the TKO club in it. I kept refreshing and logging on and off until I was sure they were gone.

Then I remembered Destiny had shared them and who knows who else shared hers. I panicked. Jumped on Google and luckily figured out that deleting got rid of the shared videos too.

After they were deleted, I grabbed my camera and deleted everything on that as well. And then I thought about my computer. Everything was on there too. Should I delete my hard drive? *Yes.*

I was losing my mind.

In that moment I thought of Destiny. I couldn't lose her. I needed to talk to someone and the only someone who might understand was royally pissed off at me.

I texted anyway.

Me: *R we ok?*

I sent it off. I waited. And waited. No response.

She was normally quick to answer. That was it. I could take a hint. I didn't want to go back to having no friends. I'd let her chill twenty-four hours, then try talking to her again.

I could call up Mom. She'd be at work, all stressing as she usually does. What was I gonna say? I know what Dad would say: *Your problem, you deal with it.*

And that's when somebody pounded on my door. "Open up, police."

My heart stopped. I looked out my second-story window. I could jump. Maybe onto a car so I didn't break an ankle. I pictured my mom getting a phone call about how either I broke both my legs from the jump or I was in jail or—

Then I heard someone snickering.

Jesus. I walked closer to the door and now the person was laughing pretty hard.

I peered through the peephole. Prince was standing there,

his head shaved.

I flung the door open and smacked him in the shoulder. "You scared the shit outta me!" I hissed.

He held up his hands. "'*Spensa*—my bad, Fish. I couldn't help myself. It was too easy."

I gawked at his pale skull. It made his whole head seem smaller. "Nice look, by the way."

"Gotta adapt," is all he said as he walked past me. His eyes scanned the room. He was not impressed. "I really had you scared, didn't I?"

Why was he here? "How come you're not in jail?"

"How come you're not in school?"

I tried not to look panicky. "I wasn't feeling good."

He shrugged. "They couldn't pin anything on me. It was dark. They showed my picture to a couple of witnesses, but they were old and didn't see so well, so they couldn't pin it on me. Besides, Destiny was my alibi. We were 'studying' together that night."

I didn't want to know what that meant. "But it was you, right?"

He smirked. "Got any beer?"

I crossed my arms. "It's morning."

"Doritos?"

I shook my head. "What. Do. You. Want?"

He crashed on our couch, spreading out. "K sent me."

"K sent you? Aren't you on his shit list?"

He glared at me. "We had a talk." He grunted painfully as he sank into my couch. "He's seeing things more my way now."

"Really." I said. "What's he want, then? He can't text anymore?"

He shrugged. "Just being safe. Don't know when the cops're listening." Prince cleared his throat. He didn't act so cocky. "Our idea is not to pull back."

"What does that mean?"

"It means, we go out again on Saturday." He leaned forward. "Play Knockout. *BAM!*" He performed an epic knockout punch for me.

I stared at him for a good ten seconds. "Are you. . . as stupid as I think you are? Didn't you just get questioned by Jamison and that cop?"

He was annoyed by my questions. "Yeah, and what happened? *Nada.* K said what you said. At first. Then I reminded him that the Knockout King don't run from nobody. See, they expect their little threat will be enough to scare off the Tokers. But not K and not me. Are you kidding? We thrive on that shit."

"Yeah, well you can count me out. I'm done."

He was trying to see if I was bluffing. "Destiny's coming," he said.

"Bullshit."

He leaned back again, shaking his head. "You got *huevos,* I'll give you that. If I had my own crew, I'd want you on my side too. Though I hear things are not so good for you at the moment."

"What does that mean?"

"Well, I personally could give a shit one way or the other. But if you're not there, I'm sure Destiny will step up and take your spot."

I narrowed my gaze at him. "You'd like that, wouldn't you?"

He stood and moved toward the door, stopping just short. "Tell me. What did you feel when I pounded on the door and yelled 'Police'? You probably thought of all kinds of crazy shit. Should I grab a knife? Hide? Jump out the window?"

He saw my reaction to that last one and smiled. "Uh-huh. At that moment, *anything* coulda gone down. One minute you was just sitting there, the next—you were a *chola* thinking of becoming a fugitive, right?"

"That doesn't mean I like it."

He didn't believe me. "I seen that look in your eye, when you hit that metal detector guy. The way you stayed behind with K on the roof."

"So?"

"So you like it. Don't lie."

He opened the front door. "I'll tell ya something else: *chinga la juda*—fuck the police. They don't scare me. They want to change the rules? Fine. We can change too." He poked me in the chest. "We're making a statement on Saturday, so you better show up next to the library on Grand Avenue. Eleven a.m. Otherwise, those who don't play, *get played*."

"Is that a threat?"

"You're smart. Figure it out," he said, walking away.

26

At nine o'clock, Mom woke me up. It was already bright out; for a second I thought I'd overslept.

"It's Saturday," she said. "I made breakfast. Come eat before I go to sleep."

I stumbled out of bed and plopped myself down at the kitchen table. She'd made pancakes. When she served me, she paused for a second, looking at something on my neck.

We sat there eating in silence, but something was on her mind. Finally, she said, "What's on your neck?"

I touched it. "What?"

"Looks like a hicky," she said, raising an eyebrow.

My face felt hot. "I probably bruised myself when I fell the other day."

I should've had a better comeback. "I used to fall too, when your dad first dated me."

"It's not like that."

She sighed. "Well, it was going to happen, so . . ."

She wasn't mad, maybe a bit sad. "One day, I'll wake up and

have missed all your teen years." She put her hand on my arm. "You know you can talk to me about anything, right?"

Probably not anything. "Yeah . . . ," I said.

"Even boys. Especially boys."

I rolled my eyes. "I'm almost sixteen, Mom. I'm not a baby."

She nodded. "I know. I was talking to your dad yesterday. I was thinking about inviting him here for Thanksgiving."

"I wouldn't get my hopes up," I said.

"I think he wants to come. He feels like he's missing out on your teen years too."

I almost laughed. "He can have them."

"Don't say that. I mean, I know it can be hard. There's no doubt, you wind up doing some crazy . . . stuff. You're going to mess up. That's almost your job as a teen, to mess up. It's *our* job to make sure you survive those years. He just wants to be involved."

She didn't know the half of it. "I'll survive, Mom. You'll see."

She stroked my hair. "I hope so."

"Me too."

***

After Mom went to sleep, it was almost 10:30. I sat on the couch, reminding myself that there was no way I was gonna go down to the library. No way she'd be bailing me out of jail tonight.

My heart jumped around like I'd just downed four Red Bulls. I tried breathing slowly, closing my eyes the way those yoga people do. Breathe in, breathe out. Let go.

Something skittered across the window like hard rain. I opened an eye. The sky was gray, but it wasn't raining.

I closed my eyes again. Something hit the window.

I got up to check it out. Peering down to the street, I saw Tyreese standing there by himself. He spotted me and waved me down. I shook my head, but he wouldn't leave. Finally, I opened the window.

"Come on; you gotta come!" he said, worried, maybe even scared.

"No, I'm staying," I said as loud as I could without waking Mom. "You go."

He shook his head, waved me down again. "Something's gonna happen. You gotta come!"

He was talking too loud. "Hold on." I pocketed my camera like always, heading downstairs. When I opened the door to the front of the building, Tyreese was standing there. He had the face of a kid whose teddy bear was just stolen.

"Look, I can't go," I told him. "I got a million things to do, and besides, they shouldn't even be out playing, there are too many eyes—"

He took three steps and wrapped his arms around me. "You gotta come, Fish. K's doin' something that ain't good."

"What?" I asked. "What's going on?"

"Maybe you can stop him before he gets in too much trouble."

I felt his tears soaking my shirt. "Tyreese, what's he gonna do?"

"He's going after the bullhorn man. I think he's gonna do something bad. Just come with me?"

Jesus. It's like he wants to get caught. Either that or Kalvin thinks he's invincible and he loves rubbing it in. "Is he at the library?"

He nodded. "Come on; he'll listen to you."

I doubted that. But somebody had to do something.

27

We reached the library around eleven. The wind was picking up: you could almost feel a storm was coming. I threw up my hoodie and walked faster. We had passed a group of Watchers a few blocks back. Not a good sign.

Tyreese spotted Prince and five Tokers sitting on a bus bench from across the street. It was an odd scene—the skinhead Latino with five black kids. When Prince saw us coming, he gritted his teeth and nodded. "Yo, make way for the queen and her little *puto*! Good job, Tyreese."

I looked at Tyreese, who grew quiet.

"What's going on? Where's Kalvin?"

Prince gestured toward the library just as Kalvin was making his way out. He paused when he saw me and walked calmly across the street, even though cars were coming. They honked and swerved out of the way, but he didn't care. He had his eyes on me.

"Well?" asked Prince.

"He's in there," said Kalvin, his green eyes blazing bright.

"Who?" I asked.

He scowled and spat on the street. "Joe Lee, of course. He needs a little reminder of who runs this 'hood."

It was like talking to a child. "Why are you being so stupid? He knows who you are," I said, stating the obvious. "Why do you have to always push the line? It's so dumb."

C-Jay piped up. "Don't call K dumb, bitch."

Kalvin slapped him upside the head. "A little respect, Toker." He glanced at me and smiled. "Things were getting too routine anyways. A little excitement gets the blood going. You know how it is."

I did, but I wasn't proud of it.

Prince stared at Kalvin. "A rat's gotta be taken care of or next thing you know, there'll be a plague."

Kalvin fist-bumped Prince. "He's in there. When he comes out, we'll give 'em a first-rate Knockout Game experience, courtesy of the King hisself."

He kissed his fists and acted out a slow-motion pounding.

I moved in close and whispered, "Can I talk to you for a second?"

He stopped his act and glared at me. He slowly exhaled, then took me by the arm and walked me over by a closed-down bakery.

"What?"

I had to choose my words carefully. "I thought the main rule of the Knockout Game was to pick a totally random stranger."

He nodded. "It is. But sometimes you have to send a message that outsiders shouldn't interfere. They need to know we can't be stopped."

"Well, then it's not really a game, is it?" I whispered so the Tokers wouldn't hear.

He shrugged. "It's all a game, don't you know that? School. Work. Life. We're all being played by someone. Might as well be a *playa* than be *played*, ya feel me?"

"I know you're smarter than that. Why can't you just stop? I mean, what's the big deal?"

I pointed out how all his boys were awaiting his word. They'd do anything he asked.

"Well the thing is . . . " he started to say. "I saw this TV show once about sharks. It said that they can never stop moving 'cause they need oxygen to keep flowing through their gills or something. That means if they stop, they die."

"So, what, you're the shark? If you stop attacking people, you'll die?" I asked, unconvinced.

He bit his lip, his eyes studying me carefully. "Look." He held up his fists. "Knockout King. That's who I am. That's all I ever been good at. And I'm fine with that. I'm not gonna go to college and do something big. I don't want to waste time flipping burgers, so I'm doing this. It keeps me sharp."

"Kalvin—" my brain was reeling. "I think . . . there's a good person . . . inside of you. You can change—"

"What are you, one of those white movie characters trying to save the black guy from wasting his life away? Fuck that. I don't wanna change; don't you get it?" He held me by the shoulders so he could look me straight in the eyes. "You. Can't. Change. Me. I come as is. I accept that. So should you." He paused a moment, waiting to see if I'd say anything.

I had seen enough. "I'm sorry, then. I can't do this anymore. I thought I meant something to you."

"Hold on," he said. He seemed puzzled. When I began to walk away, he just said, "You do. 'Course you do. But these are two different things."

"No, they're not. You were with me because of TKO. Because I had a camera. Because I knocked someone out. But that's not me. I'm not that person. And if this is the real you— then I'm out."

"Out? Out of what?" he asked.

"Everything," I said.

He squared himself. "You can't just leave."

"Why not?" I asked.

He took a step toward me. "Because you can't." His body was all tensed up.

"Or what? You going to *hit me*?"

He blinked, almost surprised by the idea. He licked his lips as he considered it, but then he softened his stance. "Don't be like this. I like having you around me. I need you here. Just . . . play along, will ya?" He reached out and gently took my hand in his, staring at the bruises. "I know you have doubts," he said. "I know that. It's cool. You're looking out for me and the Tokers, and you want what's best. I see that." He nodded as if trying to convince himself. "But what you don't see is . . . they got us pegged, the cops. Even if we did nothing, they'd always be stopping us, blaming us for this or that. *You* don't know what that's like. They don't stop a white girl, make you get on your knees, cuff you in front of your own home."

"That's just an excuse. How many times has that happened to you, really?"

"Enough." He made a funny noise in his throat, like he swallowed something that he didn't like. "Ask my moms. The last time they hassled me, Mom was there and they made her get on the ground, spread out on the sidewalk, a knee in her neck, just to get me riled enough to throw a punch. That was the one time I didn't, 'cause I knew they'd go to town on me. After that, I decided to play by my own rules." He paused thoughtfully. "I just want to be with you." He was still holding on to my hand. He placed it on his chest. "Feel that? That's my heart racin'. That's you." He put his hand over my heart. "Yours too."

"The difference is, yours beats fast because you like the hunt. Mine beats because I know something's wrong here."

His eyes grew darker. I could see the disappointment. "Fine. Then you might as well take that camera of yours and give the cops what they want. I mean, if you don't want to be with me anymore, why not?"

He was testing me. That was the last thing I wanted to do.

"Go on, take it out," he said.

I put my hand on my hoodie pocket and he knew I had it on me. He simply reached over and helped me pull it out. He turned it on and pressed Record.

He held up my arm so the camera aimed at him. I wanted to leave, but part of me wanted him to confess everything. Maybe this was the way to stop him. To save him from himself. And to save Joe Lee too.

"Yo, everybody. Knockout King at your service. 'Bout to go deliver some justice. Them's my boys back here, awaiting my word. Ain't that right?" he asked me. He dropped his hand and started walking. "Come on, let's get on with it."

I couldn't help it; I followed him. I had to see what was going to happen. Maybe the camera would actually *prevent* him from doing something bad. He could always blame my presence as a way to save face. And if that didn't work, I could warn Joe what was coming.

Prince whistled and pointed toward the library. "*Orale*. They're leaving."

"What do you mean, *they*?" I asked.

"Him and his bitch. It's like a twofer one," he said excited.

We all spotted the couple at the same time, their backs turned to us, walking away. It was only then that I knew Mrs. Lee was in for it too.

"Kalvin, that's Mrs. Lee," I said panicking.

"So? She knew what she was getting into when she hooked up with him."

"But she's my teacher," I said.

Kalvin looked at me in disbelief. "Yeah, well, she's also the one that expelled me from school."

"Bullshit. That's Mr. Jamison's job." I stared him down. "And it's not like you want to go back anyways."

"She was behind it. She's not innocent."

He was serious. I pointed the camera at him. "So what are you gonna do then, Kalvin?" I asked.

"Be a shark," Kalvin said. His eyes were blazing, the green in them almost glowing. He gestured to the Tokers and they all got up and started across the street toward Mrs. Lee and Joe as they turned down the alley—just another couple walking home from the library.

The hairs on my neck rose; my muscles tensed up. I had to warn them. Kalvin and the crew sped up, leaving me a few steps behind so I got cut off by a couple of passing cars. By the time I reached the other side, they were moving faster and faster down the bleak alley—an army about to charge the hill.

Next thing I knew, Kalvin was sprinting like the cheetahs he watched on TV. I opened my mouth to yell something, but my throat closed up tight and all I managed was a weak, "No!"

It all happened so fast. Kalvin leapt into the air and his fist came crashing down into the back of Joe's neck. The man tumbled, his bag of books went flying. Kalvin's muscled body landed right on him and he made sure it hurt. He tumbled off Joe's body, but got right back and slammed him in the kidney. Mrs. Lee stood in shock, shoved aside by Prince, who landed a few kicks of his own at Joe.

I somehow got closer than I'd planned—right in the middle of the action. I saw Kalvin get right up into Joe's ear, almost choking him, hissing, "Didn't your mother ever tell you if you can't say something nice about someone, you should just shut the fuck up?" He was about to deliver his final knockout when Mrs. Lee came out of nowhere. She shoved me out of the way, spraying pepper spray right into Kalvin's eyes, screaming out of control. Prince jumped at her, but he got it in the eyes too. Suddenly, they were both down, cursing and shouting, "Get that bitch!"

She froze when she saw me. A look of confusion passed over her face. When she saw the camera and the boys coming for her like a pack of wolves, she raised the pepper spray again.

At *me*.

My instincts jumped in. I grabbed for her hand. I had my back to her as we wrestled for control of the canister. I didn't want to hurt her; I just wanted the pepper spray, but she wouldn't let go of it. I thought if I could get it away from her, I could save her from the others, maybe even pull her away from all the mayhem.

But it was like trying to save a person from drowning. She fought back so hard, she was dragging me down with her. I found myself struggling just to keep her under control.

"Mrs. Lee, stop!" I yelled and for a fraction of a second, she did. It was too late. I heard Tyreese yelling, his body flying by me fist first. Everything slowed down at that moment; the sound turned off. I got pushed to the side where I landed on Joe, his eyes open but gazing into another world. I scrambled like mad to get off him and tumbled back to the ground. In my right hand was the pepper spray.

Tyreese almost landed on top of me. I rolled out of the way but my hand landed in something wet and sticky. The next moment was frozen in time. I gazed down at the sticky stuff—dark red, like syrup. Blood. My eyes drifted over, following the trail.

Mrs. Lee was lying at an awkward angle. Her head rested on a curb, blood trickling from some unseen area under her hair. Her lips were turning blue in front of my eyes.

No—

Tyreese took a step back, his face in shock. "I didn't mean to," he mumbled, rubbing his fist.

C-Jay came up and put his arm around him and whispered, "You took care of business." Tyreese nodded, but I don't think he believed it.

Kalvin and Prince were writhing around in agony trying to wipe the pepper spray from their eyes. But my eyes remained frozen on Mrs. Lee's face.

Her eyes were gazing right at me. But they weren't bright and clear like I remembered—they were cloudy and gray like the sky overhead. I'd never seen a dead person, but I was pretty sure that's what a dead person looked like—the life just sucked out of her and only the hollow shell left behind.

Tyreese started to cry.

C-Jay grabbed my arm. "Come on, we gotta get outta here!" He was dragging Tyreese and the others. They started running. I just stood there staring at the blood on my hands.

Finally, Kalvin wrapped his arm around me. "We have to go," he said. His eyes were red and teared up. "We have to go!"

I stayed rooted in my spot. "She's dead."

"No, she's just bleeding."

"I killed her," I said. Crazy talk.

Kalvin bent down and touched her neck. "She's still alive. Come on; we gotta go!"

We had to step over Joe. He was groaning and made a feeble attempt to grab my leg. Kalvin kicked him, pulling me away. We ran.

I was crying now. The tears made it hard to see.

Kalvin pulled me this way and that. He stopped suddenly. "We can't go to my house. Someone might come looking. Come on."

I didn't remember anything, just that we were moving, moving, moving—down alleys, across parks and vacant lots. It began to rain.

The only thought I had was that I just wanted to lie down in my bed and curl up into a ball.

28

Why I brought him here, I don't know. I wanted to go home. He somehow came with me. The last place I wanted to be with him was in *my* house. But Kalvin could talk you into anything if he wanted.

Luckily, when we got there, Mom was asleep. It was her day off. She slept all day and nothing could wake her up. The fire alarm went off a month ago and she'd slept through the whole thing.

I told Kalvin we could stay here a few hours, but he'd have to leave before she got up. I pulled him into my room and locked the door. He sat on my bed, wet from the rain, but I didn't know what to do. I thought about showing him my drawings, that's how out of it I was.

I started crying instead.

"Come on," he said softly. "Come here."

"Fuck you. Did I tell you? Didn't I? Why don't you ever listen?"

I had so many mixed feelings. I had been running on

adrenaline and now it was all tapped out. Looking at Kalvin, his eyes red, his face ragged, his fists bruised. I knew the game was over.

"Come *here*," he said a little more forcefully.

"No," I said, wiping my eyes.

He got up and took my hand in his. It felt hot; he was on fire. My fist was still clenched up in a ball and when he unfurled it, I saw I was still holding onto Mrs. Lee's pepper spray. We both stared at it for a long while. "We have to get rid of that," he said.

I knew he was thinking it was evidence. I'd seen enough crime movies to know they always got you with the evidence. But that's not what I was thinking about.

"I killed her."

"Hey." He lifted my chin until my eyes met his. They didn't appear so green surrounded by all that red. In fact, one of them was brown now.

He was wearing colored contacts, and one had fallen out.

"You didn't kill nobody," he said. "We don't even know that she's dead."

"I saw her eyes. They were staring at me."

"When you get knocked sideways, your eyes do crazy shit. She was unconscious. We don't know she's dead. And second of all, Tyreese hit her. You think that little punk can take someone out?"

I remembered the moment. "She hit her head. I heard a crack when she hit the ground. There was blood. A lot of blood."

"The head bleeds a lot, even from a little cut—"

"No." I pushed his hand away. "He hit her because of me, because she was fighting me off."

172

"He was trying to save you. You were just doing what you thought was right."

"No!" I hissed. "Why are you doing this? I wouldn't be in this position if it weren't for you. And I know somebody had to have seen us—"

"Nobody saw us."

"Joe did. He knows it was you. You don't think he's going to the cops?"

Kalvin got up and started pacing. "He won't remember. They never saw us coming. Shit, we should've taken their money, then the cops would think it's a mugging."

I couldn't believe what I was hearing. "I told you. I told you it would be bad—I TOLD YOU!" I was shouting now, hitting him in the chest.

He hushed me up. "Keep it down. You don't wanna wake your mom, do you? What's she gonna think when she finds out . . ."

I stopped listening. I saw myself in jail, my mom broken down by it all. When someone dies, you can't keep it secret, can you?

His phone went off. It was Prince.

"Where the fuck are you guys?" Kalvin hissed. "What do you mean you're at my house? Get the fuck out of there! Go somewhere else fer fuck's sake! I don't care. Go visit your cousin on the east side. Just don't be seen!"

Kalvin listened for a minute, getting more and more frustrated. "You tell that little shit to forget about turning himself in," he hissed. "Just keep the little dude contained till I get there. I'll come tonight. Promise me, you won't let him outta your sight."

I could hear Prince babbling on, freaked out. "Fuck, you think his parents are gonna notice he ain't home for dinner? You think they give a shit? Just lock it down and we'll take it from there. We'll find out by tonight what the cops know."

He hung up and stared at his phone. "Fucking Tokers."

"Maybe if you hadn't pushed them so hard, they wouldn't feel they had to prove themselves to you so much. You're just like your dad. . . . "

I knew as soon as I said that he wouldn't like the comparison. His face darkened, his muscles tensed—

"Erica?" Mom. "Do you have someone in there?" she asked.

I glanced at Kalvin. He cussed to himself, stuck his hands into his pockets to cover his bruises. He knew he had to check himself. Quick.

She knocked on the door. "Erica?"

She tried to open it, but it was locked. I shrugged at Kalvin and went over to unlock it.

She saw my face and my red eyes, and knew immediately I was upset, despite my attempts to smile. But her expression completely changed when she pushed the door open wider and found Kalvin standing by the window.

I could read her face: Black man. Disheveled. Alone with her daughter.

"Mom, this is Kalvin. He goes to my school. He had some bad news this morning and was pretty upset. He was just telling me about it. I'm sorry if we woke you up."

I knew the more I talked, the less she would think. Kalvin was already distraught, so it didn't take much convincing. "I'm sorry if I got worked up. It's just . . . it's just . . . " He wiped his eyes, which might've been a bit much, but then I saw that . . . he was actually *crying*?

My mom's face softened. She was recalculating. But something about Kalvin changed. Maybe everything was catching up to him and he was starting to break. I struggled myself not to start crying again.

Mom sighed. She was too tired to get into it. "Kalvin, I'm sorry if you're having a hard time. You can stay . . . for now. But the door stays open."

She glared at me with that look that said *we are going to have a talk later.*

"That's OK," said Kalvin, clearing his throat. "Maybe I should go."

I said *no*; Mom said *ok.*

Kalvin smiled a little. "I'll text you."

Now I had to make sure to erase all his texts in case she wanted to check up on me. "OK, we'll talk later."

He stuck his hands into the pockets of his hoodie as he passed Mom. She did not approve of him.

"Your daughter's a good person," he said without looking back. "She's someone you can trust."

We watched him go. Mom didn't have to say anything. She was doing the slow burn on me, but I just burned back.

"He's a friend is all."

She nodded. "Maybe a little more than a friend?"

"No. Not anymore." I meant it.

She walked over to the window and waited until he left the building. "I don't trust him."

Neither did I.

"He doesn't tell the truth," she said.

I didn't argue. "Mom . . . " I saw I had blood on my shoe. I looked a mess, my shirt ripped, my knee scuffed up. What was she thinking?

I wanted to tell her everything. But the whole story seemed so crazy when I tried to put it into words. Where would I start? How could she accept me after what I'd done?

She watched me arguing with myself. Her face became twisted. "You're not . . . *pregnant*, are you?"

Oh my God. "No! Why would you even *think* that?"

Then I had the horrible thought: *What if I was? He hadn't used a condom. I'd have his baby in prison?* I buried that thought deep inside me where I wouldn't have to think about it. I couldn't, not with everything else to deal with.

Mom acted relieved, but certain there was something else. "I'm sorry. I've just been screwed over too many times by men, I guess."

I knew the feeling. "Things are a bit . . . complicated right now," I said. "I can't even begin to tell you. But one thing is for sure: I'm done with this camera. I'm done filming—"

I dug around in my pockets for my camera like I was just going to throw it out the window or something. It wasn't there. I did a quick scan of the room, my mind traveling back to the last time I saw it.

And suddenly, I was back in the alley, shooting the attack when Mrs. Lee stopped in her tracks and pointed the pepper spray at me.

That's when I dropped the camera.

29

As soon as I hit the sidewalk, I saw there were more of those Eyez papered on the trees up and down the block. I ripped them off as I passed. I didn't want anyone watching me now.

I knew I'd need help on this and there was only one person to help me.

Destiny lived in the worst block in Tower Grove South. Even though I was used to hanging out with Kalvin and the crew, I began to notice I was the only white person here. And without TKO around, I started feeling out of place and a bit nervous.

So I put on my game face, hid under my hoodie, and kept walking. The streets were wet from the rain but it had let up, so people were out and about.

"Wussup, girl? You lost?" Some dudes with their pants hanging around their butts were giving me a hard time. I ignored them.

"Come on, girl. Wha'cho got for me? How 'bout a taste?"

"Man, check out that hair! Mmm, girl, you ghettofabulous!"

They started to follow me. I had no time for this shit. I stopped in my tracks and spun around. "Listen, fuckheads. You want some of this? The only way that's happening tonight is if you jack off in bed, dicks!"

They stared at me in shock—then burst out laughing. "Did you just call us 'dicks'?" one of them said. "Oh, damn, she called us *dicks*!" They circled around me. "We ain't dicks, honey. But we got some if you want. . . . "

He got real close. I could feel his breath on me.

"Come on, bitch. You came down here for something, am I right?"

I was about to crack him in the face. Then I saw Destiny standing behind them.

Thank God. "Destiny."

The boys stopped and turned toward her. They knew each other.

She popped her gum and folded her arms. "Don't mind me. My TV's broke, so I got nothing to watch."

What? She was going to play me *now*?

"I was coming to see you," I said as the boys turned back to me.

"So? Now you seen me." She turned and started walking away.

There was a moment when I thought, they'll find my body and then she'll feel bad she hadn't said something. Maybe I deserved it, but—

I stared down the wolf pack. That wasn't going to happen today. "Fuck . . . *OFF*," I told them, slowly and deadly. I meant it too. And in that moment where they didn't know what to think, I just walked right through them and followed Destiny to her house.

They backed away, muttering "Dykes!" as they headed back to their den.

"Thanks for nothing," I said to Destiny's back.

"You a big girl. Looked like you could handle yourself."

I had a comeback. But I swallowed it. "I need your help," I said instead.

"You sure about that?"

"Please?" I asked.

She took a few steps, then stopped and turned. She looked me over. "You look like shit."

I glanced at my torn clothes. There was blood on my shoe.

She sighed. "Come on."

"No," I said. "We have to go to the library."

I could tell by her reaction that she'd heard something. She didn't question me, just nodded. "Let's go this way."

We walked away from the boys and headed down an alley. I stopped her. "No alleys."

The alley was empty and overgrown. "I told you to stay away."

So she did hear. "Where were you? Prince said you were gonna be there."

"Shit, and you believed him? He was just playing you." She quickly walked down another street toward Grand Avenue.

I had to catch up. "Destiny, are we still friends? I'm sorry if I . . . did something I wasn't supposed to."

"You sleep with him, shit happens. Did he use that *I usually carry a condom* line?" She stopped when she saw the look on my face. She sighed, pulled me along by the arm. "Forget it. It's just . . . me. You were just being yourself and I guess I got a little jealous."

"Of me? I'm nobody."

She shook her head. "You ain't nobody. You *my* Fish, remember?"

"I wasn't gonna go along this morning, but he just . . . I don't know."

"He knows how to push your buttons and get you to do what he wants," she said like she'd experienced it many times herself. "Shit, the things he had me do. It's fucked up."

Like what? I thought.

"I'm sorry I dragged you into all of this," she said. "I don't know what I was thinking. I just didn't want to be the only girl in the crew anymore. . . . " She drifted off, deep in thought.

"It doesn't matter now," I told her, burying my head in her shoulder. "I got big problems."

She eased up, came to a stop again. "So it's true," she said, looking me dead in the eyes. "Prince texted me that some woman died, but I thought he was just full of shit."

"It was Mrs. Lee!"

It took her a few seconds to process that. "What?" she whispered.

"I didn't know she was going to be there. It was Kalvin's fault—"

"Are you sure she's . . . ?" she asked.

I buried my head in my hands.

She paced back and forth a few times. "I never liked her, but still—that's sooo messed up."

I had to say it. "I recorded the attack."

She made a face like she didn't want to hear any more. "After all a that, you still went ahead—"

"No, that's not the worst part."

"What? What could be worse than that?"

I gathered my thoughts. "When she grabbed me, I . . . dropped my camera. It's . . . still there."

She froze. "And the whole thing . . . is on that camera?"

"Yes."

"Girl. You *are* fucked."

We stood there in silence, heaviness in the air.

"Shit, Fish, come on," she started walking again. "It can't get much worse, so we might as well try to get your stupid camera back."

I hurried after her, afraid of what we might find when we got there.

30

As soon as I saw the crowd surrounding the crime scene, I knew it was over. There was just no way we could sneak in there now.

Only a few hours had passed. The alley was taped off. They had to have collected the evidence by now. Maybe my camera was here somewhere and hadn't been carted off yet. Maybe no one had noticed its content yet or figured out who the players were.

A couple of local news teams were getting ready to do an update. There were two things going on in my head. I wanted to find that camera and I needed to know if she'd survived. There was a big difference between assault and murder.

The reporters had to know something. I tried to listen in to what they were talking about, but it was only about makeup and lighting.

My eyes scanned the scene for some kind of evidence box. On TV, the cops always put each bit of evidence into a plastic bag and then into some kind of evidence box usually marked with big stenciled letters spelling EVIDENCE.

I was waiting to hear the reporter go live, but Destiny recognized another girl from school and dragged me toward the crowd.

"What's goin' on?" she asked the girl.

The girl was wearing a shower cap and taking pictures with her phone. "Ain't you heard?"

Destiny rolled her eyes. "Now how would I have heard anything if I just got here?"

The girl looked around, then whispered. "Some couple got jacked but word is, it wasn't no accident."

"What do you know?" Destiny asked.

The girl pointed to the back of the library which lined the alley. My eyes traveled up and saw it: a surveillance camera.

Fucked again.

"You don't look so good, girl," she said to me.

"She's sick," said Destiny. "You saying they ID'd someone?"

She shrugged again. "I just heard 'em talking. I kept hearing the word *knockout* and I thought of your boy K. But you don't know nothing about that, do you?"

Destiny was about to deliver some major attitude when a bright light lit up the scene. I turned to see an Asian reporter counting down as she stood in front of the camera with her mic.

"Three, two, one . . . Tragedy struck here outside this Tower Grove branch library when a couple was brutally attacked this morning after exiting the library. The woman is reportedly in critical condition after a traumatic head wound left her comatose and bleeding heavily. There are no known witnesses, but detectives suspect this maybe one of the so-called Knockout Games that have plagued this area in recent years—"

The reporter paused, putting her finger up to her earpiece. She nodded gravely, like someone was talking to her. "It has just been confirmed that the woman who was attacked here in the scene you see behind me has died."

The light from the camera was burning a hole in my skull. The reporter's mouth kept talking, but no sounds reached my ear except for the scream coming out of my mouth.

Destiny grabbed me and quickly pulled me from the crowd, hustling me away from the cops and the cameras. It was murder now.

I was gonna be sick.

We headed toward the library door. I didn't make it. I puked into the bushes.

I didn't care if anyone saw me. Some things you can't control.

Destiny held my hair back. "We gotta get off the street, Erica," she whispered in my ear. "We gotta get you inside—"

She stopped talking, then I heard a man behind us say, "She OK?"

Destiny's hand tensed up. "She . . . she never seen blood before. She's from Arkansas."

I hurled one more time.

"Yeah," said the man. "I never get used to it either."

I spat and glanced back. An older black man in a suit. A badge on his belt. It was Rodney Graves, the cop who came to our school.

Destiny stroked my back. "I should get her inside so she can clean up. Come on, girl, let's go." She helped me to my feet. I didn't want to look at the cop because then I might *really* lose it. I swore I was never coming to this library again.

Destiny guided me to the front door, Graves watching us the whole way through his sunglasses. "Come on, we're almost there," she whispered.

We walked inside, past a pasty white security guard who looked like he should have been retired. He took notice of my sickly appearance.

"She's not feeling well," said Destiny, and we immediately hustled downstairs to the bathroom.

"If they have a recording of me from two different sources, then I'm dead." I was gasping for breath.

"Just shut up till we get in the bathroom," she said. She spotted a family restroom and she got me inside, locking the door behind us.

I washed my face off and looked at myself in the mirror. Then it hit me. I was still wearing the same clothes from this morning.

"Shit." I tore off my jacket and stuffed it into the trash can.

"What are you doing?"

I took off my shirt. "Switch with me."

"I ain't giving you my shirt!"

I wasn't gonna negotiate. "If they see a white girl wearing a blue hoodie with a yellow T-shirt in the video and that person is still at the library, guess what happens next?"

We switched shirts.

"Give me your pants," she said.

"I can't fit in your pants," I said.

"Bullshit. Have you seen my butt?"

We switched pants but I had a hell of a time squeezing into hers. "You gonna watch or help?"

She helped me into the pants, but I could barely walk.

"Dang, girl. Well, they sayin' tight jeans is all the rage. I guess you're ragin'." She checked me out, then took off her cap and put it on me. "Gotta cover that red mop; it's a dead giveaway."

I looked at myself in the mirror. "It's not really me."

"Jailhouse orange suit you better?"

I kept the hat on. We slowly went upstairs again but spotted a group of cops talking in front of the building. The security cop was there too. That was the only exit, so we headed back to the teen area to wait them out. No adults allowed.

We found a corner, hidden behind a row of bookshelves.

I couldn't help it. I started crying again.

Destiny held my arm. "Keep it together," she whispered.

I wiped my face with my sleeve. "There's no way we're gonna find that camera. And when they see that, they'll find me. What am I going to do?"

"Maybe you dropped the camera somewhere else, while you were running away? Do you remember losing it for sure?"

It was all a haze. "I remember looking at both my hands because there was blood on them."

Destiny watched the scene unfolding outside the window in the alley. "But did you see it fall?"

"I think so."

"Well, let's pretend they haven't found it. That leaves the surveillance camera, which is on the corner of the building. You guys were walking away from it."

"We can't pretend, Destiny."

That didn't stop her. "So maybe it saw only your backs, not your faces. What happened, happened down aways, right? Maybe the camera didn't see it."

I put my head in my hands. "I hate this."

When I looked up, Rodney Graves was standing about ten feet away, studying us closely. "I'm collecting statements. Something tells me maybe you saw something I should know about. Am I right?"

My mouth went dry. Destiny didn't move.

I did the first thing I could think of.

I ran.

31

Rodney Graves might be too old to run, but he'd radio the other cops and they'd be right on my ass. I ran and didn't look back. Away from the crime scene, down Grand Avenue, trying not to act suspicious as I sprinted for my life. Just an everyday jogger . . . dressed in tight jeans.

There were Mrs. Lee's Eyez posted everywhere around the library. And they were all looking at me, like she was still alive. I couldn't breathe. I had to get out of there. I took another left and saw my escape: a bus. I frantically waved as the door was closing.

The driver frowned, but opened the door back up for me.

"Thanks," I said, totally out of breath. There was enough change in the pants pocket to pay the fare. I ducked down in my seat and waited for a squadron of police to charge the bus. But the bus pulled out and no one else came after me.

Destiny would be fucked. This'd definitely get her a Level 6. They probably had her locked in some interrogation room, doing the whole good cop/bad cop thing. She was tough, but could she stand up to them?

I thought about just taking this bus out of town all the way back to my dad in Little Rock. I'd cross state lines and buy some time. Since he was a bail bondsman, maybe he could get me a good lawyer. Or at least arrange bail.

I knew I could cross the river into East St. Louis and Illinois. But Arkansas? I dug into my pockets. Five bucks. That wouldn't get me far.

The bus was headed downtown. As soon as we turned up Seventh Street, I saw the Gateway Arch looming up ahead. The clouds were breaking up, so the Arch caught the sun, a giant silver horseshoe against a cold gray sky.

I needed to clear my head, to get perspective. I kept staring at that Arch and decided I'd finally go up to the top of it before they locked me away forever. It would buy me some time, and maybe seeing the world from that height would help me figure out what to do.

If not, I could always jump.

About fifteen minutes later, I got off the bus at the park that surrounds the Arch. I thought about calling someone who could loan me some cash. But the only person I could think of was Mom—that wouldn't fly.

The only other person was Kalvin.

That made my stomach hurt, which made me think about the possibility that I was carrying Kalvin's baby. It was just one more terrible thing to consider.

I sat down in the park under the Arch and tried to think. My whole situation seemed so hopeless. But somehow, sitting there, watching families running around on the grass, gave me space to breathe, at least for a little while. I just needed some perspective.

It felt like there was only one place to find some of that from here.

When I got to the base of the Arch and gazed up at the tiny windows at the top, it seemed impossibly big. It made no sense how someone could build such a thing. I walked down below to the visitor's center, where they had all kinds of exhibits and movies and stuff. But I just wanted to get to the top of that thing.

They charged five dollars to ride the elevator up there. Well, that was the end of my cash. I stood in line for a good ten minutes to get past the ticket taker. I pulled my hat down and tried to act casual, though I could tell a fifteen-year-old by herself was a little suspicious. When we went through the metal detector, I almost lost it because it kept beeping. *What is it with me and metal detectors?* I was sure they'd pull me into a special room and within minutes figure out who I was and that'd be it.

I emptied my pockets and when they waved the wand over me, I realized it was my phone again.

When the security guy saw me pull it out, he kind of smiled and waved me through.

I swear I almost died. I quickly moved past to where the line stopped on a series of steps. People were standing in front of these tiny rectangles on a cement wall. A dead end? But then those rectangles opened and I saw they were tiny doors to the tiny elevators—I almost freaked again. These little pods were so small, I had to crunch down in my seat so my head wouldn't hit the roof.

A family with two little kids joined me after I sat down. They were so excited. "We're going to the top of the world," the boy said to me.

I smiled and the elevator doors closed, making it even smaller. We began to move. Sideways. My eyes fell onto a sign that said TAMPERING WITH DOOR WILL RESULT IN PRISON AND A FINE.

Were those claw marks on the door?

A drop of sweat fell onto my hand, panic rising in my throat. The father looked at me like maybe he shouldn't have let his family in here with this crazy girl.

My phone vibrated. It was almost too tight in there to reach into my pocket. But it kept going off, so I dug my sweaty hand in there just as the elevator suddenly lurched to an abrupt stop.

"What happened, Daddy?" asked the boy.

"Oh, sometimes these things get stuck. They'll fix it and we'll be on our way."

I stared at the phone display. Destiny. "Well, aren't you gonna answer it?" the boy asked. *When I get to the top*, I thought.

I stuck it back into my pocket and waited for it to go to voice mail.

The walls were closing in on me. Why wasn't this thing moving?

My phone went off again. I pulled it out. Now Destiny was texting.

Where tha FUK r u????

Was this a trick? Were the cops all standing around waiting for me to answer so they could track my location?

I deleted the text.

"Why don't you wanna talk to anybody?" asked the kid.

I looked away, the sweat kept building on my forehead. *If that kid asks one more question, I'm gonna—*

"Maybe she doesn't want you listening in on her phone call," said his dad.

"That's silly," said the boy. "Texts don't talk!"

I glared at the tiny door, about to tear it open.

The phone went off *again*.

This time it was a call. My mom. I took a deep breath and answered.

"Hello?"

"Erica. Where are you?"

"I'm stuck in an elevator. Why aren't you sleeping?"

There was a long pause.

"You better come home. The police are here and they want to talk to you."

My heart stopped. "What?"

Now she was whispering. "They found your camera."

"How do they . . . know it's mine?" I asked innocently.

"Your name and phone number were engraved on the bottom, remember?"

I did now. *Thanks, Dad.*

32

That stupid elevator never did reach the top. After a half hour in that tin box, I about had a nervous breakdown. Finally, it started moving again.

Back *down*. Something about high winds.

Forty-five minutes later, I was home. I stood outside for a another ten minutes more, trying to walk through that front door. Then I saw Mom staring at me from the window above. I took a deep breath and went in.

"Erica, we meet again," said Rodney Graves, rising up to greet me, along with a nicely dressed woman who looked like a lawyer. "Have yourself a good run?"

I didn't even have time to say anything to Mom because they were all sitting there in the living room waiting for me. I'm sure they grilled her all about me, but she really didn't know anything, so they probably learned nothing.

"I wasn't feeling good."

He nodded. "You go to Truman, right? You probably remember me from school?" he said in that soft Southern lilt.

"I'm the Special Investigator for the Juvenile Division. This here is my partner, Ms. Hallstrom, from the Family Court Prosecutor's office. She makes sure we do everything by the book." He winked, tapping on his notebook. He was well-dressed and had a kindly but weary face—the deep lines in his brow said he'd been doing this forever. "Your friend Destiny. She wasn't too pleased that you ditched her and left her holding the bag."

"What bag?" Mom asked.

"It's just an expression, ma'am, you know?" He stared straight into my eyes like he was trying to suck the information from my head using telepathy. "I already know that you know something about the events from this morning, so you might as well start talking before things get ugly. We have your camera and that alone says a lot. Right now, you could either be a potential witness to a serious crime and or you could be a suspect. One is a lot better than the other—"

"I didn't do it." The words just came out. "I ... I ... " Mom looked at me, confused by it all. "I need to think."

"I think you've had plenty of time to think this afternoon. Where did you go?" he asked.

"Is that important?" I asked.

"It is if you went to visit the suspects in a murder investigation."

The words sunk in.

"I went to the Arch."

Mom looked at me, surprised.

"Funny time for sightseeing," said Mr. Graves.

"What did Destiny say?"

Mom put her hand on mine. "Erica, if you know something,

you have to tell him. A woman died today! She could be some-body's mother. What if it had been me?"

I imagined Mom lying in a pool of blood. After seeing what Kalvin was capable of, I knew anything could happen if I talked.

"She's right. This needs to stop, now," said Mr. Graves.

Mom panicked. "Was that Kalvin involved?" she asked.

I tensed up. Graves noticed.

"Who's Kalvin?" he asked.

"A boy from school," I said.

"What's his last name?"

I wasn't ready to say anything; I was so stunned. I just shrugged. "I don't . . . even know. Everyone just calls him K."

He scribbled some notes. "Does the name 'Knockout King' mean anything to you?" He looked for a reaction from me.

I dug my nails into my arms to see how much pain I could take. Mom noticed I was about to explode.

"Is she under arrest?" Mom asked.

He stopped writing, glancing at Hallstrom. "Not yet." He seemed to confer with the woman lawyer telepathically. She nodded. "But perhaps . . . it would be best if you all came down to my office. We could take a formal statement and, as you have the right to an attorney, especially considering her age—"

"I didn't do anything!" I said, the tears flowing.

A lie. That stupid camera would betray me. I wished Dad had never given it to me. I wished he and Mom had never divorced. I wished we'd never come to St. Louis and that my video had never impressed Destiny. Then I wouldn't be stuck in this mess.

***

Assured that I wasn't about to skip town, they gave us until tomorrow morning. Mom said we'd come down after she called Dad. He knew lawyers. I almost screamed from the tension in the room, but Mom kept a firm grip on my arm until they left.

"*Please* don't call Dad," I begged.

She grabbed my shoulders hard and hissed, "You think I *want* to call him?! I can't afford a lawyer by myself for whatever you've gotten yourself into. So it's either him or you're on your own!"

I could see I would lose this one. I was tired of fighting. "Fuck it."

Her face screwed up. "What happened to you? You used to be such a sweet girl."

"I moved to St. Louis," I shot back.

She gritted her teeth. We'd been through this many times and she didn't want to go through it again. She spoke very slowly. "Now . . . you're going to tell me and your father everything. No more stories, just the truth. Because the police are surely going to get to the bottom of this and we are the only two who have your back. Certainly not that Kalvin."

I nodded to Mom. She called Dad, who was too busy until she told his assistant that I might be going to jail. That got him on the line.

I heard them arguing for about half an hour, blaming each other for how I turned out. Finally, she came in and put Dad on the speakerphone.

"Erica."

"Hi, Dad."

He sighed and then there was silence. "I don't really know what to say to you. I was getting ready to come in a few days for Thanksgiving."

"Are you still coming?" I squeaked.

There was a long pause on the other end. I knew he was trying to hold it in. Finally, he said, "Yes. I will save my sermon for tomorrow when I'm there. But right now, you need to tell me everything. And I mean *everything*."

Of course, I couldn't tell him *everything*—just some of the highlights. I made it look like I'd been sucked in, and that I was innocent. I didn't tell him about the other Knockout Games, but let him know that it was an accident gone bad and that I didn't do anything but try to save her.

Mom's expression was bad enough. She'd read about the Knockout Games and was horrified to see it hit so close to home. "He was in your *bedroom*," she said over and over. I lied again, told her he'd never touched me, that he was a mixed-up boy who wasn't so bad.

"Not so bad?" Dad started in. "Your mom said they were doing this game for fun! Do you think this is fun?"

No, I told myself. "It wasn't like that . . ."

"Why would you even attack another human being? It really makes me sick—" he paused for a few seconds, the anger building up in him. I heard something break. Finally, he took a deep breath. "To know that you were somehow involved in all this just makes me sad. I liked you better when you used to sit by yourself and draw, not—" he couldn't say it.

So much for saving the sermon for tomorrow. "Maybe if you hadn't divorced Mom—"

He cut me off. "Don't even go there, Erica. You're close to becoming an adult and it's time you learned that we cannot clean up after all your messes. I take responsibility for mine because I know life is messy. This one, you'll have to deal with the consequences. Whether you like it or not."

I was done talking. So was he. He said he'd make calls to his lawyer acquaintances and be here tomorrow first thing. We'd plan on a strategy where I had been coerced by the others, but I had never actively participated. I did not tell him about Metal Detector Man. He said if I testified against the others, I could probably get probation or community service.

This is a conversation I never expected to have with my dad before my Sweet 16.

33

Dad showed up at ten in the morning. His lawyer friend, Mr. Tillman, did not look like the lawyers I'd seen in the commercials. I found out later he wasn't even a criminal lawyer, but that's all Dad could come up with overnight. Tillman was short and balding, and probably needed glasses because he squinted at everything. Dad said the guy owed him one, though he wouldn't say why. When you owe a bail bondsman one, it's usually not a good thing.

Tillman had already done some digging. "They're not after you. They really want this Knockout King guy. You give them him, and we can negotiate. At your age and being that you have no criminal record, you might get off lightly."

"I don't know if I can do that," I said.

Dad was confused. "Why?"

I sighed again. "You're asking me to snitch."

My parents were about to say something, but Tillman cut them off. "Right now, Erica, you still have a future. But you've hit a major fork in the road. One way is a dead end. That road goes nowhere and you can ride it with all the others who were afraid to speak out. The other road is filled with obstacles, but at least it goes somewhere."

"Where?" I asked. I wanted to know.

"That's up to you."

Dad stared at me, confused. "Are you in love with this guy or something?"

"What?" The question caught me off guard. I was sure my face was turning red.

He rubbed his temples, unsure. "Do you . . . care for him?"

I felt my stomach. I imagined something alive growing in there. But even with that possibility, I wasn't sure about this.

"No."

He turned back to Tillman. "Can she get off with probation?" asked Dad.

Tillman shrugged. "Possibly. Or a few months in juvie."

"There goes college," said Mom.

I shot her a look. "Thanks for caring."

"Push for probation," said Dad. "Or no deal."

"Do we know what's on the camera?" Tillman asked me.

I sighed. "Enough to get Kalvin."

"Good. Then we have something."

"But if they have that, why would I still have to testify?"

He turned to my dad. "They'll probably want to build a bigger case than just second-degree manslaughter. If they can show that he was the leader of this gang and that he got young boys to do all his dirty work *and* that it was premeditated, then it's conspiracy to murder. They'll try him as an adult. That's the only way to really keep him off the streets. Otherwise, he may just go to juvie for a few years, get out, and *then* you'll have a problem."

***

When we arrived at the Juvenile Division, things were not so easy. Rodney Graves sat behind his metal desk, perfectly groomed in his dark suit and calmly laying out crime photos of Mrs. Lee on the table for me to see. Dad turned pale. I couldn't look at them. But I knew they were there.

Mr. Graves was going to show us the surveillance video from the library. Dad made Mom wait outside, but it was bad enough having Dad see this.

The black-and-white video showed Joe Lee and my teacher walk past, holding hands. You could tell they'd been together a long time. They didn't talk. But they still held hands, something my parents were definitely not doing right now.

"And here come our suspects." Mr. Graves watched closely, even though he'd seen it many times before.

Everybody's back was to the camera, Kalvin and Prince in the lead. The only one that turned around, just for a second, was yours truly, but the black-and-white video was blurry so you couldn't even tell the color of the clothes or my hair.

"That doesn't look like her," Dad said.

But it was. Seeing us on this video with no sound, where everything was so matter-of-fact, made what was about to happen feel even worse. I suddenly wished I could rewind my life just like this tape and start over again. But that wasn't going to happen.

"They're so young," Dad said to himself. "Just babies."

"Middle-school kids. Sad but true," said Mr. Graves. "It's been going on for years. They seem to outgrow it by the time they reach high school, except for a few, like the Knockout King."

The video was just too grainy to get much detail. The lens was pretty dim from all the bad weather it had seen. On top of that, Kalvin was wearing a hoodie, so you couldn't see his face.

Kalvin just took off, out of frame. Prince and the others followed. Only I was left on-screen, holding my camera and struggling to catch up. It was strange seeing how tense I was. Everyone else ran out of range and I followed.

The camera caught none of the attack. After about thirty seconds of staring at the cement, Tillman interjected.

"That's it?" said Tillman.

"Hold on," said Graves. Another unbearable minute passed, then a rush of Tokers came running back. Another twenty seconds later, me and Kalvin skirted the edge of the frame. Graves froze the video. It looked like just a blur.

"Really? You got nothing there," said Tillman.

"Looks like Erica and the Knockout King to me."

Dad squinted at the image. "Bullshit. No jury's going to believe that. What about Erica's camera?"

"So you're saying it's hers?" asked Mr. Graves.

"You know it is," said Tillman slowly. "What I'm wondering is why you didn't lead with that? Unless, of course, her camera had nothing on it." He stared down Graves.

Mr. Graves stopped the video.

"There's an issue with the camera," he said, hesitating.

I perked up.

"It was damaged in the scramble and—" he glanced meaningfully at me—"my guys say blood and memory cards apparently don't mix. They're still trying to get some reliable footage off the camera."

Tillman slapped his hand on the table, ignoring my

sickened expression. "So you have nothing, then." He shut his notebook. "I think we can go now, Erica."

Graves eyed him wearily. "Mr. Tillman, I don't want to put Erica in lockup if I don't have to. Rest assured, we *will* get the video off that camera. But what I really need is a witness who can testify to these crimes and help put an end to these Knockout Games. If she can be of help, then—"

"*Help.* There's a word you usually don't hear unless they have squat," said Tillman.

Graves looked like he'd eaten something bad. "You can help or we can drag this thing out."

"Help with what?" said Tillman.

Graves turned back to his computer and opened another file. It was the same surveillance camera, but later in the day when the investigation was happening. That's when me and Destiny walked back into frame looking for answers.

"Erica returned to the library a couple of hours later with this other girl, Destiny Jones. That's where I first encountered her." He reached down into a box and pulled out my jacket, which was in a big Ziploc bag.

"This was found in the trash around the same time. The security guard saw them run down to the bathroom, where he discovered it later." He looked at the video and then at the jacket. Same jacket, of course. "These dark stains here? Blood. The lab—"

Tillman held up his hand. "I need to confer with my client. Alone, if you don't mind."

Mr. Graves nodded. "Take your time."

Dad waited for Mr. Graves to leave. He turned his focus on me, studying my eyes for any kind of reaction. "So?"

"What?" I said.

"What else haven't you told us?"

I stammered. "I didn't think they'd find the jacket."

"I say we go back to the original plan," said Tillman. "We play friendly; they'll be friendly back. We testify and shoot for full exoneration."

"And between now and when they pick up Kalvin? What if he comes after her?" Dad asked. "Is he capable of that?"

Tillman shrugged. "It happens. But if they nab him quickly enough and he's certified as an adult, chances are more in your favor that he'll do real time. . . ."

I couldn't get that quote from Kalvin's Facebook page out of my head: "A disobedient child shall not live his or her days to the end."

"He'll come for me," I said.

Dad leaned back in his chair and closed his eyes, wishing it would all go away. "So what should we do?"

"Are you licensed to carry?"

Dad nodded.

"Just keep an eye out. That's what I'd recommend," said Tillman. "Those boys'll be keeping a low profile for now."

"Carry what?" I asked. "Will you just stop for minute? This is all happening way too fast."

Dad turned to me. "I'm sorry; we're just trying to make it through this mess. If your teacher meant anything to you, you have to do what's right. Even if it's not fair. You need to step up for the good of everyone."

My eyes accidentally fell upon the photos of Mrs. Lee that were spread out on the table. They were horrifying, even worse than I remembered. It hurt to see her like that. "If I do this . . .

what will happen to Tyreese?" I asked. "He's still a boy."

Tillman studied his notes. "He's too young to be tried as an adult, and you could corroborate that he was manipulated by Kalvin. I think they'll lock him up in juvie until he's eighteen and then, maybe probation after that."

"But he didn't mean to . . ."

Dad pointed to the pictures. "Tell that to her."

***

Tillman made the deal. I'd testify in exchange for charges being dropped against me—two years' probation with community service. I had to sit in front of a stack of yearbooks for Truman and Joplin and ID each member of the TKO Club. I knew no one's last name or where they lived, except for Kalvin, Prince, and a few others. I told Graves about the club and the Rec Center and Kalvin's home.

I almost lied to protect Tyreese, but the detective sensed me hesitating and didn't let up with the questions until I buckled. I guess they're good at that.

When I came to Kalvin's photo, he was smirking like school was all a big joke.

Graves said, point-blank, "We know he's the Knockout King. Will you back us on this?"

I stared into those green eyes, which had been dulled by the black and white of the photo. Without those piercing eyes, he looked like an ordinary punk. Even then, all I could think of was our night on the roof. I could almost feel myself lying in his arms and yet, my only memento of that night was that I still hadn't had my period yet.

Graves sensed my reluctance. He was patient. "Take your time. It's an important decision that will affect a lot of lives."

I looked at Kalvin's photo for the longest time. I wondered where he was right now. Did he know his fate was in my hands?

"I can see you're like my daughter, " mused Graves.

"I doubt that."

"My daughter likes to dive off the high dive sometimes. It's all she talks about. But when she gets up there, she still freezes up. Sometimes, she just needs a little push." He pretended to poke her in the back.

Seeing I still wasn't sure, he pushed himself away from the desk. "I know we have a deal and everything, but sometimes, the proof is in the pudding. Let me show you something."

He started walking down a long cold hallway. At the end, there was a series of doors. He looked up to the camera and the door buzzed. I hesitated. "Come on," he said to me. "Let the doors slam behind you."

We walked through two metal doors and each time they slammed shut so loud it made me jump. He kept walking and I could see we were in the prison side of the juvie center. Through some windows, I saw kids in a classroom. They all wore matching jumpsuits, either red, yellow, or orange. A girl spotted me and watched me as we walked by. She was my age.

I didn't know they had school in juvie, but I guess it made sense. We passed through another metal door and by the time the echo of the slam died down, we were standing in a closet-sized room with a tiny window high out of reach. It was empty except for a metal bed and someone's flip-flops on the floor.

"This is where he'd be staying. Locked up, out of sight. He wouldn't escape from here, if that's what you were worried about."

"No, that's not it."

A mattress was shoved underneath the metal frame and board. He noticed me staring. "Some of them sleep underneath their beds. It makes them less afraid at night."

His walkie-talkie went off. "'Course, you wouldn't want to find yourself on this end of things, just so we're clear." He answered his call and while I was imagining some kid sleeping under his bed at night, he walked out into the hall and let the door slam behind him.

I jumped, but I knew what he was doing. I didn't panic and start banging on the door for him to let me out. I just sat down on the bed. In there without all the clutter and confusion, I just stared at the light coming through that tiny window. I felt empty inside. So empty, I just crawled underneath and laid on that mattress in the dark.

When my eyes finally adjusted, I could make out that some-one had scrawled the word SORRY in the metal bed frame.

34

It was Thanksgiving weekend when Dad moved in with us. Not exactly a Norman Rockwell moment. He was just going to stay until things calmed down, whenever that would be. Nobody was in the mood to celebrate, but Mom went down to Schnucks and picked up a turkey dinner, and we all ate it in the attic that we lived in.

Dad wasn't happy about the whole situation. Not happy with missing work, not happy with me, and not happy with the place Mom and me lived in. The couch was in bad shape, so the first thing he did was buy us a new one, because he was going be sleeping on it.

Since we moved here, he had never visited or asked about our circumstances. He'd lost a lot of our money and there was that thing about another woman, so I figured maybe he was too ashamed to show his face. But he was here now and trying to be "Dad" again.

He and Mom talked about me staying home from school, but Dad was determined that I act like everything was normal.

"Only a guilty person hides," he said.

Mom was concerned for my safety, but after speaking to Principal Evans, he assured them that Mr. Jamison would escort me between classes. That way I could at least finish out the term. Dad would take me to and from school, so I was covered. Other than that, I'd be grounded. No phone, no friends. And no contact with TKO crew.

Mom had been reluctant to go to work that first day I went back to school, but Dad said he had it under control. It was weird waking up Monday morning for school and seeing Dad in the kitchen. He was already on the phone making calls when I walked in. While I was eating breakfast, I saw him going through his briefcase and that's when I saw he'd brought his *gun*. I almost choked on my Froot Loops.

"Really?" I said, pointing.

"Tillman thought we should have some protection. Hopefully, I won't need it while I'm here. But according to you, I could be knocked out by a twelve-year-old at any time. If any of your little boyfriends tries that on me . . . " He took out his gun and checked the chamber. One bullet.

I don't know what was scarier, the idea that we might be attacked or that my dad was packing. I knew he'd never fired that gun in real life, except at the shooting range. In fact, he always kept only one bullet in it at any time. *You can do a lot of stupid things with six bullets*, he'd say. *One forces you to make a real choice—and to choose wisely.*

The gun was just for show, something to impress all the sketchy characters that came into his business at one in the morning looking to bail out their buddies. But he did go to the range and had made it a point to take me before we moved here, so I'd know how to shoot it as well. He suggested we get one for the house, just in case, but Mom wouldn't have anything to do with that.

Maybe she wouldn't be so against it these days. Dad had gotten a newspaper before I even got up, and Mrs. Lee's death was on the front page. TEACHER KILLED BY KIDS read the headline. *Are Today's Youths Incapable of Empathy?* read another opinion piece. Details were being withheld pending investigation, but seeing Mrs. Lee's photo in the paper made me dizzy.

Alice Lee, fifty-four, an art teacher and community organizer, a mother of two, both in their twenties now. Her husband, Joe, had been a medic in the Iraq war; he had been wounded and retired.

They didn't seem like the reactionaries I imagined them to be. They lived near the library and went there a few times a week. Friends and colleagues said she loved her students.

That last detail got me. I wondered what she was thinking when she saw me with all those kids attacking her and her husband. Did she still love us then?

I wondered if she had any inkling that morning that it'd be her last. Is that something you can feel coming, like right before a storm when the wind kicks up and the air turns heavy? Or was it a complete surprise?

Her husband Joe was in the hospital. He had a broken jaw and swelling on the brain. They said he didn't remember anything. One minute, he was at their favorite library; the next, he woke up and his wife was dead.

I felt sorry for him. I remembered Kalvin saying, *What do you care what happens to them? You don't know them. They could be child abusers for all you know.* But they weren't.

I thought about our other targets and wondered what had happened to them. Were they afraid to go out anymore? Did they hate the world because of us?

Then, I saw that Mrs. Lee's funeral had been set for Wednesday. I tore out the notice and put it in my pocket. There was going to be a candlelight vigil tonight as well. Maybe I'd go to that.

Dad saw me reading the piece, but didn't say anything. What could he say?

35

When we arrived at school, the word was already out. I could tell because everyone looked at me like I had rabies or something. When Jamison and his crooked eye came marching up to talk to Dad, I spotted Prince and some others watching me and I knew they knew. They were thinking the same thing: *snitch bitch.*

"This isn't gonna work," I said.

Dad corrected me. "This *will* work. I know it's not a perfect situation, but Mr. Jamison will escort you everywhere you need to go."

I looked at Jamison. I couldn't tell if he was looking at me or my dad.

"That's the problem." I scanned the front lawn. "The whole student body is staring at me. They already know I sold them out."

Then I spotted the flowers piled up around the flagpole in front of the school. Some students were signing a poster with Mrs. Lee's picture on it.

"I think we should go home," I said.

Dad saw what I was looking at and put his hand on my shoulder. "I think you should think of her and not yourself. I know it's not easy. But you are doing the right thing. That's not always the popular thing. Believe me, I know. I see plenty of losers in my line of work."

"So I should stay?" I asked.

"We have to carry on. Despite everything. Just remember, you are my daughter. And believe it or not, I still love you. As long as you are protected, you'll go to school."

He kissed me on the head. "Just think of Mrs. Lee when things get tough. She'd want you to go to school."

He said good-bye and drove off. Jamison gave me the once-over. I could tell this was not his idea. "It's a sad day. And you should know, I'm only doing this for Mrs. Lee. If it was up to me—"

"It isn't." I wanted to be clear about this. "And I know. Let's just . . . get on with it, OK?"

He decided not to challenge me. "There's going to be a memorial for her today. A big assembly with both the middle school and high school, out in the bleachers. Other than that, you go to your classes and I'll escort you in between. Questions?"

"What if I have to go to the bathroom?"

He frowned. "Save it for your breaks. If you go during class and I'm not around, you'll be on your own." He started walking.

First thing I saw once I got past the metal detectors at the school entrance was a poster that said, *Today is Mrs. Lee Day: Respect and be kind to your fellow humans!*

A voice hissed, "Snitches get stitches."

I wheeled around, but the hall was so crowded I didn't see who said it. People were watching me, so it could've been anyone.

"Come on," said Jamison. "I'm not waiting on you."

We headed to my homeroom, the one where Destiny sat behind me. When we got closer, I spotted her waiting outside the door. She saw Jamison, shook her head, and went in.

Jamison put his hand out to stop me. "Hold up."

Now what?

"Just so we're clear here: no drama."

Too late for that.

I sat in homeroom trying to ignore people's stares. Destiny was burning a hole into the back of my head with her eyes. Finally, I felt her nudge my elbow when the teacher had her back turned. A note.

I need to talk to you!

I wrote: *Ok, but Jamison is watching.*

There was a long pause. The note came back: *Sit next to me at the assembly.*

I nodded.

***

The assembly happened after third period. Thank God. That was the period where I would have had to sit through art class without Mrs. Lee and I don't think I could've handled going there. Instead, we were told to report to the football field even though it was freezing. Jamison said he hoped it would wake us up.

Students walked in herds, making their way from class.

When we reached the bleachers, I saw a stream of middle graders coming from the opposite end of the field, which bordered their school. By then, of course, everyone knew about Mrs. Lee. There was an oversized picture of her by a mic stand in front. People were somber and upset.

I spotted a few of the TKO Club: C-Jay and Tyreese and some others. Tyreese seemed super nervous and C-Jay kept a hold on Tyreese's shirt as if to keep him from running. They didn't see me, and I ducked into a row to avoid them. The rows filled in; I kept my head down, covering myself with my hoodie.

"No hoodies," Jamison said.

"It's cold. Everyone else is wearing hats," I pleaded. He backed off.

Destiny sat next to me. "That was fucked up what you did," she said, instead of hi.

"Which part?" I knew she was pissed. "I'm sorry I ran out on you," I added. "I just freaked . . . big time."

Her jaw was clenched. "Yeah, well, you left me to deal with that stupid Mr. Graves and his crew. They kept me for two hours. My *mom* had to come get me. They were gonna take me in unless I told them who you were."

"You gave me up?"

"No!" she hissed. "What do you think I am, a snitch?" She eased up. "That cop noticed your name on the bottom of your camera."

"Well, I got screwed, if it makes you happy. My parents know everything. My dad drove in from Arkansas. I got a lawyer and—"

Destiny cut me off. "I hope you didn't say nothing."

I couldn't look her in the eyes. I just shrugged it off.

"Erica . . ."

"What am I supposed to do? Mrs. Lee is dead and I'm an accomplice!" I hissed as quietly as I could. "I can't just let it pass."

"And Kalvin?" she asked.

I didn't answer.

The principal gave a heartfelt tribute to Mrs. Lee. She'd been at Truman long before he came in and he recounted how she'd made him help paint a school mural with the students as a way to bond with them. She was always involved and always pushing for more after-school programs and arts funding and was willing to do almost anything to get them. She would be missed. The principal called for a minute of silence and we all stood. Jamison stood at the end of the row, head bowed.

After the longest minute in the history of mankind, the principal said we all needed to take a good hard look at ourselves and added that we should take a pledge of nonviolence and goodwill toward our fellow humans. We didn't have to stand up with our hands on our hearts or anything for that, but he asked us to think about our teacher and what she meant to the school. I'd already done plenty of thinking.

When he mentioned the Knockout Game, I winced. Even though they had spoken about it before, he had a special speaker he wanted us to hear from, a young black guy who could've been a senior here. The guy acted nervous and uncomfortable in his suit and tie as he stepped up to the mic. Even his glasses and close-cropped Afro seemed out of place.

That's when Destiny went pale. "Oh shit," she said.

"My name is Tuffy Jones."

"What?" I whispered.

She got all quiet. "That's my brother."

I studied the guy. He did look kind of like her. "Why's he talking?"

She didn't answer.

"You didn't know he was going to be here?"

She was grinding her jaw. "He called me the other day in the park and wanted to make things right. But I could tell he still had a thing about Kalvin and he was trying to pry information from me. I didn't know . . . that he'd show up here. . . ."

Tuffy seemed awkward up there behind the mic. I could tell he wasn't used to speaking in public. "I went to school here three years ago. Mrs. Lee tried to keep me on the straight and narrow, but I didn't graduate 'cause . . . I was in detention. And I don't mean the kind after school."

Everyone quieted down.

"I went to Joplin Middle too. That's where I started playing the Knockout Game."

I glanced at Destiny: she had a look of horror on her face. She turned pale, her eyes drained of life. I'd never seen her look so worried.

Tuffy cleared his throat again and gathered himself. "In my head, it was funny—knocking people out. I liked the thrill of proving I was a man, even though I was just a kid, really. I used to have marks on my wall for how many knockouts I got. For real. We did five knockouts in one night once. By the time I came to Truman, I was top dawg—the Knockout King."

Someone giggled behind me and someone else tried to shush him. I heard, "The real Knockout King would whup that boy's sorry butt."

I ignored them. I felt like Tuffy was somehow going to speak to me in a real way. I was sitting fifty feet from him but in my head, it was a close-up, the sounds of the crowd dropping away. He was talking to me at that moment, like I was sitting in an empty theater staring at the big screen.

He looked right at me. "What y'all is doing now is stupid. I mean, we was some badasses but we never did no old heads and definitely never did no teachers. Never. Mrs. Lee is the only teacher who took a interest in me. What happened to her ain't right. It ain't right by a long shot."

All I could hear was the sound of my heart beating in my ears. Until . . .

"I thought he failed that class," said the guy behind me. "Dang, you go away for a while and you get all weak in the head."

"Jesus, shut up," I said under my breath.

Tuffy was staring into the sky. "I remember lying in my bed at night, all pumped up from all the excitement. Whenever I thought about my targets, I just pushed it outta my head. Hell, I didn't know 'em, why should I care? But when I was in ninth grade, I stopped. I saw this guy I'd KO'd a year before. He had to walk with one of them walkers now. He was real messed up and had kids too. I couldn't stop thinking about him. But I was just a kid myself . . . so I had to do one more before I stopped and that's when I got caught."

"'Cause you stopped thinking straight," whispered the dude behind me. "Sellout."

I was about to let him have it.

"Now, I just got out," said Tuffy. "I never graduated. I got a record. I can't get no job. I'm basically fucked." Evans glared at him. "Sorry, but you know how it is. I ain't got no future. You guys, though, you still got a chance."

"Who gives a fuck if he has no future? He was top dawg and he fucked up. He makes me sick."

That was it. I turned around. "What the fuck is your prob—"

A girl was sitting there looking at me. She pointed down to her feet. I glanced down and saw Kalvin, Prince, and a few others standing underneath the bleachers staring at me through the slats.

"Oh, you heard that?" Kalvin said calmly. "I was running out of shit to say. Takes you long enough to get pissed off."

I shot a look at Destiny. She kept her eyes glued to the ground.

"Don't look at her. She's a good soldier."

"What are you doing here?" I asked, confused. The girl sitting behind me got up and moved to the next row. I looked over to see if Jamison was watching, but luckily, he was distracted by a couple of guys goofing off on the next bleacher.

Kalvin touched my ankle and I recoiled. "You won't return my texts. How else am I supposed to talk to you?" Everyone was still focused on Tuffy, so Kalvin spoke softly, leaning his head to the edge of the bench. "I really..." he struggled for words. "I was really upset when I heard that you had visitors this weekend. And I'm not talking about your dad."

He had been watching me.

"Then I heard you went down to juvie? And I asked myself, why would she do that? She wouldn't ... she wouldn't rat us out, would she? Not after what she'd done herself? No, I couldn't believe that, despite the fact that Prince here thinks you're a snitch. No, I said, she's a good girl, just confused; seeing a dead person probably freaked her out, am I right?"

I nodded.

He traced his finger softly up my calf. "I've seen a few myself and it's not a nice thing. Still, I wondered what you talked about? I mean, I know that the surveillance video didn't show shit, and for some reason, they couldn't get anything off your camera that you happened to *leave behind*." He scowled at me good, then shook it off. "So I figured it out. They needed a witness, someone who knew not only everything that went down that day, but everything about *us*." He took a deep breath, exhaled.

"But I wonder if that person remembers that she wasn't the only one with a camera and maybe some *other* videos might be making their way into the wrong hands. . . . " He was neither threatening nor angry nor confused. He was certain—certain that everything would go bad for me . . . if I didn't play ball.

"Did you talk to Rodney Graves?" he said, matter-of-fact.

I had lots of answers in my head and things to get off my chest, but before I could, Jamison caught my eye and glared at me for talking. Kalvin ducked back into the shadows. I turned back around and sat there, making sure I didn't look like my crazy ex was standing underneath me. Jamison stood there for the next fifteen minutes, until Tuffy finished his story. Kalvin had stopped talking, but I could feel him breathing on my leg the whole time. I pressed my hands to my stomach and prayed that I would get my period soon. I tried not to imagine the other possibility.

Destiny practically jumped out of her seat the second it was over. She didn't want to talk to her brother or Kalvin or me for that matter.

When everyone else stood to leave, Kalvin reached out and slid something into my hand. "I can't let you take away everything I've built. I just can't. I need you to understand that."

He and his crew disappeared into the shadows. I looked in my hand. It was Mom's driver's license.

36

I freaked. Called home. Voice mail. I dialed Dad's cell. When he picked up, I started rambling a mile a minute. He'd been out all day, had not seen Mom, and was trying to interpret my incoherence as to why I was calling him before lunch. I made him come pick me up. He heard the panic in my voice and came right away.

Evans said I could leave, but only after I told him that I had been intimidated by someone. When he asked by whom, I just said people that shouldn't be here. He caught my drift.

As soon as we pulled up to our house, I raced upstairs. The front door was unlocked.

I ran into Mom's bedroom.

Empty.

"Mom!" I cried out. "Mom!"

"Hello?" she answered from the bathroom.

I stood there, my head spinning. "Are you . . . OK?"

The toilet flushed and my anxiety dropped away. "Jesus." I collapsed onto her bed.

Dad walked in. "Now would you mind telling me what this is all about?"

Mom shuffled into the room half asleep. "I thought I was going to get some rest today...."

I took out her license and handed it to her. She blinked. "What's that?"

"Um, your driver license?"

She looked puzzled. "Why are you handing it to me?"

"The real question is who handed it to *me*?" I said.

"What are you on about? Why aren't you in school?"

"That's what I still want to know," added Dad.

"Mom, focus. Did you leave the door unlocked?"

"No, I don't think so," she seemed unsure. "Why?"

I hugged her. She was surprised, but I didn't want her freaking out more than I was. "He was here, Mom. He was in this room."

She tensed up. She understood immediately.

"Who was here?" asked Dad.

"Kalvin. Kalvin came to school this morning with a message. A warning, more like," I answered.

Dad got it. He walked straight to the front door and checked the lock.

"Are you OK?" I asked Mom.

She felt her clothes like she was checking for stab wounds or something. "Yeah," she nodded.

Dad came back in, visually sweeping the room, looking under the bed. "I'm reporting this," he said.

"What are you going to say?" I asked. "That he stole her driver's license?"

"How about breaking and entering, for one? Threatening

a witness? He'll be behind bars today if I can help it." He took out his phone and called Mr. Graves.

Mom was in shock. "I can't believe they were in here. Watching me." She shuddered. She looked tiny and frail in her nightgown. When I thought about Kalvin standing over her and what he might have done . . .

"It's all my fault," I said, hugging her again.

She hugged back, but didn't disagree.

***

Dad put us on speakerphone as he told Graves what had happened. I added the part about my encounter at the assembly. Graves said they were going to bring in all the suspects tomorrow. They needed extra time to work out the details because the crew were all minors. But they would try to pick up Kalvin tonight just to be safe. After tomorrow, things would be alright again, he assured us.

"And in the meantime?" he asked.

"We can send a squad car over to stay with you, if you like."

"No thanks," said Dad. "Just do your job and I'll do mine." He patted his chest. I could see his holster strap under his jacket.

Mom leaned into the phone. "Send the car," she said.

***

Dad stared silently at the squad car parked outside our apartment. He ordered the locks changed, but in the meantime, I took a chair from the kitchen table and propped it up against the front door. When it was jammed in good and firm, he asked, "So we're on lockdown?"

"Yep."

I wanted to talk to Destiny about everything, but Dad wouldn't let me. At some point, I was getting too antsy. Even though I was grounded from communicating with the outside world, Dad allowed me to go online. I got onto the *St. Louis Post-Dispatch* site and saw the candlelight vigil was happening tonight, right outside the library. I showed my dad.

"Maybe we should go?" I asked.

He put his hand on my head, something he used to do when I was tiny. "I don't think it's a good idea with all this going on. It'll be dark, with lots of people. You never know who will be in that crowd."

I agreed. Maybe they'd have a live feed online or something.

I checked my e-mail. Nothing from Destiny or any of the others. But there was a Facebook notice that I had been tagged in a video. I clicked the link.

A page came up and a video called *Heavy Metal Mama*. I clicked Play. A serene image came up of a park somewhere on a crisp sunny day. And then I saw him: Metal Detector Man—and me coming up behind him.

I shut the laptop. Dad looked at me funny, but I tried to act normal. I opened the laptop again and untagged myself, but now I knew Kalvin still had the video. Something would have to be done.

Mom got up for dinner, which Dad actually cooked—a first. Even though it tasted horrible, I could see he was trying. We didn't talk about much. I suggested that maybe I stay home tomorrow, but Dad said if they got Kalvin tonight, it would be good to show my face, to show the rest of them that I couldn't be intimidated. "It makes a difference in court," he said.

"How?" I asked.

He didn't answer.

Mom suddenly got brave after being cooped up with us two. "I'm going to work, then. He's not going to make me a prisoner. What's he going to do, march into the lab? We have security."

So we all drove to Mom's work. The squad car followed us and it felt like having our own Secret Service detail. We dropped her off, and Dad said he'd come pick her up in the morning.

On the way back, Dad took a different route. "Where are we going?" I asked, but as soon as I saw the crowd, I knew.

We drove by the library and there were about three hundred people standing in silence, the candles lighting their faces. Some people had signs saying DEATH IS NOT A GAME and SHE DIED FOR PEACE. They marched in a circle in front of the library. There were pictures of Mrs. Lee on each sign. Someone was singing "Imagine" and playing a guitar.

Dad stopped across the street, but kept the engine running. He just wanted me to see it.

"Snow," I said. The snow was falling gently and silently, making the whole scene angelic.

After a minute, someone startled us by knocking on the window. It was one of the cops in our Secret Service. "Just wanted to let you know that they apprehended Mr. Barnes, sir. Still, we should probably get back to your home."

"Did he go quietly?" Dad asked.

"He gave us a bit of a chase," said the officer.

I imagined Kalvin flipping them off and hitting the streets like one of those parkour guys, hopping walls and jumping off bridges.

"They caught him hiding in the bushes."

So much for parkour.

37

The next morning I woke up and felt like I was going to puke. I sat staring at the toilet and thought: who feels sick in the morning? *Pregnant girls.*

Shit. I wanted to pretend all the stress was keeping my period away. This was the last thing I needed in my life. I prayed the stress would go away, along with everything else. There was only one kind of blood I wanted to see now.

***

Dad drove me to school. He was in a better mood. "With Kalvin behind bars, I think this whole thing will crumble now. You just have to stick to the plan and everything will work itself out."

Jamison was there to meet us. I got the same stares, same comments behind my back. But around 10:15, Jamison came into my class and told me to come with him. Someone hissed, "Busted. . . ."

We ended up in the principal's office. Evans was dressed in a dark suit like he was on his way to a funeral. He gestured for me to sit, while he just sat there behind his desk, staring out the window. Something was going to happen; I could feel it in the air. "We're expecting visitors," he finally said. "I thought it best that you stay here until they finish with their work."

He didn't say anything more until I saw four police cars and two black vans pull up quickly in front of the school. They skidded to a stop and the doors burst open. About fifteen cops jumped out, dressed in black riot gear. Half of them went to the middle school; the other half came running into ours.

Evans handed Jamison a list he had handwritten on a piece of paper. He told him to go give it to the cops and to make sure they didn't cause too much of a commotion.

"What's going on?" I asked.

"Taking care of business," he said, watching. "It'll be over soon."

I heard them marching down the hallways. Classroom doors were opened; names were shouted; scuffles followed. After ten minutes, I saw them marching back out with three students, including Prince Rodriguez and a couple other Tokers. They had plastic bands tying their wrists together.

Suddenly, I saw Tyreese sprinting across the grass. He had seen the cops coming out of the high school and took off—a gazelle trying to escape a mob of hungry cheetahs. The cops sprinted after him, but he moved fast, slipping in and out of their grasp. When they surrounded him on the front lawn, he spun around, running them in circles until he slipped on the grass and went down. Three cops pounced on him and it was over. He squirmed about as they tried to pin him down, but eventually they dragged him off to a van. They had seven other middle schoolers, including C-Jay and Doughboy. Then as quickly as they came, the cops hustled everyone into the vans, and just like that, they were gone.

"Well, that made a statement," said Evans.

"Can they do that?" I asked.

He ignored my question. "Hopefully, our students won't forget this little show and it'll be more effective than Kindness Day. Unfortunately, you all tend to respond more to getting caught than having empathy toward the victims."

"And what about me?" I asked.

He studied at me with lizard-like eyes. "It seems you have a little more breathing room for now. I would still keep a low profile, if I were you."

I left his office a bit stunned. It had all happened so quickly. I expected Jamison to escort me back, but Evans' secretary told me he hadn't returned from the raid. Besides, they said the threat was gone, so I was on my own.

I found myself alone for the first time in days. It was eerie. I started down the hallway until I felt somebody watching me.

I turned and saw Mrs. Lee. The poster of her from the assembly was standing outside her office. It was a blowup of one of those bad yearbook photos everyone had to take, the ones where you had to look optimistic and hopeful. I gazed at it for a long time, hoping it would wash away the images burned into my brain from the crime-scene photos. This was a much better way to remember her.

***

During lunch, Destiny found me alone, shivering on the bleachers. I didn't mind the wet seat; I wanted to feel numb again.

"You know they got this thing called indoors, right?" she said.

She waited for me to say something. When I didn't, she zipped up her jacket and sat down next to me. We sat there in silence for a good couple of minutes, until she meekly said, "Are we still friends?"

I shrugged. "Oh, now *you're* asking," I said.

She bit her lip. "I didn't . . . set you up. I guess I just got caught up in everything . . . and then my brother showed up. . . . "

"Well, if it means anything to you, I'm not seeing Kalvin anymore."

We both looked at each other and busted out laughing. It was such a stupid thing to say.

"Was it the prison duds that turned you off?" she said, barely able to get it out.

We laughed until we couldn't anymore. Then we got serious again.

"So, I guess I should say thanks," she said. "Seems someone left me off the TKO list."

I had managed to overlook her picture in the yearbook. "I'm always saving your ass."

She was about to say something back, but nodded instead. "I remember when my brother made me swear I'd leave the TKO club," she offered.

"And why didn't you?"

She scrunched up her face. "I wish I had, way back when.

I was too young. But I guess I was no different than the rest of 'em. . . ."

"You're like me. Too stubborn to listen to anybody who tells you not to do something. Besides, if you had left, we wouldn't be friends now."

She nodded, sheepishly. "I didn't know K was gonna be at the assembly."

I believed her, but didn't say so. We sat in silence.

"You gonna testify?" she asked finally.

I shrugged. "Someone's gotta stand up for Mrs. Lee, right?" I said, mostly to myself.

She put her arm around me in a sisterly way. "You do what you gotta do. I got your back."

I was surprised. "Really?"

She shrugged. "I don't know; I have a thing for losers. If I don't stand with you, who will?"

"Thanks." I put my hand on hers and felt the warmth of her skin. "You wanna ditch school with me?"

She did a sly double take. "Now? Aren't you supposed to stay out of trouble?"

"I can't stay here. There's something I have to do. And I want you to come with me."

38

St. Matthew's Cemetery was only a short bus ride away. When we got off and she saw where we were headed, she shot me a look.

I nodded. When she saw the news crews in the parking lot, she got it. She saw I meant business. "Whatever you gotta do. . . ."

We waited under a tree for about twenty minutes. People began to arrive. All kinds of people. Much more than just family and friends. The community was turning out for this one. Evans and some of the staff were there too. I didn't care if they saw me.

We walked in with the rest. Everyone was dressed in black, except for us. As we headed up the hill, a funeral procession of black cars turned into the main gate, led by a hearse. We watched them pull up to a freshly dug grave at the top.

I saw Joe Lee emerge from his car. It was hard for me to breathe. He looked like he'd aged ten years in three days. When I turned away, Destiny put her hand on my back.

"I got you, remember?"

It was a gray and unforgiving day. The priest did all the things that he usually did every time someone died. Then the mayor got up. With him was a man leaning on a cane with a bandage on his nose. He was probably that city councilman Prince hit. There were a lot of people there that looked important. Destiny said she saw some sports stars there too.

The mayor spoke about being "appalled" by Mrs. Lee's violent death, and of feeling "helpless" to prevent more of them. He gathered himself and continued, "But seeing everyone here today and the responses in the paper and online has given me hope. Maybe Alice Lee didn't die in vain. Maybe her death has a deeper purpose behind it. To bring people out of their shells so they don't accept random violence as a way of life. We are better than this. The great Gateway Arch that you see in the distance is not just a tourist attraction. It's a doorway—a doorway to a greater future of unlimited possibilities. We cannot let the acts of a few ruin the acts of the many. We are better than that, and Alice Lee will stand as beacon of hope when all is said and done. Enough is enough."

Many people spoke after that. Some knew Mrs. Lee well; others knew her only by her community work. The only one who didn't speak was her husband Joe. He had to be assisted to his chair beside the grave. He had a neck brace, and bruises on his face. Maybe he couldn't talk.

Finally, a man stood up with a card in his hand. He introduced himself as Joe's brother. "Joe asked me to read this. He thanks you for all your support and prayers, and says that if Alice was able to talk to us today, she would forgive those who did her wrong."

A murmur ran through the crowd.

"Joe admits that although he had the right intentions, perhaps his own pride helped spur on those who ended his beloved's life. For that, he is sorry." The brother cleared his throat. "But Alice would still feel the need to reach out and help all of those kids because that is what she did her whole life: help kids. Her students were everything to her. She never judged them and always gave them the benefit of the doubt because she believed there was good in all of them, no matter how troubled they were. And now, she'd ask all of you to be open to the possibility of forgiveness too. Thank you."

I wish I could feel that about myself.

**

As they lowered the coffin into the ground, one by one, people rose, grabbed some dirt from the pile, and dropped it gently into her grave. I started walking.

"Where're you going?" whispered Destiny.

I didn't answer her. I just kept moving until I was standing in a line of about ten people, each moving slowly toward the grave. I grabbed a handful of dirt from the pile. As I moved closer, I knew that dirt would be the dirt that buried her forever.

When it was my turn, I stopped short of the edge of her grave. I'd never seen a coffin up close before. My hand began shaking; my legs weakened. Suddenly, it felt like the grave was sinking deeper into the earth, sucking me in too.

A hand grabbed my arm.

Joe.

Seeing him up close was shocking. One eye was really swollen and bloodshot. The bruises on his face and his broken jaw made him look like he was wearing a Halloween mask.

He grunted, guiding my hand over the grave. I dropped the dirt. It landed with a soft thud on her coffin.

He was unsteady, but he was staring at me intensely.

I wanted to tell him I was sorry. I wanted to tell him it shouldn't have happened. I wanted to ask for his forgiveness.

But my mouth went dry.

His brother came up and took his other arm, guiding him back to his seat. "Come on, Joe, you need to sit."

He let go of my arm and moved slowly back to his seat. But he kept staring at me as if he knew something.

39

Afterward, Destiny walked me home, where we ended up shivering in front of my house. "I still can't believe you live here."

"It was cheap, what can I say?" I said.

She looked around at the empty lots surrounding our house. "You gonna be OK?" she asked.

I shrugged. "I just have to wait things out, I guess."

"And hope things don't get worse."

I laughed, but she wasn't joking. "What do you mean?"

"Nothing," she said, hesitating. "It's just things haven't exactly gone your way lately." She didn't know the worst of it.

Destiny kicked at the sidewalk. "I kind of worry for you is all."

"I worry for me," I added, wondering where she was going with this.

She had something else on her mind. "What if ... things go bad at the trial?" she asked.

"How do you mean?"

"Um," she cleared her throat. "Like what if ... Kalvin and them ... get off?"

I didn't want to think about that. "Did you hear something?"

"It's just that it kinda . . . happened before."

This was news to me. "When?"

She kicked at a rock in the dirt until it skittered across the sidewalk into the tall grass. "Why do you think they're so hot for Kalvin?" she asked. "Three years ago, there was a knockout where some old guy ended up in a coma. Rodney Graves happened to be the one who found him. He had just passed this group of kids who did it. When he was waiting for the ambulance, he noticed a girl watching from her stoop. She had seen the whole thing; she knew those kids too. Graves convinced her to be a witness. Checked up on her every day to make sure she was still willing to do it. It was an open-and-shut case. This was back when my brother was king."

Heavy. "Is that how come he ended up in juvie?"

She laughed bitterly. "No. An hour before the trial, the girl disappeared. The boys had gotten to her, convinced her to not testify. Kalvin . . . made me hide her at Prince's cousin's house till the judge had to finally throw out the case, a mistrial. Everyone got off, made a big show of it. People were pissed."

"So how'd they get your brother, then?"

"'Cause he was an idiot. Thought he was invincible. He hit a reporter who asked the wrong question, right outside the courthouse! In front of everybody!"

"And that's how Kalvin took over?"

"Yep."

She kept kicking at the ground. "They're not going to take any chances this time."

"Who? Kalvin?"

"No, the city. If they're not 100 percent convinced you can

win the case for them, they will drop you and walk away. They can't afford to be embarrassed again."

"And why didn't you bring this up *before* I agreed to testify?"

She gave me the stink eye. "Um, because you ran away?"

Right.

***

Dad was drinking coffee and working at the kitchen table when I walked in.

"The police raided the school today," I told him.

He nodded. "Graves called me. Quite a list of charges they had. Assault, collusion, witness intimidation, second-degree murder."

I'd never get used to hearing that word *murder.* "How did they know Kalvin intimidated me?"

Dad studied me for a moment. "Not you. Joe Lee."

"What?"

"Online stuff. Plus making threatening calls and leaving messages in his mailbox. Stupid stuff."

I thought of Joe sitting by his wife's grave. The man had no recollection of the attack, but still, they had to make sure he got the message.

"So what do we do now?"

Dad collected his papers and put them in his briefcase.

"Now we wait."

We were told it'd take two months for it to go to trial. The prosecutor was hoping a few of the younger ones would turn on Kalvin, after spending some time in a cell. There was very little evidence, I guess, so the case seemed to rest with me. They needed more, but no one else was coming forward. Even Joe was hesitant to say anything, because his memories were playing tricks with his head.

Meanwhile, life went back to normal, except all I had was time to think about what I was doing. Graves checked in with us every few days, making sure that I wasn't getting cold feet. He'd just drop by, as he was always out patrolling the neighborhoods, looking for certain kids before they got too deep into their criminal ways. He always brought us something: donuts, candy. And he always had the same message: "You're doing the right thing."

I wasn't so sure.

40

Graves wasn't the only one counting days and checking in. I finally looked up online how long you could go without a period and not be preggers. Ten days.

Today was the tenth day.

***

I called Destiny. She knew it was important because I was calling, not texting.

"I haven't gotten my period yet," I told her.

She knew what that meant. "Are you late?"

"A little. . . ."

She thought about it. "You been under a lot of stress. That can fuck with your insides."

I didn't say anything.

"If you're worried, we can find out. If you want to."

I swallowed hard. I had pushed this out of my head long enough. But now it came roaring back in.

She was not one to bullshit me. "Come on, no use adding extra worry to that head of yours. The last thing you need is to be Kalvin's Baby Mama."

***

She took me to a drugstore where we headed for the home-pregnancy-test section. She scanned the selection and picked one in a blue box.

"You seem to know what to look for," I said.

She gave me a glance that said it wasn't her first time in this aisle.

"Come on." She led me back to the bathrooms.

"Aren't we gonna pay for it?" I asked.

"You don't think you been paying for this yet?"

She came in with me and locked the door.

"How come we always end up in the bathroom together?" I asked.

"'Cause you always fucking up," she answered without thinking. She tore open the box and pulled out a plastic ther-mometer-looking thing and held it up to the light. "I didn't mean that. . . . "

I took it from her. "I know." I looked at the "thermometer." Two options: *pregnant* and *not pregnant*.

"You gotta know," she said, seeing my hesitation. "You don't wanna be carrying around his seed in you."

"Nice way of putting it."

"Just—"

"I'm gonna do it," I said. "Fuck . . . " I stuck the thing in my mouth.

She just looked at me like a child and pulled it out of my mouth. "You *pee* on it, idiot." She handed it back to me.

I knew that.

I waited for her to leave, but she stayed put. "You just gonna stand there?"

She sighed and turned around. "You ain't got anything I don't."

I sat and waited for the pee to come. "What if—"

"There is no *what if*. There's only *what is*. But either way, there's options."

I closed my eyes and tried to relax. I thought back to that night on the roof. It felt like forever ago, but everything changed in three weeks. I remember staring up at the moon with him. This was not where I expected to be.

Destiny stood there waiting for that plastic thing to reveal the truth. I saw her eyes straining for the answer.

"Well?" I asked.

"Hold on . . . it's coming."

I couldn't take it. "Tell me!"

Her face was all tense and then . . . she dropped it and took two steps toward me and wrapped her arms around me tight.

I looked down at the thing on the ground.

Not pregnant.

The next day, I got my period.

41

Christmas happened, but I can't say it was merry. We did our best to have a normal family holiday, with the gifts and the tree. It even snowed for about twenty minutes, but soon that turned to brown mush.

For a present, Dad got me some fancy drawing paper and new pens, hoping maybe I'd take up drawing again—like that would cheer me up.

As soon as I could, I'd donate it all to the new art teacher.

***

My phone vibrated with a blocked ID. I answered anyway.

The operator said there was a collect call and then I heard this tiny voice say, "It's me. Tyreese." An image of him curled up under his bed in that cell flashed in my mind.

The operator asked if I'd accept the charges, but I couldn't bring myself to do it. He'd just make me cry, and I was tired of crying.

"Sorry, wrong number."

Shortly after, I received an e-mail from Destiny. I guess it was too personal to text.

She'd talked to Tyreese. He told her how hard it was in juvie. Fights broke out all the time. The juvenile authorities kept trying to get him to turn against Kalvin. But Kalvin was there too, waiting to be transferred to an adult facility, so that made it impossible. He was sure Kalvin was out to get him in his sleep or something.

Kalvin kept telling Tyreese that in Missouri, a twelve-year-old could be tried as an adult for murder (it was true; I Googled it). Tyreese was begging Destiny to help him. He promised he was done with the TKO Club, done with fighting. He said he couldn't stop thinking of Mrs. Lee—it had been an accident; he just wanted to knock her out, not kill her. He was scared, scared that Kalvin would do something if he said any more.

After that, I saw Destiny less. Seeing her made me think of Kalvin, which made me think of Tyreese. Instead, I tortured myself by watching all those movies we never finished with Kalvin—*A Clockwork Orange, Butch Cassidy and the Sundance Kid, Bonnie and Clyde*. Now I knew why we never saw the endings: things ended badly for the "heroes"—all winding up dead or in prison or brain damaged. Now suddenly, I could see the movies for what they were: tragedies.

I guess the joke was on us.

***

A couple days before New Year's, I was walking home from the market when I saw Joe Lee struggling to carry his shopping bags. He no longer had a walker or the neck brace. But his arm was wrapped in a sling and he limped so badly, he needed a cane. It was a fight just to carry his three plastic bags.

It was cold and a little icy. I was going to walk away before he saw me, but after watching him struggle for a few seconds and seeing nobody was offering to help, I found myself next to him.

"Do you need some help?" I asked.

He had two bags on the ground and was leaning against a light pole, resting. "No thanks. I'll manage."

"Really?" I said.

He laughed at that. "No. I just . . . doctor won't let me drive yet and my brother couldn't make it and you know . . . gotta eat!"

I looked around for a taxi or a bus he could take home. "Well, don't they have one of those dial-a-ride things?"

"That's for old people. I'm not old."

"But you're—" I was going to say disabled, but he grunted. "So . . . how far are you going, then?"

"Oh, not far. Maybe five blocks or so—"

That's when he looked at me for the first time. "Do I know you?"

My shoulders tensed up, my feet itching to run. But I held my ground. "No. But I know you. I . . . came to your wife's funeral?"

"I remember you." His hand reached out for my arm. I had that same panicked feeling as when he was lying on the ground and grabbed my leg. My hand turned into a fist. I was shocked to feel my body ready to hit him to get away. His hand gently held my fist as he used me to help regain his balance. "You came to say good-bye."

I relaxed my fist. "Yeah. She was my teacher."

He looked into my eyes. "She had that effect on you young people. They flocked to her. . . . " he paused, struggling to remember.

"I'm sorry," I said so quietly, I don't think he heard me.

"I still don't get much sleep," he said. "Nightmares. They keep you awake."

"Do you remember much?" I blurted out. I don't know why. Did I want to know if he remembered *me* at the scene? "I mean, it's not my business."

He glanced up. "No. Nothing. They even showed me a surveillance tape and it was like watching two actors in our place." His gaze fell to the ground. "I am grateful that my last memory of that day is of her, in the library. Her smile. That's what I remember." He choked back the thought. "But I regret getting so caught up in my cause that I forced their hand. Some of the things I said . . . stupid. I should have just—"

"No, you were right," I said. "It was right to stand up."

He went silent, lost in his own head. I needed to tell him.

"I was there," I said suddenly. "When it happened."

He seemed confused. "What do you mean?"

I caught my breath. "I . . . saw it happen."

I could see all kinds of thoughts racing around his brain. "You *saw* it?"

"I—"

He moved toward me. "You saw them? You know who they are?" He was getting manic. "Did you tell the police?" He was only a foot away now. I could smell his desperation.

I nodded slowly.

Then his eyes went wide. "*You're* the one who identified them?"

I nodded again, unsure.

He wrapped his arms around me and started crying. "Thank you, thank you . . ." he kept saying, rocking me back and forth. "You will help keep these boys off the streets so that it doesn't happen again. And then we can start the healing process, help bring them back from the ignorance that's set in their minds—"

"No!" I said. "No, I—it wasn't like that—"

I pushed myself away from him. I couldn't bring myself to say it.

"It wasn't like . . . that," I said again.

"What do you mean?"

I was one of them.

I started to back away and he just stared at me, confused.

"Where are you going?" he asked.

It was my fault.

"Where are you going?"

Suddenly, I couldn't face him anymore. I turned and walked away quickly.

"Don't leave!" he shouted.

People in the parking lot had their eyes on me. I didn't want to face any of them.

"Hey!"

I ran. Hard and fast. I slipped and fell, scraping my knee.

"Wait!"

But I got up and kept going until I couldn't hear him anymore.

42

I don't know how I made it home. I was shaking badly when I stumbled through the front door into Dad's bags.

"Where have you been?" he asked.

"Are you leaving?"

He seemed distracted. "I have some work I have to attend to back in Little Rock. I'll be going back and forth until the trial." He gestured toward the couch. A woman in a suit was sitting there. "This is Ms. Hallstrom. Remember, she's the one from the family court? You do what she says and you'll be OK."

"Where is Mr. Graves?" I asked.

"I'll be handling your case from now on," she said, slightly dismissing her partner.

Great. The last thing I needed was another handler. I was still trembling when I shook the woman's hand. Hers was dry and steady.

"Erica. We have a little problem we need to clear up."

We sat. She took out her iPad. "There's this video—"

I knew what she was talking about. Metal Detector Man.

"Now's not a good time."

Dad was in a bad mood. "Erica, I need to get back. If there's a problem, we need to deal with it while I'm here."

"I don't feel good," I said. I didn't want him to see the video.

"Erica—" Dad said.

The woman interrupted him, calmly but firmly. "Would you mind if I speak to Erica alone?"

Dad was offended. "Yes, I do mind!"

Hallstrom remained calm. "It's my experience that sometimes clients are unwilling to talk about certain issues in front of family members."

"Her lawyer's not here."

She was short on patience. "We're on the same side, sir. We all want what's best for Erica, if she's to be our main witness."

Dad was having none of it. "What do you mean *if*?"

"It's OK, Dad. I'll talk to her," I said. Better her than him.

Dad huffed and puffed, arguing with himself. "That's not how things are done, Ms. Hallstrom. I am in the business, you know."

She was steady and sure, but lowered her eyes. "Which is why I'm asking. Please."

Dad grunted, held up his hand. "Five minutes. I'll be downstairs loading my bags. If you do anything illegal, there'll be hell to pay."

Ms. Hallstrom let him rant. "I work for the family court. I'm bound by oath and common sense."

Dad grunted again and made his way to the front door. "Five. I'll be counting."

When the door shut and we heard him go downstairs, Hallstrom turned to me. "Actually, there's more than one problem."

Not a good way to start. "I got sucked into it. I didn't think it would happen."

"What?" she asked.

"Um, that I'd hit that guy?"

She made a face. *Wrong video.* "Yes, there's that one. It's generally not good to have visual evidence of a star witness doing the same crime the perp is up for. But that's not the video I was talking about."

She held up her device and pressed play. Immediately, I heard the sound of myself moaning and I knew what it was. For those few seconds, it wasn't at all like I remembered it. There was an overweight girl, awkward and fumbling to take her shirt off. When the boy pulled it off for her, she got stuck in the neck hole, her pale skin flabby and white even in the dark. She noticed her back scraped up from rolling around on the roof, her hair matted with sweat, her cheeks flushed—

"Turn it off," I said.

She did. "Your parents haven't seen this, I assume?"

I shook my head, "No. Where did you get this?"

"Kalvin's computer."

I guess it shouldn't have surprised me that he backed it up. Was all that struggle to get him to delete it just for show?

"I'm afraid it will come out in the trial," she said. "The defense will use everything at their disposal to discredit or embarrass you. But one thing's for sure, the judge will not like it."

"My parents won't either." I buried my face in my hands. "Everyone will see it?"

"All evidence has to be shared by both sides and the first thing they'll notice is that you and Mr. Barnes appear to be . . .

closer than we thought," she said. "It will show up in the trial; you can be sure of that."

"I was . . . confused, OK? He . . . set me up. . . . "

"Set you up?" she asked, skeptically. "That's not what it looks like. I need to know how serious this was."

My face was getting hot. "It happened once and then . . . I ended it. I didn't like who he was becoming."

"Did you fight?"

"I guess . . . yeah. We had words."

"Did you hate him for using you?"

"I do now. What's it matter?"

She leveled her gaze. "It matters because the defense will try to get this case thrown out, saying you have motivation to get back at Kalvin."

I began to panic. "Why would I do that?"

"Jilted lover? Angry at being kicked out of the club? I don't know. What *are* your motivations?"

I couldn't believe this. "Isn't trying to make things right a good motivation?"

She sighed. "In my eyes, yes. In the judge's . . . it's questionable. I have to be honest, Erica. I don't like finding these things out after you've said you told us everything. I need to know what's in that head of yours before we continue walking down this road. What else aren't you telling us?"

I thought about my encounter with Joe an hour ago. I didn't want to get into that. But then Dad came back before I could answer. "Are we done?"

Ms. Hallstrom looked at me. I nodded. "There's one more thing," she said. "This one, you should see."

Dad sat down, all his bluster gone.

"We finally got something off your camera. It wasn't the whole video, more of a snippet. But I should warn you, it's not easy to watch."

She scrolled through some videos and brought up the one she was looking for. She pressed Play. The images were a far cry from my usual work. It was broken up with glitches and skipped around. It began with me running, the camera all over the place. The sound cut in and out, and you couldn't make out anyone clearly.

But then the image froze on Mrs. Lee. She had fury and fear in her eyes. It stuck there for a moment and then speeded up again. The camera fell to the ground and settled on a scurry of feet. I was struggling with her. We were both screaming when the sound cut out. Then there was a blur and we were both knocked out of the frame. The video ended with part of her body blocking the lens.

Hallstrom turned it off and let it all settle in. "It doesn't look good, does it, Erica? I don't think you've been entirely honest with us and that's not a good sign. The defense will jump all over us, and you in particular, and they *will* show all these videos—"

"There's more than one?" asked Dad.

"There might be a lot more than one." She leaned over and looked me dead in the eye. "I need you to really think hard about this, Erica. I know we will be. I'm pretty sure there's a hard drive somewhere with all kinds of videos you haven't shown us. The lead prosecutor would like a sit-down tomorrow in our office. With your lawyer."

Dad appeared worried for the first time. "What's going on here? This is my daughter. We've risked a lot coming this far. I don't like what I'm hearing."

Hallstrom put away her iPad and closed her briefcase. She was all business, but I could tell she was exhausted. "We will reassess where we stand and discuss our decision tomorrow morning."

"*Reassess*?" said Dad.

She got to her feet and shook my dad's hand. "I don't like wasting time, sir. And neither does the State of Missouri. We'll see you tomorrow."

By the time Dad walked Ms. Hallstrom to the door, I'd locked myself in my room. I couldn't bear to tell him what she told me.

43

I guess it was no surprise that everything fell apart. Our meeting did not go well. It was New Year's Eve day and the office was half empty. The prosecutor, an older man who was all about winning, told Tillman and Dad that I'd become an unreliable witness and that too much was riding on me. He'd met with the judge and the defense. The defense let them know that, in no uncertain terms, they were going to expose me as unreliable, misleading, and someone who could be easily manipulated.

The prosecutor's office was backing out.

When Tillman raised hell, Ms. Hallstrom reminded him that I was lucky not to be charged as an accessory, something that it was still possible. Maybe worse.

Dad's shoulders slumped. "But you've left us exposed. They'll come after her."

She knew. "I have to deal with a city that's crying out for justice. Trials are never that easy. We can get him tried as an adult, but there are things clouding the investigation. No one else is talking. Even Mr. Lee's memory of previous incidents is cloudy at best. If we mounted a big trial and it goes bust, it'll be twice as bad. We can't go down that road again. I'm sorry."

She got up to leave, but before she reached the door, she stopped. "Oh, I almost forgot." She reached into her briefcase and produced my camera. "Just returning your property since . . . well, it's no longer required for evidence. The guys managed to get it working, at least."

She put it on the table and we all stared at it like it was a ticking bomb.

***

After the deal was officially declared dead, all the lawyers left my dad and me alone in the room. We were silent for a long time.

"What are we going to do, Dad?"

He stopped and turned to face me. "I'm going to undo the biggest mistake I ever made. I'm taking you and your mother back home. You'll get back on track, go to your old school, graduate, then—"

"Then what?" I asked. I really didn't know.

His eyes couldn't hide the doubt. "Then . . . we'll pretend this whole thing never happened."

We waited for the elevator. I could see he didn't believe his own words. I reached over and held his hand. He kept staring at the elevator door, but squeezed my hand back.

***

We had a family meeting. Actually, it was more like a fight, but after a while everyone calmed down. During a lull, I got a call from Destiny.

"They're being released. I just got a text from Prince," she said.

"That was fast."

"What are you gonna do?" she asked.

I listened to my parents. "We're fighting about it now."

"We are not fighting," said Dad. "We're discussing."

"Are we?" asked Mom.

I held up five fingers, asking for a break. They didn't notice. I walked away to my room and closed the door. "We might be moving back to Little Rock."

There was a long pause. "That would suck," Destiny said. "For Little Rock, I mean."

She still knew how to break the ice.

"There is one other option," I said. "But my dad would kill me if he found out."

"Like that's better than Kalvin killing you?"

I shuddered. "I really don't think Kalvin would do that. He'd be the first one the cops tracked down. Besides, I got him off, didn't I?"

"Technically. I don't think he'll see it that way."

She paused for a long time, weighing the options. "Do you need help?" I didn't want her getting sucked into this. But I did need one thing.

"You can help me arrange a sit-down," I asked.

"A sit-down? What're you, a mafia guy?"

I shrugged. "Even the mafia knows you have to respect a sit-down, especially with your enemies."

"You know you're crazy, right? That's just in the movies."

"I know . . . but will you just . . . text him and ask? Somewhere public. For tonight? Before we move away?"

"It's New Year's Eve," she sighed. She was thinking it over. "Fuck it. Might as well ring in the new year with a bang."

I hoped it wouldn't come to that.

She called me back ten minutes later.

"Tonight," she said. "Taco Bell on Grand. Ten o' clock. But I'm coming with you. You'll need backup."

"Fine. I just have to sneak out. I'm pretty sure we'll be on lockdown tonight. My mom might even stay home from work."

"So how are you gonna pull that off?" she asked.

"Uh, I'll think of something. Did you talk to Prince? What're they doing?"

"Celebrating. You should see the TKO page. They talking shit like they're political prisoners set free. Say they gonna sue the city and all that kind of stuff. K's talking about how they're the Trayvon Martins of St. Louis."

"Jesus. I know he doesn't believe that shit. He's just saying whatever will get him on the news."

"They're already on the news. They've been the lead story today. You should check it out."

I turned on my TV, flipped a few channels until I saw the news showing the crew emerge from juvie. Even their parents were out there cheering and high-fiving each other.

A reporter cornered Kalvin. "Of course, the case got thrown out," he said. "They're always trying to profile us, 'cause of the way we dress. Some people get attacked and who do they look for? Black teens."

The reporter asked him what he felt about the victim. "I

don't hold no grudges. I feel sorry for Joe Lee and his wife. It's sad. Whoever did this is messed up."

So what were they were going to do now? He shrugged. "Celebrate. Be with my family and start the New Year free. Just be happy to be out. I'm going to Taco Bell first thing."

He looked into the camera and winked. At me.

44

Mom and Dad didn't say too much during dinner; we just resigned ourselves to the idea that we'd probably have to leave St. Louis. We'd sleep on it and talk more in the morning. Dad felt we'd be OK tonight, that no one was stupid enough to come after us on the day they got out of jail.

Still, just to be safe, he'd use the chair under the doorknob trick. And he'd be sleeping on the couch. With his gun.

Mom and Dad wanted to stay up and watch the ball drop in Times Square on TV. When 9:30 rolled around, I pretended to be tired and said I was gonna crash. Before I locked my door, Mom and Dad each came in and gave me a pep talk.

Mom was gentle. "I stare every night through a microscope at these cells, knowing that couples are out there praying for fertility. And some of them will go on to have babies and it's a miracle. But what I think about now is how they can never imagine what it's like when that baby grows up and something like this happens. You can get mad, say you'll disown them, but in the end, you're still our child. No matter what, we'll do what's best for you. We aren't going to let somebody else ruin our lives. The new year will bring us better things; you'll see."

Dad took a more direct approach. "I almost hope that bastard tries something, because I'd be perfectly in my rights to shoot that son of a bitch. That'd be my New Year's resolution." But then he let the bravado slip and he put his hand on my head. "We'll get through this, kid. And then we'll start over, OK?"

Each followed with a hug and a kiss and a good night.

I locked the door behind them.

When the TV in the living room came on and was loud enough, I opened my window and listened to the distant sirens coming out of this huge city. Then it sank in: how stupid was I to meet to meet Kalvin at night? They could be waiting for me in the parking lot to jump me.

"Hey!"

I looked down and saw Destiny standing on the sidewalk. "Are we doing this?" she whispered loudly.

I'd snuck out once before, shimmying down the drainpipe and almost killed myself. But I knew I'd caused all this. I brought this on my family. It was up to me to do something about it. To fix my own mess, as Dad always said.

I had no plan, just a feeling. I grabbed my camera, took a deep breath, and reached for the drainpipe.

***

When I walked into Taco Bell, I could see why Kalvin had picked it. It wasn't too crowded, just some teens loading up on burritos before hitting the parties, and a few homeless people escaping the cold. I didn't see Kalvin at first, but he was around the corner, back toward the bathrooms, sitting in a booth. Just him and Boner. He had his leg hanging out the side and I spotted my homemade tattoo faded and almost gone.

I expected him to be pissed, but instead when he saw me, his eyes lit up. He was all swagger. "Bet you didn't expect to see me again."

Boner was wagging his little tail at me. Out of the corner of my eye, I spotted Destiny outside the window behind him. She hung back out of sight.

"I don't think they allow dogs in here," I said.

"You kidding? He's the Taco Bell Chihuahua, ain't that right, Boner?" he said. Boner barked and Kalvin gave him some of his Burrito Supreme.

I slid into the booth across from him. I decided I'd just cut to the chase and took out my camera, putting it on the table between us.

He looked at it and chuckled. "Like old times, huh? I suppose you expect me to confess on camera or something? *Please . . .*" He picked it up and turned it on. "I am innocent," he said into the lens.

Then he just sat there staring at me, trying to read my mind.

"What?" I asked.

"No New Year's Eve kiss?"

I started to leave, but he laughed it off. "It's a joke. Just trying to make this less awkward."

"That didn't help."

"Fine. Come on, why don't you sit next to me," he said. "I won't bite."

He wasn't going to make this easy. I glanced quickly over at

Destiny lurking in the background. There were enough people around that he wouldn't make a scene. Plus I spotted the surveillance cameras in the corners.

"Come on, I need to be careful," he said.

"I'm fine here."

"Suit yourself." He got up and moved into my side of the booth. I was about to climb over the back, but he reached out and held my hand. "That's not the way to treat the guy you almost fucked over for life, is it? Just relax."

I slid up against the wall. He smiled, then leaned in and touched the zipper on my jacket. I flinched.

"Don't worry. I need to see if you're wearing a wire," he whispered.

"I'm pretty sure minors can't wear a wire," I said.

He shook his head and slowly pulled the zipper down. "Still. Can't be too careful, no?"

I took a quick look over my shoulder. Destiny wasn't outside the window anymore. Kalvin slipped his hand inside the jacket, where it came to rest on my chest. I lost my breath, panicked, and scanned the main room, where I spotted Destiny sitting at a table near the front door. She had a confused look in her eyes, wondering why we weren't talking.

Kalvin watched me closely as he moved his hand down my front. When his fingers touched my breast, I caught my breath. I was sure he could feel my heart racing.

He sighed. "Memories. That's all I got."

He cupped my breast for a few seconds and smiled to himself. Boner watched me with his big eyes, trembling. Then Kalvin's hand continued to wander down, over my stomach. He paused when he came to my belt.

I looked him in the face, but his eyes were closed. His hand slipped down into my panties, but I jumped, grabbed his arm, and pulled it out.

The dog jumped down and hid behind my feet. Kalvin shook his head, disappointed. "Sorry, you never know where they'll hide a wire these days. "

"I'm not wearing a fucking wire," I said, cold as ice.

He sat back, almost admiring me. "If I hadn't slept with you . . . I might think you were a guy. You got balls, girl."

I wasn't sure if that was a compliment or a threat.

He picked up my camera and began fiddling with it. I noticed it was still on. "Normally, if someone tried to fuck me over like you did, that person would be in the hospital. Or worse." His eyes bore holes into mine. "You'd find out pretty quick what pain was."

I let him talk. I suppose that's the least I could do. At least the camera would record everything.

"I'd probably do it myself too, even though I try not to get my hands dirty these days. Just got a manicure today," he joked.

I didn't laugh.

"So, we're sitting." He leveled his gaze at me. "What do you want, Erica? To say you're sorry? To say you didn't mean to do it, but they made you confess? That you wanna rejoin the crew? Get back together?"

I stared him down. "No. I want to know what I have to do so you'll leave me and my family alone."

He slowly nodded. "A deal. You came to make a deal. Without even apologizing?"

"You mean for how you manipulated everyone to do what you wanted . . . including me?"

264

He didn't seem offended. "You're stronger than you think, Erica. I didn't *make* you do anything. You *wanted* to do it. You were just afraid to admit it. I'm living the life most people don't dare to. A life that ignores the rules. A life that knows we're all animals inside and acts on it. That's the only difference."

"So by that way of thinking, maybe you agreed to show up because you thought I'd . . . sleep with you again?"

That kind of caught him off guard. "Oh, that's cold." Then he thought about it. "You'd sell your body just for me to leave you all alone?"

"That's not what I said."

He pondered that thought, then he let out a long sigh. "Maybe that's what you meant, though. But as much as I'd like to take up your offer—and it's a good one—" he looked me up and down again. "I had something . . . different in mind."

"OK . . . what?" I knew it had to be good.

"One more game."

At first, I didn't know what he was talking about. Then it sunk in.

"That's what you want? For me to play one more Knockout Game?" I had to make sure he wasn't playing me.

"It's only fair. That's the TKO rule. You want out, you gotta fight your way out."

I was skeptical. "TKO has rules?"

"Jesus, girl. 'Course it's got rules. No stealing. No drugs. No messing with gangs. And if you can't handle it anymore, you gotta prove yourself before you walk away."

I had to ask. "And if I don't?"

He leaned forward, looking me straight in the eye. "Then *you* become the next target." He meant it.

"And if I played along, you'd leave us alone?" I asked, coolly.

"Forever. I wouldn't give a shit about you no more. Not that I do now, but seein' as you're asking, *that's* the price."

It wasn't cheap. "And how would it work?"

"We'd meet up, just you an' me. I pick the target and you gotta deliver."

"You want *me* to knock someone out."

"Hey, I've seen you do it. Plus I taught you all the secrets." He leaned back, put his hands behind his head, and waited for an answer.

"You know they'll be watching you, right? I mean, the police are just waiting for you to do something to take you down."

He nodded sagely. "Which is why *I'm* not doing anything. *You* are."

"My dad wants me to go back with him."

He laughed. "To Arkansas? You think that'll keep me away? That's not so far. I've always wanted to see Little Rock."

He pointed the camera at me. "Well, what's it gonna be, Erica? Wanna play? Or do you wanna end up like what we did to poor ol' Joe and Alice?"

I glanced over at Destiny, who was mouthing, *What the fuck is going on?*

"Don't look at her. I saw Destiny before you walked in. She ain't gonna give you the answer. So what's it gonna be, Fish? Are you gonna take the plunge?"

I was already in over my head. "OK, but then it's done."

Kalvin got up. "Oh, it'll be done, alright." He toggled through the camera and deleted what he just shot. "I'll text you the location in the morning." He scooped up Boner, passing

Destiny on his way out. He handed her the camera. She took it and rushed over to my table.

"Well?" she asked.

"I gotta do one more thing."

She watched Kalvin disappear into the darkness outside. "Well, whatever it is, you'll need backup. I'm coming with you."

"No. This one I have to do alone."

She shook her head. "Bullshit. Me and Tuffy will take his ass out."

I smiled. I knew I wouldn't win this argument, so I told her I'd call her in the morning.

I don't think she believed me either.

As I walked home, the fireworks went off overhead, climaxing at midnight. I could hear parties going on in people's houses, and saw some people kissing in the streets. My only New Year's resolution was to be true to myself. No more lies. No more hiding.

The new year starts now.

45

The phone vibrating on my nightstand woke me up. Kalvin. All he texted was for me to start walking east on Grand by eleven a.m. He'd text the location then. He added: *Happy New Year!*

I hated mystery. It sounded like a setup but what could I do? I had to get this over with.

I thought I'd woken up before everyone, but when I peeked into the living room, the couch was empty. But Dad's briefcase was still on the coffee table and he never left without it.

I heard a strange noise coming from behind Mom's door. I pressed my ear to it and listened in.

Dad was snoring.

Whoa. Last night was crazy, but I guess I missed the real party. I know it happens—they always got sappy and sentimental on New Year's Eve. Still, I didn't want to visualize it. It probably didn't mean anything.

I kept staring at Dad's briefcase. It was the first time I'd seen it without him around. If I was going to do what Kalvin wanted, I'd need some protection. I kneeled in front of the briefcase, listening to Dad's snores. I knew the combo: 9/6/98. My birthday.

I cracked the briefcase open, trying not to make any sound. And there it was—Dad's gun.

It had been a long time since I'd held it, back when he took me those few times to a shooting range before Mom put a stop to it.

It was cold to the touch. Heavy, like it meant business. Dad kept it clean. It looked new even though it was at least ten years old.

I played with the safety, made sure it was on (first rule). I popped the cylinder and checked the chamber to make sure it was loaded. There was one bullet.

Then I remembered Dad's bail bondsman motto: one bullet forces you to make a real choice—and to choose wisely.

There were no extra rounds in the briefcase.

That was a stupid motto. What if I had to use this and missed?

I tried tucking it into my pants, but it felt like it'd fall out. They made it look easy in the movies, but this wasn't working. Finally, I just threw on my hoodie and hid it in my jacket pocket. I checked myself out in the mirror to see if it was noticeable. I was surprised to see I didn't look scared.

I put a Post-it in Dad's briefcase. It just said, "Sorry." Anything more would only make it worse. I locked the case, grabbed a bagel, and headed out into the cold morning.

***

I moved uneasily down the icy street. Some people were out scraping off their windshields, others huddling at the bus stop with their shopping bags. To them it was just a normal Saturday.

Destiny answered my call on the fifth ring. She had been asleep. "It's Saturday. Do you know what time it is? That's why we text."

"Sorry. I said I'd call, so I'm calling."

She remembered. "What's going on? It's too early for this shit."

"It's not that early. I think the library's open."

"Fuck the library," she said. "What's the plan?"

"Destiny?"

"Yeah?"

"I just wanted to say . . . well, I guess, thanks."

There was a long pause. "What the fuck for?"

I laughed. "For being my friend. In the beginning. You know, when nobody else would."

She grunted. "You coulda told me that later. Like at dinner. When we'd laughing about how nothing happened today."

"I had to tell you now. Just in case. . . . "

"In case . . . what? What's going on?"

"I made a deal, that's all. And now I gotta do something. Alone."

"See? I knew you'd pull this shit. When people say things like that, bad things happen." She sounded awake now.

"You watch too many movies," I said. "Besides, you got me in and out of enough trouble. I have to do this on my own."

Now she knew she wasn't going to win this argument.

"Erica. Just don't do anything stupid." She sounded worried. "OK?"

"Too late." I didn't want to get into it. "I gotta go, 'bye."

"But—"

I hung up. Turned my ringer off. She tried calling again, but I ignored her.

I headed down Grand and started to feel bad that all I left my parents was that stupid Post-it.

I opened a new text message on my phone.

Mom Dad.

Im sorry I failed u. I know u tried. At least I didnt do drugs right?

Lame.

I switched over to the voice recorder mode and pressed Record.

It took me a few seconds to figure out what to say. Something like this isn't like leaving a message saying that you're going out to dinner. So I just began talking.

"OK . . . by now you noticed that I . . . took the gun. It's for protection . . . just in case. I'm going to meet Kalvin and hopefully settle this so we can . . . get on with our lives. I decided even if we leave St. Louis, I don't want this hanging over our heads. It ends today." I paused it, trying to think where I was going with this.

"If something goes wrong, or if I end up in jail or the hospital or worse . . . just know that . . . I'm sorry for how things turned out . . . and that I wanted to do better. I wanted to do better by you, but even more by me." I paused to gather myself.

"For a long time . . . I just felt numb inside. Now I can feel pain. I know I am alive. I want to keep it that way. If you are listening to this, it means the police gave it to you. I'm not gonna send it to you because then you'll panic and be searching the

271

streets. If you never hear this message, then things worked out, but just in case . . . I'll say it: I love you. Yeah. Really."

I wiped away a tear, then laughed that I was doing this. "If I'm reincarnated as something else, I will do better with my life. I know you tried, so now I will too. I can't stop talking for some reason, so I just will. Stop."

I saved it and kept the recorder mode open on my phone as I buried it in my pocket. I hoped nobody would ever have to hear it.

It started to snow again.

46

Kalvin's second text said he wanted to meet her at the library. He knew how to push her buttons. The Watchers had to be on the lookout for him, but the weather was shitty and the library closed for the holiday, so the streets were pretty empty.

None of the other Tokers were in sight, not even Prince. No Watchers either. Just a guy walking his dog. Someone riding his bike. Then she spotted somebody with a hoodie covering his head, pacing in front of the library. She zoomed in. Kalvin.

When he saw her, he ducked into the alley behind the library. Erica put her hand on the bulge in her pocket. She looked jumpy, glancing around and checking over her shoulder.

It was Boner who snuck up on her and licked her foot. She leaned down and petted him. He looked scared and just sat there whimpering.

"When all this is done, you should think about moving in with me instead," she said. She made her way into the alley,

Boner on her heels. She saw Kalvin standing in the spot where Mrs. Lee had died. He was hovering near a small memorial on the fence, surrounded by sad little flowers, candles and cards, all soggy from the snow. When she moved in closer, she saw him staring at a photo of Mrs. Lee and her husband.

"You know, it might surprise you, but I do feel bad about that woman," he said. "She didn't deserve what happened. She just . . . got in the way."

"She didn't deserve to die, you mean," Erica said. She zoomed in tight on his face. He smiled slightly at the sight of her camera.

"She was a willing player. You saw her, at Joe Lee's side. She was no different from him."

"He thought she was better than him."

Kalvin grunted. "That's not saying much. If he'd a kept his mouth shut, she'd be alive today. People make choices."

"So it's *his* fault?"

He leaned down and picked up a candle that had fallen over. "It doesn't matter. Sometimes a shake-up is good. I'll bet he's appreciating life a lot more now."

"No. He doesn't."

He studied her. "And how do you know?"

"I talked to him."

He scoffed. "I suppose you apologized too. Maybe begged for forgiveness?"

"No. I was a coward. Just like you."

He stood up, his hands balled up into fists.

She didn't flinch. She could see he was breathing hard in the cold—his face pale, his eyes dull, less threatening.

"You have a free pass, you know?" she said.

He shrugged. "What, you mean retire? Just walk away from TKO while I got my freedom?"

"Something like that, yeah. Don't you think it's time to grow up?"

"Oh," he said, considering the idea. "Is that what you are now, grown up? Did all your crazy shit and now you're ready to become a responsible citizen?"

She let the camera stay on him without answering.

"You wanna play games, is that it, Erica? Outthink me, get me to confess to my sins? Turn that shit off," he said, pointing to her camera.

That was the first time she ever heard him say something like that. She pretended to turn it off, but kept it running in her hand.

"So why don't you stop, Kalvin? Haven't you had enough of all this? Haven't you knocked enough people out?" she asked.

He didn't answer. It was deathly quiet, only the sound of the snow falling gently on the ground. *Pat. Pat. Pat.*

"You know, I've had Prince do a little surveillance work of his own. Turns out our friend Joe is a man of habit."

"So?" she said.

"He likes to come here every day at 11:30, the moment they were gamed. To visit the site where his wife died like that? That's real loyalty. I can respect that."

"Are you saying I'm not loyal?"

He stared her down. "What do you think?"

"I think you can't stop because you think you have some kind of rep you need to uphold. And that rep is only held together by the loyalty of your crew and you're worried that what I did created, like, a 'disturbance in the force.' And now you have to show you can control me by making me do something I don't want to. Is that about right?"

He wasn't amused. "Really? A *Star Wars* reference? Well, doctor, the rest of your theory is bullshit. We play the game because we can, and there's nothing they can do to stop us. We'll keep knocking out people and if someone tries to stop us, they might end up like poor Mrs. Lee. Like I said before, we meant to take out her husband, but hey, shit happens. Which is part of the reason we're here now."

She glanced at her watch. 11:30.

And that's when she had a moment of clarity, of what this was all about. He didn't want her to knock out just anybody; he wanted somebody special—

"Right on time," he said, glancing over her shoulder.

Down about a block away was Joe Lee. Wrapped up in an Army jacket and limping his way into the alley. He was carrying flowers.

"It's touching. I mean, it really is, that you of all people will be the one to take care of business on this very spot. It's almost what they call ironic."

She glared at him. "Leave him alone."

"Oh, *I'll* leave him alone. *You're* the one who's gonna take him out. I got him started, but you can finish him. He's barely on two legs—"

"What *happened* to you?"

He ignored her. "He's getting closer. He hasn't recognized us yet. Probably lost in thought—"

"Jesus, Kalvin . . ."

His eyes searched hers. "You don't want to find out what'll happen if you back out."

She looked back. Joe was getting closer, but was still out of hearing range. He hadn't seen them yet.

"I said, leave him the fuck alone."

"Or what?"

He noticed her fists balled up and the look in her eye that said *enough*.

He raised an eyebrow. "Oh, now's she's ready! You'd like to smack *me*, is that it? You'd like the chance to knock my face in?"

"The difference is, you'd deserve it."

"Well, come on then. Take your best shot. Now's your chance. I won't even protect myself."

He put his hands behind his back and just stood there.

"Come on, Fish, *do it*." It sounded like he wanted her to. Boner began yapping, running back and forth between them.

She raised her fist.

"There you go! See? You *are* like me, Erica. Don't you get it? You were so hopeless and defeated when I first met you and now, you got spirit, you got rage, and you want to let it all out. You're just like me, Erica!"

Erica slowly breathed out and lowered her fist. "I'm nothing like you. I don't know what happened to you, but I will never be like you. There's something broken in you, Kalvin." She opened her hands and shook them out. "And fuck you if you think I'd ever stoop to hitting that man. He has suffered enough, but to you, he's still a joke, a thing to be played with. Well, I'm done with this game. And so are you."

She glanced over her shoulder. Joe was about ten yards away, watching them. He recognized her. She looked Kalvin in the eye. "Now just walk away, before it's too late." She stuck her hand in her pocket. There was an audible click.

He rolled his eyes. "It's never too late." He took a step toward her.

She took a deliberate step to put herself between him and Joe. When Kalvin smirked, she pulled out her gun and pointed it at his face.

He froze, his eyes wide with surprise. Then he kind of laughed. "Damn, girl. Is that thing for real?"

"As real as it gets."

"Have you ever shot a gun before?" he asked. His voice wavered.

Erica swallowed. "Don't have to be a sniper to hit something from this range."

He took a step back, admiring her. "Look at you. You're one tough motherfucker. And I mean that in the best way. I'm impressed."

"I don't give a shit. Start walking."

Now he was getting pissed. "You really think you're gonna shoot me, right here? On the very spot where that woman died, the one you helped kill?" He said it loud enough for Joe to hear.

She cocked the gun. "I didn't kill her. But I think the police would say I was acting in self-defense if I shot you. They might even find it fitting that it happened right here."

He seemed unsettled for the first time.

When she heard the footsteps coming up fast behind her, she spun around—Joe rushed toward her, holding out his hands.

"Don't do it!" he shouted. "Don't! Please! It's not worth it!"

She froze, distracted. She felt a *pop* in her head and everything went white and blurry. All she heard was the ringing in her ears as the ground came rushing up to her face.

47

A loud bang startled me awake. My face was numb. I couldn't feel a thing. For a minute I thought I was still in bed, but that didn't make sense because why would my bed be covered in snow? When I tried lifting my head, my cheek was kind of frozen to the ground. I had to peel it off slowly and that's when my face started burning and the world began to spin. I dry heaved, but nothing came up. My jaw hurt like hell. I tried to open my eyes, but they felt frozen shut and crusted over. I could smell flowers. And candles. I could feel the snow falling gently on my face.

I heard some whimpering and Boner started to lick my face.

Stop it, I tried to say but I couldn't get my mouth to work. The dog came right up to me and licked my left eye. I let him. It felt good. I forced my eye open. Everything was blurry, but I could see Boner's nose, then his big eyes staring at me. For a second I saw the reflection of a zombie in his pupils. The zombie had red hair.

I felt my face. It was like touching my lip at the dentist—I couldn't feel it. From the swelling, I probably looked like the Elephant Man, all puffy and distorted. I rubbed the crust off my eyes and looked at my hand.

Blood.

I tried getting up, but it was like the earth was tied to my back. So I pushed myself to the fence next to me and pulled myself up into a sitting position.

I almost heaved again.

Fuck, what happened?

I was in an alley. Why was I in an alley?

Then I saw footprints leading away from me. There were little droplets of blood splattered in the snow.

It came rushing back.

Kalvin.

Joe.

There was a gun. My gun. But now it was gone. Boner was yapping in my face, which fried my ears and sent a train roaring through my head.

"Shhh . . ." I croaked. Even saying that stung my brain. Boner grabbed my jacket sleeve in his little teeth and tried to yank me up.

My camera was still in my hand, the strap around my wrist. I got onto one knee and pulled myself up on the fence. It felt like climbing a ladder made of ice; I kept slipping and catching myself.

Once I was on my feet, I had to rest my head against the fence. I was burning up. The cold felt good on my skin. I opened an eye and searched the empty alley. The little drops of blood looked like red bread crumbs sprinkled along the white snow.

OK, think . . . call someone. . . .

I fumbled for my phone and managed to get it out of my pocket. But I couldn't think straight. I thought about calling Destiny, but it was too much to find her number.

I dialed the only number I could think of. Each ring made my head vibrate with pain.

"911, how can I help you?"

When I tried to open my mouth to talk, a pain shot through my jaw. I couldn't move my mouth. No words came out, only garbled sounds. I managed to croak, "Gun."

"Ma'am, I'm afraid I can't understand you. Are you in distress?"

I nodded.

"Ma'am, I'm showing that your service provider carries a Public Safety Answering Point device in your phone. We can locate you to help. Do you need assistance?"

I managed a "Yes."

"Keep your phone on. Assistance is en route."

I shoved the phone into my pocket without thinking. I looked at those footprints and the trail of blood. It looked like there was a scuffle, then like someone ran.

***

Each step sent a wave of pain through my jaw and into the space behind my nose. But I was not going to let Joe down again. He deserved to live. It felt like I walked a hundred miles. The pain absorbed my head, dulled my thoughts, set me on autopilot. My body knew how to get there. Just follow the blood.

Somehow it did. Boner ran around me in circles, excited I

was taking him on a walk. Stupid dog.

Two smaller boys passed me on their bikes and almost crashed into each other when they saw me stumble by. A homeless person gawked at me from the inside of a refrigerator box he was living in. I heard him say, "You OK?" But I kept walking.

Then I heard voices. I wasn't sure if they were real or not. The footsteps led into the yard of a partially torn-down house. The voices were coming from in there.

I spotted them immediately.

Kalvin, his back to me, had Joe cornered against a tall gate. He was pointing my gun at Joe.

I could finally hear them over the pounding in my skull. "—don't have to do this," Joe said painfully. His arm was bleeding.

Kalvin was out of breath, like he'd been talking a long time, psyching himself up to do something.

"*Fuck*. I'm *tired* of this shit," he said. "Why you making me look bad? If you don't keep your mouth shut, I'll have to shut it for you!"

"How can I be silent after what you've done?" he said. "I have nothing more to lose."

"You can lose your life."

Joe didn't have to think about it. "I already have."

That pissed Kalvin off even more. "Jesus, you really are fucking crazy."

"Go ahead then, do it."

"Stop saying that!"

They were both breathing hard, their frozen breath huffing into the air like smoke signals. Neither seemed to know what to do next.

Kalvin was looking for a way out. Joe saw me out of the corner of his eye and cringed. I must've looked pretty bad. "You can do like that girl said—just walk away. From everything. You have your whole life in front of you still. But once you pull that trigger, it'll be murder. Then it'll really be over."

"Over for you." He saw Joe look at me and glanced over his shoulder.

"You got a witness now," said Joe. "You kill me, then you'll have to kill her too."

Kalvin wiped the sweat from his eyes. "Shut up. I'm sick of you!" He took a step forward and stuck the gun in Joe's face. "Take back what you said."

Joe didn't cower. "I can't. I remember now. As soon as you pointed that gun at me back there, it came flooding back. I remembered you attacking me and my wife—"

"You can't remember. Your head, it's not right. You're making things up."

Joe looked exhausted. "I'm tired of running. . . . "

"You want me, you're going to have to turn her in too. She was the one who did it."

Joe looked at me. "I don't believe that. I know she was there, but she's not like you are. You're responsible for all of it."

"Fuck you, you racist piece of shit!" Kalvin was panicking, swinging the gun wildly. "Listen. Take your own advice and walk away. Why would you even want to stay here with this hanging over you? Leave, and then I won't have to kill you."

Joe thought about it, but I could see it wasn't going to happen. "This was our home. I refuse to leave it because of you. You committed yourself to this trap. I'm going to keep speaking out. So, you might as well take the next step. You seem to want to destroy everything, including your own life. So do it."

"Maybe I will." Kalvin shook his head, his body tensing up like he was going to do just that.

"Kalvin," I said through gritted teeth.

He didn't look back. "Go away."

I struggled to speak. "I called . . . the cops," I managed to say.

His shoulders slumped. "You people don't know how to play . . . ," he said quietly.

"It's not . . . a game." Each word stung like ice picks. "Let . . . him *go*."

He had the muzzle of the gun resting against Joe's forehead. "I can't."

I stepped closer. I could taste the blood on my tongue. "You . . . can."

"No, I can't. Stay back."

"Kalvin," I said. I swallowed the pain and reached out to put my hand on his shoulder.

"You don't understand."

I was trying to talk him down, all the while thinking, *did he already fire a shot?* "I think . . . I do. Now . . . let him go." I wrapped my arms around him.

"Fuck," he said to himself.

I made eye contact with Joe, motioning for him to leave. He slowly put his hands down. "Look at me . . . Kalvin."

He gazed over his shoulder, lowering the gun.

Joe moved away as quietly as he could.

"Give . . . me . . . the gun."

"Can't do that, Fish."

Far in the distance, I could hear the sirens coming.

"You . . . are better . . . than that."

"Am I?" He listened to the sirens coming. He shrugged himself out of my arms. "You know, everything was good before you showed up."

I saw the gun slowly swing my way. I could hear voices in the background.

"You don't . . . believe that."

He stared at the gun. "Wouldn't it be a great ending to our movie? I shoot you, then blow my own brains out and nobody ever catches me."

"That would . . . suck . . . as an ending. I thought . . . you only liked . . . beginnings?" I stared into the barrel of the gun. *Was that a bullet in the chamber?* "You have a chance . . . to begin again. Turn yourself in—"

Something caught his attention. He looked past me. "What're *you* doing here?"

"Trying to keep her from doing something stupid." Destiny.

Kalvin was pissed. "What'd you do, invite the whole world? I been knocking people out for four years now, training my Tokers how to do it right. And now you want me to turn myself in? I wasn't gonna kill him."

Joe suddenly collapsed against the house. There was so much blood on the snow.

"Did you . . . shoot him?"

He shrugged. "He tried to get away. I couldn't let him escape after all this."

The sirens were getting closer. Destiny moved slowly toward us. "Put the gun down, K."

He grabbed me by the shoulder and spun me around so I

was facing Destiny. He wrapped his arm around me, the gun resting against my neck. "Don't tell me what to do."

Destiny froze. "It's gonna be OK, Fish. Trust me."

"Why should she trust you?" he spat.

My face was on fire, but I had to keep him talking. "She was the one . . . who took me . . . to get tested," I said.

He kind of fumbled. "Tested for what?"

"I thought I was . . . preg . . . " I couldn't say the word.

His face dropped. "You're pregnant?"

I could hear the sirens coming down the alley now. I didn't know what to say.

"I'm gonna be a daddy?"

I looked at Destiny, then shook my head. "No."

He took a step back. He didn't know what to do.

"I wouldn't want . . . to have . . . your baby," I said.

He was looking at the gun, cradled in his hands.

"You and me . . . we coulda been like Bonnie and Clyde. On the run with our own little Toker."

"I watched the end . . . of that movie. Clyde . . . dies," I said.

He blinked. "So does Bonnie." He cocked the gun. I could smell the residue of smoke.

"Mutherfucker," said Destiny. "You put that gun down before I—"

He pointed the gun at Destiny.

"There're no more bullets," I said.

His grip got tighter. "Fuck both of you," he said and pulled the trigger. *Click.*

Destiny turned pale, piss slowly spreading down the legs of her pants. She stood there, frozen.

Kalvin looked at the gun again, not sure why it didn't fire.

"Fuck this." I pushed away from him—he raised the gun to strike me. I steeled myself, but looked him straight in the eye. "You can't hurt me . . . more than you already . . . have."

He hesitated. "There's always more pain. Just when you think you've had all you can handle, there's always more."

The sirens were getting closer. I thought of my mom. "Pain . . . is a gift," I said.

Kalvin looked confused. "You're crazy."

The sirens were deafening now.

He took a few steps back. "I gotta go now. Maybe I'll drop by later for a visit." He looked at the gun. "I'm sure your dad would appreciate it if I reloaded this before returning it. Next time, we'll have a blast."

He put the gun in his pocket and glanced at me one last time. He looked nothing like the self-confident Kalvin I first met. "See ya when I see ya," he mumbled, reaching for the fence gate behind him.

He opened the gate and that's when I saw Tuffy Jones. Before Kalvin could even think, Tuffy sent his fist crashing into Kalvin's face and Kalvin dropped like a ton of bricks, his head bouncing off the snow.

Tuffy stood there rubbing his fist. He shot Destiny a look. "Now we even, D." He shook his head at the sight of my face. "I was the first Knockout King. Now I'm the last. It's done." Then he just turned and walked away.

Destiny came running up and grabbed me. "I brought the cavalry."

"How did you know . . . ?" I slurred.

"You said the library was open and then it hit me—of course, *that's* where Kalvin would ask you to go."

I looked back at Joe, who was leaning against the fence, holding his arm and looking as pale as the snow.

"Are you . . . OK?" I grunted.

He lifted his hand and winced at the bullet wound. "Seen worse in the war. You need to worry about yourself."

I felt faint. Destiny grabbed me as I buckled to the snow.

***

Maybe I passed out for a bit. My mind drifted and for a few seconds I could see everything that was happening. I was floating high overhead. I saw myself in Destiny's arms; I saw Joe drag himself over and look into my eyes. Tuffy was walking away, his hands tucked in his pockets as a cop car rushed by. It pulled up in front of us and two cops jumped out. One radioed for an ambulance; the other, at Joe's urging, went over to check on the Knockout King, who was spread out, facedown in the snow. It all felt like a dream.

Then the pain woke me up.

***

It turns out life is not like a movie. It doesn't have a happy ending where the hero defeats the villain and rides off into the sunset. Life is more like a puzzle. With a few pieces missing.

When Kalvin came to, his wrists cuffed, his face bloodied, he looked shocked and confused. At that moment, I saw the real him for the first time—just some kid who pretended to be a tough guy with a heart of gold—a character in his own movie. For a few months, we all existed in that movie—a stream of hi-def moments that proved we could leave our mark in this world. The TKO Club was digitally immortalized—just like Alex, or Sundance, or Bonnie and Clyde.

But then the real world came crashing down on us, and now, his movie would be replaced by a new one.

My camera had recorded everything that day. There was now enough evidence and eyewitness testimony to get convictions. Tyreese broke down and confessed to his actions. The judge tried him as a minor, but he was found guilty on second-degree manslaughter. He will be in juvie until he's eighteen. Some of the other Tokers ended up doing two to four months, then transferred out to Grant Remedial.

Unfortunately for Prince, after doing only eight weeks for aiding and abetting, he tried to knock out a Watcher who happened to be an off-duty cop. The cop was packing. Prince died before he reached the hospital.

Destiny and Boner were the only two who got away unscathed, but I knew they both bore their own scars. They were the only good things to come out of this whole mess.

As for me, after a period of house arrest, I got probation and enough community service to fill up the next couple of years. I knew why. I was not innocent. I would never be innocent again. I had to skip the rest of my sophomore year, and was forced to repeat it again the next year. That was alright by me because the do-over kind of allowed me to pretend that it never happened. And after I turn eighteen and have my record wiped clean, maybe it never did.

Kalvin, the Knockout King, was found guilty in adult court for attempted murder, assault and battery, possession of a stolen firearm, and conspiracy. Since it was his first conviction, he only got twenty years— still, longer than he'd been alive. But Tillman warned me that with all the efforts to relieve prison overcrowding, Kalvin could be out in ten with good behavior.

I would be twenty-six by then.

I hoped I would be far away from here when he got out. I didn't want to think what he might do if he showed up on my doorstep. I still didn't know why he'd chosen me. Was it just because I had a camera? Or did he really have feelings for me? Maybe he thought I could save him from himself.

When the doctor finally removed the wires from my broken jaw and checked my busted nose, he told me, "You're gonna look like a fighter for a while."

I was a fighter. And I was determined to remain standing until the last bell.

EPILOGUE

I finally made it to the top of the Arch. It was September and I no longer had to wear an ankle bracelet, so as a way to celebrate my sixteenth birthday, Dad thought we should do something fun for a change. We were still struggling as a family but, despite everything, my parents were there for me. We were never gonna be one big happy unit—we were too flawed and broken in our own ways for that. But I think it brought us closer together. Maybe pain really was a gift in that way.

The top of the Arch was a narrow curved room with windows on both sides and slopes to lie on as you gazed out. I'd invited Destiny, who smuggled Boner inside her jacket. We lay down together by the middle window and when I saw how high we were, it took my breath away.

It was impossibly beautiful up there. The river was beaming under the late summer sun. Ships made their way up and down the Big Muddy like little toys in a rain puddle.

Boner licked my hand. Sometimes, Destiny brought him over to keep me company at night. She knew I had a hard time sleeping. Every night when the lights went out, I thought of Mrs. Lee and felt the hollow in the pit of my stomach. Some nights, I cried myself to sleep. Other nights, I'd lie there in the dark, thinking of Joe, all alone.

I don't think that kind of regret ever goes away—you don't forget things like that.

At least I can't.

"Look how tiny those people are down there," Dad said, lying next to Mom in front of a window.

"They look like tiny toy figures," said Mom.

"They look like ants," I said, winking at Destiny. I was no longer angry at the ants. They all had worries and pains. I was no different in that way.

"Dang," said Destiny as she switched windows. "You can see everything up here. That's the stadium. And there's the freeway we came on. Hey, isn't that our school way over there?"

Our school. That sounded good to me. I was back, starting over as a sophomore again. But this time, I played it differently. I grew my hair long, stopped hiding behind a hoodie, showed off more of my curves. I didn't care what anybody thought of me. I was doing my own thing.

Sitting up there in the Arch, high above the world, I tried to imagine all the incoming middle schoolers out there, roaming the neighborhoods, looking to impress the older kids. I knew that the TKO Club was disbanded. But every once in a while, I'd hear about some idiot playing Knockout. It seemed amazing to me, after everything that had happened, that anyone would be stupid enough to copycat. But I guess nobody remembers anything for long.

Some kids end up in gangs, some become bullies, some hit random strangers.

But if I ever hear of another Knockout King in my neighborhood, they'll have me to deal with. And that's a promise I intend to keep.

The King is dead.

Long live the Queen.

AUTHOR'S NOTE

In spring of 2012, I visited St. Louis to do some school visits organized by the St. Louis Public Library. The librarian in charge wanted me to visit a specific school and a specific branch of the library system. She kept saying there was a reason and finally, as we drove there, she asked me: "Have you ever heard of the knockout game?"

I had not. I had worked with gangs, been to all kinds of urban inner cities throughout America, but I had not heard of the phenomena she was about to tell me about. The middle school we were visiting had been recently raided and several arrests associated with this game were made. And right outside the library where we were going that night, a knockout game ended in the death of an elderly man.

The rules of the game were simple. A group of kids, mostly middle school–age, gathered in some random spot and picked a random passerby. One of the teens was given the task of approaching the stranger and trying to knock him out with one punch. The kids did not steal their victim's money. It was simply something they found to be funny—perhaps a way to escape their boring lives and prove their manhood.

There were several high profile cases, one of which was thrown out when a thirteen year old failed to testify at the last minute. The TKO Club was back out on the streets. Citizens were up in arms but the police were helpless. There was no pattern, no rhyme or reason. People were getting seriously hurt, both physically and emotionally. These kids had the run of the streets. It was like the *Lord of the Flies*, only instead of Piggy, they preyed on citizens.

This was crazy stuff, but what also grabbed my attention was that this was not a gang-affiliated activity. It was more like a social club. Fight Club for young teens, if you will. And sometimes there were girls in these groups.

I was immediately drawn to this unknown world. Who were these kids and why were they doing this? How could they think it was funny? How could they make videos of their conquests? I started Googling and the attacks went back years. It was one of these closed-off worlds we rarely get a glimpse into. And the kicker was: the one real lead that tied these assaults together was a person of interest called "the Knockout King."

The librarian wanted me to talk to these kids at this school because they had responded to my book *Yummy: The Last Days of a Southside Shorty*. She wanted me to reach out to them. I did and quickly decided that the best way to have an impact was to make this story my next project. I went home and started writing.

This is that story.

ACKNOWLEDGMENTS

A big thanks:

To one of the best libraries in the country, St. Louis Public Library and its YA heroes: Carrie Dietz, Joan Smith, Patty Carleton, all of whom make me feel like a rock star.

To my early readers, for all their advice: Steven Lovy, Lynne Hansen, Joyce Sweeney, and especially Andrea Tompa.

To the St. Louis juvenile authorities: Nathan Graves and Rodney Smith, and to Principal Cornelius Green, for their stories.

To the *Riverfront Times* and the *St. Louis Post-Dispatch*, for their excellent coverage of the knockout game attacks.

To my medical expert (and along with his wife Robin, my biggest fans), Dr. Edward Schroering.

To Maurice Sendak, for saying, "Make it personal. Make it dangerous."

To April Henry, for her criminal advice and twisted mind.

To the Internet, for making research a lot easier.

To my partner in crime (and agent), Edward Necarsulmer IV, for finding the way out of this detour.

To everyone at Carolrhoda Lab, for all their efforts, especially Giliane Mansfeldt and Laura Rinne for all the design headaches they had to deal with on this one.

To my editor Andrew Karre, for not being afraid to take chances.

And most of all, to Maggie and Zola, who make my life possible.

ABOUT THE AUTHOR

G. Neri is the Coretta Scott King honor-winning author of *Yummy: the Last Days of a Southside Shorty* and the recipient of the Lee Bennett Hopkins Promising Poet Award for his free verse novella, *Chess Rumble*. His novels include *Surf Mules* and the Horace Mann Upstander Award-winning *Ghetto Cowboy*. His work has been honored by the Museum of Tolerance and the Simon Wiesenthal Center, Antioch University, the International Reading Association, the American Library Association, the Junior Library Guild and the National Council for Teachers of English. Neri has been a filmmaker, animator, teacher, and digital media producer. He currently writes full time and lives on the Gulf Coast of Florida with his wife and daughter. Visit him online at www.gregneri.com

CALGARY PUBLIC LIBRARY
NOVEMBER 2014